ONE THING AFTER ANOTHER

IFEANYI ESIMAI

CIPARUM
PRESS

PUBLISHED BY CIPARUM PRESS
an imprint of Ciparum LLC
270 Sparta Ave., Suite 104, PMB 152
Sparta, NJ 07871

ISBN: 978-1-63589-703-6 (Print)
ISBN: 978-1-63589-705-0 (E-book)
ISBN: 978-1-63589-704-3 (Hardcover)

For my father

PROLOGUE

"Put your right hand up and spread your fingers. Don't ask me why, just do it!" barked Okoro. "Now look at your fingers. Are they all equal? That's exactly-"

Okoro listened to the dial tone and shook his head. He dropped his cell phone on the table and tried to control his anger. How else could he make his wife understand he's only a detective and does not have access to the type of money her friends' husbands make. He cannot keep up with her friends — the wives of senators, high ranking government officials, and generals who send their family to Europe or America every summer. Where was he going to get that kind of money?

The last contract he did with his company registered with the police department was yet to be paid for work done. Even though as a serving policeman he wasn't supposed to do that. They called it a conflict of interest. But, the difference in opinion was overlooked after a fat envelop exchanged hands.

The personal secretary to the Assistant Inspector General of Police had assured him his file was among the next batch of contractors to receive payment. Getting his company folder to the top of the pile had cost him what was left of his savings. Now his wife wanted to go to Europe with their daughter on vacation.

Okoro was a pragmatic man, and his motto, 'No food for the lazy man' turned him into a jack of all trades, doing whatever was needed to make extra money. He wished they'd given him a more lucrative assignment like finding black market petrol sellers or smugglers, instead of finding the girls abducted from their schools by terrorists. At least smugglers have the money to persuade him to look the other way. This assignment to locate the kidnapped girls was like eating chloroquine—very bitter.

He looked at a plaque on his table an evangelical pastor had given him some years ago. Things had stopped working in his favor the way they used to. Okoro sighed, then his phone rang, interrupting his thoughts. Okoro felt his pulse shoot up. Maybe his wife was calling to shout at him some more. Reluctantly, he looked at the caller ID, and the smell of crisp naira notes clouded his senses.

In the past, he had done stuff for this caller, who he knew only as Malam. He had detained people in jail for him to soften them up. Done security work, police escort; you name it. The man was loaded, and he always paid in cash. A fat 'Ghana must go bag' delivered by hand. Okoro jumped to his feet. The big smile on his face effortless. "Hello, sir!"

Pleasantries were exchanged, and Okoro listened more than he spoke. He picked up a pen from his table and scribbled a name on an envelope. A knot tightened in his stomach as the caller wanted to know if the request was something he could do.

Okoro knew he had only one decision to make. If he declined, the caller would reach out to another detective, and all the money would flow that way. And worst of all, he wouldn't be considered for future opportunities. Okoro's house in the village wasn't going to roof itself. His wife was planning a summer vacation with their daughter for four weeks. They weren't going to trek to Europe and then sleep on the streets of London, Paris, and Frankfurt.

"No problem, sir," said Okoro. "I'll take care of it. Yes, sir. The same bank account."

Okoro hung up and shivered as a cold sensation traveled down his spine. He took a deep breath and let it out through his nose. For the first time in his career, he wasn't sure what to do.

Many had perished in police custody. Everybody understood that sometimes, things 'just happen'. And it was accepted as God's will. A knock on his door broke his thoughts.

"Who is it?" asked Okoro. The door creaked open and the constable peeped in. "What is it? Can't you see I'm busy!"

The constable opened the door wider and snapped to attention.

"Sorry sir. There's a girl out here who said her name is Ngozi Balogun Bashiru." The constable's lips spread in a smile after he said the name. "She said she's one of the kidnapped girls-"

Okoro looked at the name he had scribbled on the envelope. "What? She's outside there?"

"Yes sir."

Okoro's pulse started to race. He had planned to send his men to the girl's home and invite her to the police station, now this. A girl with the name his client had given him was at the station.

"What should I do sir?"

"Tell her to wait. Don't let her out of your sight. I'm coming right now."

The constable saluted and left the office. Okoro jumped to his feet and headed for the door. He glanced over his shoulder and read the plaque on his table. "If God is for us, who can be against us. Romans 8:31." He couldn't believe this sudden turn of events. Not only had God provided him bread, but he had also buttered it for him.

1

I paid the taxi driver and stepped out after he handed me my change. Auntie Halima would ask me for it. The main entrance of the police station looked like a car junkyard. Different makes and models of cars littered the front of the station. Most had been in an accident. Intact ones had their tires deflated.

I hurried out of the way as a big police truck, the Black Maria, screeched to a stop beside me, rattling my already frayed nerves. It had horizontal bars where windows should be—a mobile prison cell.

"Little sister, please give me money," said a voice from the Black Maria. "Anything, even ten naira is fine."

A man's face came into focus. His sad eyes peered at me. He disappeared as if yanked away from the window, replaced by a wide-eyed bearded face. The newcomer was frantic. His eyes darted around and relaxed when he saw me.

"Hey, you! Bring your toto here!"

I walked faster past the truck toward the entrance to the station. Auntie Halima had insisted I visit the police and make a report. I didn't think it was a wise idea, but I had to listen to her. A beggar has no choice. I could still see the shock on her face when I returned from Sambisa.

Inside, the reception area of the police station had been swept clean, the cement floor puckered with holes that seemed to have been patched and re-patched over the years.

A policeman sat behind a desk. "Stop there!" He raised his hand and stared at me, then returned to the ledger he was writing on.

I froze where I stood. I shouldn't have come here alone. Fatima or Maryam should have come with me. On the wall behind him were photographs of the president, the state governor, and the inspector general of police.

Propped up against the wall opposite the policeman was a wooden bench. Different-sized brownish palm imprints plastered the walls. In some spots, the paint had peeled and revealed a rainbow of layers of old paint. The current color was blue.

A gentle breeze accompanied by the smell of cigarette smoke and urine floated in through a dirty louvered window, the foul air circulated by a brown ceiling fan with telltale signs of its former white grandeur. A door led to a corridor, and conversations in Pidgin English drifted back.

After a few minutes, I cleared my throat. The policeman ignored me and kept writing. When he finally got up, his stomach spilled over the black uniform, which was two sizes too small. I thought the scowl on his face could be because of the discomfort caused by his tight uniform. He looked at a piece of paper in his hands as he walked over to a blackboard on the wall and wrote:

YUSUF HASSAN — BURGLARY
   Hafsat Amil — Prostitution

Atta Amin — Armed Robbery
Miriam Usman — Prostitution

"BELLO! BELLO!" SAID ANOTHER POLICEMAN AS HE walked in.

The policeman at the blackboard glanced over his shoulder.

"Musa, morning. Is that you?" He continued to write.

Both policemen must use the same tailor. The newly arrived policeman, Musa, ignored the question, his eyes fixed on me. I glanced away.

"Ah, who is this one?" asked Musa. His eyes scrutinized me from head to toe in one sweep. "They're getting younger and younger."

Behind him was a woman wearing a tight short skirt. Her face was made up as if she was getting ready for the masquerade festival.

"Bello, please, put her down for prostitution," said Musa in Pidgin English.

"You young policemen are always in a hurry to arrest," said the woman. "Musa, listen, let's talk first." She batted her eyes.

Musa stared at her for a second longer. "Bello, wait. Let me hear what she has to say first." He turned to the woman. "Okay, come with me."

Bello turned away from the chalkboard.

"Okay, smally," said Bello. "What brings you here?"

I told him how I was kidnapped from school with other girls. And about how we jumped out of the truck to escape. And the attack by hyenas and coming back with the other girls.

Bello raised a single eyebrow and hissed. "Have you been

drinking?"

I frowned. "Drinking? No."

"And you were there?" asked Bello.

I nodded. But I didn't think he believed me.

"Wait, what's your name again?"

"Ngozi Balogun Bashiru."

"What!" Bello threw his head back and laughed.

I knew what was coming next.

"Ngozi Balogun Bashiru. Your mother couldn't decide who your father was?"

I'd heard that before. Was he Ibo, Yoruba or Hausa? I ignored Bello as he wrote it down. "Can I go now?"

Bello sprang to his feet like a featherweight. "Go? Hmmm, the information you gave me is serious. Wait, let me call my oga. Sit on that bench." He pulled his ear to show the seriousness of what he was saying. "Stay here."

Bello dashed off into an inner office. The police are better avoided than interacted with, I thought. A few minutes later, Bello reappeared and sat behind the counter. He said nothing. Policemen and a few policewomen with their black skirts and huge hips shuffled in and out of the station.

Moments later, the same door Bello had disappeared through burst open and a large short man with a round face in a brown kaftan, faded and shiny from ironing, stepped into the room. He glanced around.

"Bello, where's the girl?" asked the man.

Bello jumped to his feet and saluted. Bello pointed at me.

The man walked over. His dark lips parted in a smile, the type of smile that conveyed one meaning while the owner of the smile had other ideas. His eyes were cold.

"Good morning, sir." I got up.

"No, that's okay." He motioned with his hands for me to remain seated. "I'm DSP Okoro.

What's your name?"

"Ngozi."

"Okay, small girl, what is it? Did somebody molest you? Steal from you?"

I didn't know where to start. I hesitated. "Emm . . . no. Yes . . . I'm a student at Akarika Girls. I escaped from the kidnappers. They . . . they killed Faith—"

"Killed? Wait! Who killed who?" asked Okoro.

"They came to our school at night and took all of us."

Eyes wide, Okoro glanced around and leaned closer. "You . . . You're from Chibok?"

"No, from Akarika Girls," I said, lowering my voice.

Okoro stood straight and exhaled through his mouth. "We've been working hard to find the girls and the terrorists." Okoro paused. "Out of all those girls, how come only you escaped?"

I frowned. "It wasn't only me. There were about twenty of us."

"Okay, come with me," said Okoro. "You'll have to write a report on what happened." Okoro pointed towards a door and I followed.

"Sir, should I put her name on the board," asked Bello.

"Yes," said Okoro.

I glanced over my shoulders at the chalkboard and felt my heart drop into my stomach.

Yusuf Hassan - Burglary

    Hafsat Amil - Prostitution

    Atta Amin Armed - Robbery

    Miriam Usman - Prostitution

    Ngozi Balogun Bashiru - Kidnapper/Terrorist Accomplice

• • •

I WAS LED INTO A ROOM SPARE OF FURNISHINGS EXCEPT FOR A wooden chair and a marred table with a pad of paper and several pencils on it. A bright naked bulb dangled from the ceiling.

"Write everything that happened after you got to school," said Okoro. "When you're done, knock on the door."

It took a while, but I wrote the events as they happened. I knocked on the door, and a policewoman came and took the paper away. Tired, I placed my head on the desk and dozed off. When the door opened again, I raised my head. The policewoman was back with a piece of paper.

"I typed your statement," said the policewoman. "All you need to do is sign it." She handed me the statement and a blue pen.

I removed the cap and ran my finger over the statement as I began to read. I stopped and reread the first few paragraphs: "I, Ngozi Balogun Bashiru, state that on April 20, I and some other accomplices broke into Akarika Girls and kidnapped . . ."

A knot tightened in my stomach. "I didn't write this!"

"Sign it," said the policewoman. "You're not leaving until you sign it." She left, and the deadbolt of the door sounded like a clap of thunder as she pushed it home.

I felt like I was back at the dormitory the night the terrorists struck. Laughter bubbled in my stomach and spilled out of my lips as a grunt. The police rescued people and did not hold them hostage. Why me? From one trouble to another. What did I do to deserve all this? My frustration turned to fear, then anger. I banged on the door.

The privacy window on the door slid open, and a menacing unknown face appeared. "If you don't stop this nonsense, I'll make you see your ears without a mirror."

I remembered Faith. Her motto was to always turn the

other cheek. It had kept her alive until I convinced her otherwise, and then it didn't. I would sign the paper, maybe it would save me. Who would I turn to—?

"Where is my client?" a voice yelled in the corridor.

My heart thumped in my chest. Are they coming for me? I heard raised voices, for and against whoever was shouting. The deadbolt to the door screeched as it slid open and the door flew open.

A tall, gray-haired man dressed in a black suit walked in, followed by a woman dressed in jeans and a T-shirt. The man in the suit was angry, the woman wide-eyed and scared.

"We do not allow civilians in this part of the police station!" yelled Okoro, bringing up the rear, his face a mask of rage. "We have dangerous criminals in custody!"

"My name is Gani Fulbright, SAN," bellowed the man in the suit. "I am Ms. Ngozi Bashiru's lawyer."

"SAN . . . Senior . . . Senior Advocate of Nigeria?" Okoro stammered. "And you're . . . her lawyer? She has a lawyer?"

I looked at the man and woman. I'd never seen them before.

"Yes, and you have her in unlawful custody," said my lawyer.

I have a lawyer!

"Unless you can produce her arrest warrant, I'm removing my client from your premises to consult with her in private."

Mr. Fulbright grabbed the piece of paper on the table and ran his eyes through it. He looked at me and forced a smile.

"Did you sign anything?" His voice was stern. Eyes cold and hard.

I swallowed. Speech deserted me. I shook my head.

"Good." Mr. Fulbright folded the paper and put it in his pocket. He took me by the arm. "Young lady, let's go."

2

"*Do you think we'll sell out today?" asked the girl in rapid Hausa. Conscious of the tray full of oranges balanced on her head, she swiped a finger across her forehead, removing the sweat that dotted it.*

"We have to," said the taller girl. "Sometimes, the day starts slow, but it always picks up." She spoke fast, almost babbling. The taller girl adjusted the tray of bananas on her head. Her eyes darted around as if she was expecting something.

Both girls wore clothes that had been washed and rewashed so much that the print design on them was barely visible.

"Oranges!" a male voice yelled.

The two girls stopped. They turned toward the voice. The girl with the oranges turned much slower, keeping her orange pyramid intact.

They were in a construction site with buildings at different stages of construction. Some had wooden scaffolds around them, some were at the foundation level, some at the decking level, and some were getting their roofs installed.

A man peeped out of a window in one uncompleted building and motioned at the girls to come. They didn't hesitate.

"DON'T GO!" MY SCREAM PIERCED THE NIGHT. I SAT UP IN bed trembling; my nightshirt clung on me as if I'd been in the rain. I looked around, still a bit unfamiliar with my new surroundings. Moments later, there was a knock on my bedroom door.

'Mom' peeped in. "Another nightmare?"

I nodded and glanced outside—darkness.

"Are you all right!"

"Yes," I croaked. I cleared my throat. "I'm fine. Good morning." The nightmares had started after the ordeal at the police station.

My new mom sat on the bed beside me, her shoulder-length braids secured in a scarf. "Good morning. It will get better." She smiled at me shyly, then looked away.

There was nothing Mom could do, nothing anybody could do. The pediatrician we saw said to come back if it happened more often. It happened almost every night, but I stopped telling my parents. I didn't want them to have buyer's remorse in adopting me. I wanted them to be happy. Only in situations like tonight when I screamed did they know I still had them.

"Try and sleep. We'll be going to the high school in the morning to get you registered. It's right here in Falls Lake, just ten minutes from the house. Your first official day will be next Monday."

"What should I wear, Ma . . . Mom?" I caught myself.

Mom laughed. "Jeans and a blouse should be fine.

Nothing formal." She patted my leg, got up, and headed for the door.

I remembered the first time I'd called her "Mom." She and Dad had just shown me the layout of their home, my new home.

"Come, Ngozi, I'll show you your room upstairs and the rest of the house," Mom had said.

"Yes, madam," I'd replied.

She spun to face me. Her smile widened, "You know, you can call me Mommy or Mom, if you like, never madam or ma, okay?"

"Mommy," I mouthed, testing the word. "Mom!" I said louder and giggled, timid. I knew it would need getting used to.

"And Dad to you!" Dad had chipped in. He ran his hand over his bald head and smiled. He had a habit of stroking his goatee while talking.

It'd been four weeks since I'd landed in New Jersey. Sometimes I had to pinch myself to make sure it wasn't a dream. It still amazed me that less than six weeks ago I was a captive, and today I didn't have to worry about terrorists or the police.

To say my life had changed would be an understatement. Somehow, I missed my old life. It was unpredictable, kept me on edge most of the time. Auntie Halima, Maryam, Peter, and Fatima. They had yelled at me, told lies about me, or threatened to beat me up. I missed Fatima. But this was better. It would only be a matter of time before I forgot them.

Sometimes I would wake up in the middle of the night and wonder where I was. It took a few days to get over waking up at odd times of the night and feeling sleepy during the day.

"It's jet lag. Your body will adjust," said Mom.

The first few days after we arrived from Nigeria, Mom had taken a couple days off to help me get comfortable.

But after that they went back to their regular routine, both were busy. My parents left the house early and didn't come back until late in the evening. They worked at different hospitals. Dad was a cardiologist and Mom a nephrologist. A cardiologist was easy to figure out—the heart—but nephrologist?

"Just call me the kidney doctor," Mom said on one of those early nights as we ate dinner.

"We sometimes talk about work during dinner," said Dad. "We'll try not to, but maybe all that talk will rub off on you."

I ran the back of my hand over my neck to wipe the sweat. Mom worried about me a lot. She wanted me to feel at home and mix with people whenever we went out. We'd visited some of their Nigerian friends for birthday parties, baby christenings, and one wedding reception. I always felt like an outsider and would sit on my own, in self-inflicted exile.

I'd overheard Dad several times talking to Mom. "Don't worry, it's natural. We took her away from the life she's always known to a different one. She's adjusting."

I wanted her and Dad to be pleased, to not regret coming to my rescue and adopting me.

My eyes closed, and I fell into a dreamless sleep.

Our appointment at the school was for 9:00 a.m. On the way, Mom pointed out the town library, police station, and a football field.

"Our house is not too far from here," said Mom. "I'm sure you'll be visiting the library."

Mom and Dad had tried to figure out the grade equivalent between the Nigerian high school system and the US's, but they couldn't. They had done all their schooling in Nigeria, apart from their postgraduate medical training.

Mr. Holden, a chubby man of average height with a bald spot, had worked it all out.

"Ngozi's grade equivalent would be the eleventh grade, junior high," said Mr. Holden. He had smiled throughout the meeting and seemed happy to make my acquaintance. I got a tour of the school—the cafeteria, the bathrooms, the gym, labs, and classrooms. Falls Lake High basketball court was impressive. It was indoors, smooth and level. There was no comparison to the one at Akarika Girls.

The whole school, the classes and laboratories, were all in the same building. Well linked; you didn't have to step outside. At my old school, we had several separate, unconnected buildings. God help you if it rained.

After the high school tour, my parents dropped me off at home and then left for their jobs. I was home alone. I started one of the books I'd bought from Amazon. Dad had tried to get me to read on a Kindle, but I still preferred the tactile feel of a book in my hands. Being lost in a book was one way I'd found to cope with all the things that had happened—to distract myself from thinking about the days at Sambisa and about Faith, Joy, and the other girls. I wondered about the twins and little Mary.

3

———

The next day, Saturday, by some miracle I'd slept through the night. I was surprised Mom hadn't come in to check on me during the night, but maybe she had and I just didn't hear her. Then there was a knock on the door—I'd spoken too soon.

"I checked on you earlier," said Mom. "But you were fast asleep, so peaceful. It would have been a crime to wake you up. I made eggs and pancakes. Come and get some when you're ready."

"Okay," I said, stretching. "Good morning."

Mom turned. "Later we'll go see my colleague, Aparna, Dr. Kumar. Her daughter Preeti is in Falls Lake High too. I think there's a Nigerian family whose kids go there. You'll figure that out with time. At least you'll know one person before you start."

Mom shut the door behind her. My phone buzzed, and I turned to the bedside table. The time on the phone was 8:00 a.m., and it showed a message notification from Maryam. I chuckled. I'd sent Maryam a text as soon as I got my phone.

Since then, she'd been texting me almost every day. Now I was her favorite cousin.

Dad had bought me the phone and given me his old, but still very new, laptop computer on the second day I was in America.

"I bought this a few weeks ago, but I don't need it," he'd said. "My iPhone, iPad, and desktop serve me well. The laptop is yours." He pushed the laptop toward me.

I hesitated. Was he joking?

"I would have reset it to the factory setting, but I just didn't get to it. Play around with it. Delete everything I have there. My e-mail, social media accounts; I have them on my other devices."

As Dad was about to leave, he handed me an envelope.

I took it and raised an eyebrow.

"Your allowance. Yours to spend as you wish."

Allowance?

The hum of the water pump brought me back to the present. Faith looked happier in a larger tank even though she was alone. We'd attended the fair organized at the elementary school in Falls Lake. The fish had been my prize for tossing table tennis balls, no, ping-pong balls, into a cup. By the time we finished at the fair, I had four goldfish.

Dad bought a small tank from the stand owner and some fish food. All the fish but one had died within two days.

"Google 'goldfish care,'" Mom had said. "I'm sure there will be something online or videos on YouTube."

I learned fast about goldfish. They don't do well in small aquariums, and I had four packed in a small glass tank. Mom took me to the pet store and bought a fifty-gallon tank. I named the surviving fish Faith. If anyone had told me two months ago I would be in New Jersey in my own room, feeding a pet fish, I would have thought they were crazy.

I fed Faith a finger pinch of food and smiled as she rushed to the surface to devour the food.

The smell of new clothes and leather rushed out once I opened my closet. I reached for the right corner where I had two pairs of jeans and some T-shirts, which were my favorites. That was about all I needed. Wrapped in a plastic bag in a corner were my clothes from Nigeria.

I grabbed blue jeans and a T-shirt and laid them out on my bed. Once in the bathroom, I turned on the shower and let the water run until it got warm. *Where was the water heater?* I wondered. At Auntie Halima's house, each bathroom had its own small water heater.

I looked at my bookshelf to see what book I'd read next.

"You're now thinking about it by trying not to think about it," I mumbled. It was frustrating.

My luggage out of Nigeria was a half-empty "Ghana Must Go" bag with an old shoebox that contained a few Polaroid pictures of me, Zainab, Uncle Thomas, and his family. There was also a photo of my mother, Matron, plus a traditional outfit, two blouses, and a pair of jeans. The pictures of my mother and uncle used to be on my shelf, but I put them back in the plastic bag. It could create an awkward situation with my new parents.

I showered, dressed, and opened the door. Mom's voice traveled up from the kitchen. I walked down the sizeable curved staircase and remembered the first time I'd arrived at the house in Falls Lake, New Jersey.

It was huge and reminded me of the large homes I'd seen along the drive when we went to complete the adoption papers, after Mom and Mr. Fulbright rescued me from the clutches of the corrupt police in Abuja.

The main door opened into a foyer as wide as our living room in Lamija. A gold-framed decorative mirror hung on the left wall, and a half-moon table with flowers carved into the edges was pushed flush against the wall underneath the mirror. Hanging from the high ceiling was a large chandelier. The whole house had a faint sweet smell, which I later learned was apple and cinnamon. There were three living rooms, each with stylish leather chairs that looked like things you look at and then sit somewhere else.

Behind the house was a bike trail that led into the woods. It seemed like a glorified bush path to me. The first time I went for a walk, I was skeptical. Was it safe? I expected to see slithering snakes or an animal jump out of the bushes and attack me.

But I only saw a peaceful family of deer and some squirrels running around. Park benches placed at intervals for people to sit on were empty. The pathway ended at a pond fed by a creek. Occasionally I would see other people taking a walk, jogging, or riding their bikes. It was beautiful and serene.

I entered the kitchen and my stomach rumbled. Mom gave me a thumbs-up and moved the cell phone away from her ear.

"It's all for you. We'll run errands, then go see Preeti, okay?" She put the phone back to her ear and headed for the stairs. "No, I was talking to my daughter, Ngozi. She starts school on Monday. Yes, it's the middle of the semester, she's not going to just stay home. Who? Ben? No, he's not home. He's on call—"

Mom shut the door to her room, and I couldn't hear anymore. So Dad was on call.

I stuffed myself. The pancakes and eggs were delicious. I was full, but there was still a lot left. At Auntie Halima's you must finish any food placed on your plate, or else . . .

I felt hot. *What do I do with the leftover food?* Then I thought of meeting new people. Would they like me? What would I tell them about myself? I chewed on my lower lip. My scalp itched, then my armpit.

$$4$$

I took a few deep breaths to calm myself as I heard Mom coming down the stairs.

"Wow, you must have been hungry," said Mom.

"No, I didn't want it to go to waste. You said it was all for me."

Mom smiled. "Oh, you poor thing. Next time put what's left in the fridge. This is your home, you can ask me anything, okay?"

I nodded. I knew I couldn't just ask anything, but I promised myself I should, instead of getting myself all worked up over something trivial.

Mom and I ran more than a few errands. Mom doted on me. *"Do you want this? Do you want that?"* she asked at every store we went to.

We arrived at Dr. Kumar's house in the early afternoon. Their home was as large as my parents'. Apart from the color and a few minor layout differences, it was very similar.

The closer we got to the door, the hotter I became, despite the perfect weather. I broke out in a sweat, not because it was hot, but because of my fear of meeting new people—of being accepted. As we climbed up the short flight of stairs to the door, it flew open.

"Aparna!" screamed Mom, arms extended.

"Nkechi! How are you?"

She was about the same height as Mom. Her long hair came down to her waist. I'd never seen hair that long.

"Aparna, you went traditional today," said Mom, beaming from ear to ear and admiring the woman's Indian outfit. The two women hugged and jumped up and down like teenagers.

"The weather's nice. I thought I'd go traditional like you. This must be your daughter?" said Aparna. "Come in. What's your name?"

"Ngozi," I said.

"I'm Aparna—"

"No, Dr. Kumar to you," said Mom.

"Ah, your culture is like ours," said Dr. Kumar. "Children don't call their elders by their first names. Come in." She paused. "Preeti! Preeti!"

The smell of food greeted us as we walked in. It seemed like they were getting ready for lunch.

"Yes, Mom!" said a voice from upstairs.

"Come down here. Nkechi is here with . . . her daughter." Dr. Kumar turned to me and narrowed her eyes. "Say it again"

"Ngozi," I said.

Dr. Kumar inhaled. "Ngozi?"

"Yeah," said Mom. "but I doubt Preeti can pronounce it."

A girl about my age and height, five feet seven, showed up. She looked like her mother, but younger.

"Hi," she said and waved at me. "Hello, Dr. Obi."

"Preeti, Ngozi. Ngozi, Preeti," said Dr. Kumar.

I had a plastered smile on my face. Mom had told me to help people out when they try to learn how to say my name right, so we came up with something close. But they didn't ask. With names like Aparna and Preeti, which were new to me, I was sure they'd gotten plenty of requests about spelling and pronouncing their names.

"I'm Preeti."

She was Preeti, but who goes about telling people how pretty they were? I nodded. "Ngozi."

"We were just about to eat lunch," said Dr. Kumar. "Why don't we all go to the dining table."

Dr. Kumar led the way. "Nalini!"

"Yes, Mommy!" answered Nalini.

"Come and say hello and eat," said Dr. Kumar.

Nalini came down and said hello. She was a younger version of Preeti. With all the yelling and the smell of food, I felt at home. It could have been a Nigerian family. The television was on, adding to the ambiance.

On the walls were pictures of the family. There was a Mr. Kumar who was also a doctor and like Dad, was on call. The food was excellent, spicy. There was white rice, chicken with yellow curry sauce, and fish fried in garlic sauce. I liked this family. They were not pretentious. I hoped they liked me too.

"Preeti, tell Ngozi about your school," said Mom. "You know, like what the people are like. Who to avoid . . . things like that."

Preeti giggled and her head shrunk into her shoulders. "Everybody is nice. I'll show you around on Monday. Do you know who your homeroom teacher is?"

"No," I said. "Not yet."

"Let's play a game," said Nalini as we sat in their living room.

Nalini was two years younger than Preeti and in middle school. Preeti, like me, was seventeen and in eleventh grade.

"What game?" asked Preeti in a tone that suggested she wasn't a fan of Nalini's game.

Nalini ignored her sister. "Ngozi, do you read a lot of novels?"

"Not . . . not too much," I stammered. My eyes darted from Nalini to Preeti, not sure where she was going with this.

Nalini sat on the rug cross-legged. Her eyes flashed from me to her sister. "Okay, I will make some assumptions here . . . that we've all read the same novels."

We can't assume that. But I didn't say that out loud.

"I'll say a quote," said Nalini. "And you'll tell me which novel it's in."

"What if we haven't read it?" protested Preeti.

Nalini ignored her. "'Not accepting yourself the way you are is a waste of your existence,'" said Nalini.

"Lame," said Preeti. "I'm sure you've butchered someone's quotes again. Okay, who said it?"

Nalini chuckled. "Emmm . . . I can't remember."

We all laughed.

Preeti threw out her hands. "See." Let's do something else. Something more measurable. What about a movie?"

Nalini's eyebrows narrowed, almost touching each other. "Quote movies or watch a movie."

I didn't have a dog in this fight. Whatever Preeti and Nalini wanted to do, I would go along with it.

"So, you moved from Nigeria?" asked Preeti.

I nodded, but I could feel my body closing. The follow-up questions: Tell me about Nigeria. Do you like it here? What's your typical day? I didn't have answers. It wasn't something I wanted to talk about. How would they react if they knew the truth?

"Is it hot in Nigeria?" asked Nalini.

"Probably like India," said Preeti, channel-surfing.

"Yes," I said, and Preeti and Nalini went about talking about their visit to India and how hot it was when they visited.

"Ngozi, you don't talk much," said Preeti.

I nodded. "But I do talk, just warming up."

"My mom says I talk too much," Preeti said. "That means you're a good listener then. We'll get along just fine."

5

"Remember, if you need directions or anything, ask your fellow students," said Mom. "If they can't help, ask a teacher, or go to the principal's office."

I nodded, afraid to speak. We'd seen Mr. Holden last week when Mom and Dad took me to enroll. My whole body was tense. The more I looked around, the more anxious I became. *Keep calm, you'll be all right once you get out of the car.* The car inched forward in the carpool as parents or the yellow school bus dropped off students. I wanted this moment to continue forever so I wouldn't have to get out of the car.

"You have the class schedule Mr. Holden gave you?"

I nodded again. I had the map of the school clutched in my fist. As it approached my turn, my scalp itched. I took a few deep breaths to calm myself. *It's only school, there's nothing to fear.* I was just lying to myself, this was a different environment from the one I was used to. Boys and girls hurried along, interacting with each other as if they were all siblings. All my life I'd worn a uniform to school. I associated uniforms with orderliness. It felt strange going to school in my regular clothes and seeing other students with backpacks and regular clothes in school.

"Here we go, Ngozi." Mom stopped in front of the school. She bit her lower lip and tried to smile. She looked as concerned as I was.

"You have my number. Call if there's any problem."

I got out of the car and patted my jeans pocket; my cell phone was still there. In my pen case was twenty dollars from my monthly allowance.

I'd told Dad I didn't need money since they'd already provided me more than enough, but he said to keep it, just in case.

Other kids in the carpool got out of the car and walked into the building. I did the same when it was my turn, as if I'd done it before a thousand times. I didn't look back as Mom drove off.

The corridors looked familiar but different. When I'd taken the tour with the principle, the halls were empty, but now, full of students, it looked and felt like another place. I went in the direction where I knew the lockers would be.

Then there were the boys. For the past five years, I attended an all-girls school. Since elementary school, I hadn't been in such proximity with a lot of boys. I felt out of place.

I glanced around, looking for another complexion as mine, but there was none. Where was Preeti? Was I alone?

"Hi!" a voice yelled behind me.

I whirled around to see a girl waving at another girl down the hall.

I didn't know whom to make eye contact with, or not, along the hallways. Not that anybody paid attention to me. Boys and girls were all over the place, smiling, hugging, or talking. I hoped that familiarity would come to me soon.

I prayed somebody would stop me and say they hadn't

seen me in school before. *Are you new? I don't think I've seen you around before*, they would ask. *Yes, I am*, would be my reply. Fresh off the boat. The chances of that happening were close to impossible.

I put my backpack in the locker Mr. Holden had assigned me. The first class I had for the day was chemistry. I followed the map and found the chemistry room. Some students were already seated. On the blackboard, someone had written: "Locate your name on the desk, and that's your spot."

I found my name, sat down, and looked around at the other students. They were talking and goofing around. A few looked at me and looked away. It was obvious they'd all known each other since elementary school. I was the new girl, out of place. I wondered if I would ever make friends.

A hand tapped me on the shoulder. I jumped.

Had I taken someone's spot?

"Sorry, I didn't mean to startle you," said a voice behind me.

I spun around, ready to apologize for any transgression.

"Hi, I'm Jennifer, Jennifer Davis, and I think we're partners." A tall girl smiled at me.

I smiled, "I'm Ngozi Bashiru . . . Ngozi Obi." Heat rushed to my cheeks. I still had to get used to my new last name. She spoke fast and seemed to have a permanent smile on her face. She was pretty, like she could be on a magazine cover. Her green eyes captivated me. I stared at her.

"Repeat it? I don't want to mess it up!" she blurted.

"Sure, it's a Nigerian name," I said. I smiled and spelled my name.

"N-gozi?" said Jennifer. She raised one eyebrow and gave the "how did I do?" look.

I gave her a thumbs-up. "That's good." Even though she just said "N" and then added "Gozi," that was fine with me.

"Don't worry about it. The more you hear and say it, the better you'll get at it. Yours is easy."

"Yeah."

"Jennifer," I said sheepishly. Last night, I'd rehearsed how I would respond when spoken to and so far I hadn't let myself down.

"You're from Africa, right? Your English is excellent. What's the language spoken there?"

"Nigeria. It's English," I said. Dad had warned me. I would meet people that thought Africa was one country, instead of a continent with fifty-four recognized countries. And Mom had chimed in that people used to comment about her English when she was doing her residency, so I expected a similar question.

"Oh, Nigeria. Did you take any classes, like ESL courses?

"What's ESL?"

"English as a second language," said Jennifer.

"No, Nigeria used to be a British colony, so the official language is English."

"I didn't know," said Jennifer. "And I thought I knew a lot about the world. I'm glad I signed up for history class."

"Most educated Nigerians speak two languages," I continued. "English and their local dialect. And sometimes a third, Pidgin English, a combination of the local dialect and English."

"Hmm," said Jennifer. "So, how many do you speak?"

"I would say two. I grew up in the north, so I speak Hausa." I wanted to add I was about to learn Igbo because that's what my new parents spoke, but I stopped. Too much information.

I smiled. "Add Pidgin English, and it would be three."

Jennifer pulled out the chair beside me and sat down. "Wow, I speak English, maybe a few Spanish words here and there. My grandparents migrated from Poland, so I know a few words in Spanish . . ."

I looked down and away.

"Is anything wrong?" asked Jennifer. "I hope I said nothing to upset you."

6

As soon as Jennifer mentioned her grandparents, I realized I didn't know my heritage. My first name was Igbo, middle name Yoruba, and my last name was Hausa. Now it's Igbo.

My expression must have changed as these thoughts went through my head because Jennifer looked stricken.

"Did I say something wrong?"

I shook my head. "No, talking about Nigeria brought back memories." I smiled. "You've received a free course on Nigerian languages."

"Thank you. Any brothers and sisters?" asked Jennifer.

"It's only me. What about you?"

"I have a brother, Ken. He's in twelfth grade. I'll point him out when we run into him. He's a pain."

The student chatter died down like a radio with the volume turned down fast. I looked up to see a man writing on the blackboard. He wrote "Mr. Robert" and underlined it. He took a roll call and started the introduction to the periodic table. I'd already taken the course in Nigeria. I heaved a sigh of relief. So far, so good.

Jennifer and I both had history for the next period, so we went together. I was glad I didn't have to pull out my copy of the map of the school again. Jennifer had been in the school from middle school and, according to her, knew it inside out. I glanced at my copy of the class schedule to reconfirm that I had a history class. I hoped I'd have it memorized sooner rather than later.

"Where's the library?" I asked.

Jennifer pointed to our left. "In that direction, you can't miss it."

"I'll spend my free period after history class there and prepare for the next one."

Jennifer nudged me on the shoulder. "Aha, an astute student."

Jennifer and I walked to Mrs. Coleman's American history class. Some students were already there. I recognized some of the faces from chemistry.

"Hi, Jenny," a voice yelled. "I didn't know you enjoyed history stories. Who's your friend?"

I turned to look as heads turned to look at Jennifer and me. Every direction I looked, I met a pair of eyes already watching. I felt hot all over. Some looked away, and some didn't. The safest place to look was the floor, and that was what I did.

"Hi, Paul," said Jennifer. "This is my friend, Ngozi, she's new. Ngozi, Paul. Paul is my brother's friend. They get together to pollute the neighborhood."

My eyes widened. Pollute the neighborhood? Jennifer must have sensed my confusion.

"They're in a band together," said Jennifer and laughed. "They practice in our garage. Noise pollution."

"Hello," I said and glanced at Paul.

Jennifer headed toward three empty desks in the middle

of the classroom. She sat on the aisle seat, and I took the middle one. Just as I settled down, the chair beside me was yanked back, and Paul threw himself into it. He turned and faced me as if I was a fascinating creature.

I stiffened. My pulse raced. I looked at the window; we were one floor up. The door was still open. Good. I could escape from there. Paul ran his fingers through his black hair.

"So, how do you say your name?" asked Paul, smiling.

"Ngozi," I said slowly. I hoped he hadn't noticed how tense I was.

He shook his head. "I still don't get it." He reached for my hand on the desk. "Can I?"

It took every ounce of energy in my body not to scramble for the door. His skin looked so pale side by side with my dark skin. What did this boy want from me? He didn't want my hand; he was pointing at my notebook. I removed my hand, and he looked at my name on the book.

"Ah, that's how you spell it. Is the N silent?"

I remembered what Mom had told me. "No, it's not. It sounds like saying sing without the S."

"Ah," said Paul. "Like ing, ing, ingozi."

"Yes!" I said, surprised.

"Hello, class!" a voice barked in front of the class.

"Mrs. Coleman is here," said Paul.

I looked up to see a black woman standing in front of the class. My mouth dropped open. Mrs. Coleman looked very much like Mama Musa, who had a store across our gate in Lamija. If it weren't for the American accent, I would have yelled out, "Mama Musa what are you doing here?"

"See you later," said Paul.

Jennifer leaned over. "Where's Alex?" she whispered.

"I don't know," Paul whispered back and scrambled away to another seat in the back of the classroom.

"Everybody find a chair and sit down," said Mrs. Coleman, her eyes fixed on Paul.

Mrs. Coleman went straight to business and didn't act like there was a new student in her class.

She talked about the first settlers in America, how Christopher Columbus discovered America. About the Bering Theory, a land bridge thousands of years ago that early hunters had crossed from Asia into America.

"European settlers' adventures to what is now the United States started in the early 1600s," said Mrs. Coleman. She paused, looked around, and continued. "A lot of immigrants have come to America over the past three to four hundred years."

"Last twelve months too!" someone shouted.

My nostril flared. Someone was making fun of me.

"Hush it!" said Mrs. Coleman and continued as if the interruption and her response were a scheduled part of her lecture. "So, today, we'll begin a project to trace our family history using a genealogy tree. Questions?"

Nobody had questions.

"Good," said Mrs. Coleman. She gave a girl sitting in front sheets of paper. "Take one and pass it along." She looked up at the class. "This is your homework. Go to the website on the sheet of paper and follow the instructions. For those of you who want an in-depth study you can ask a parent or guardian to work with you and use sites like *Ancestry.com* or *23andMe* to trace your ethnicity."

I sighed. What type of family tree was I going to make? The bell rang for the end of class, and people filed out.

"You have a free period, right?" asked Jennifer.

"Yes." I stared at the piece of paper, not sure how to tackle this project.

"I'll look you up at the library after my class."

I smiled. "Jennifer, thank you so much. You made my first day very pleasant."

"The pleasure is all mine," said Jennifer. "See you later."

I watched Jennifer walk away. She was so nice. Loud voices drifted toward me from the door. I looked up to see Paul and his gang exit. *Thank God*, I thought.

I looked at the sheet of paper again and at the front of the class. Mrs. Coleman was still there putting books in her bag. I would ask her.

Mrs. Coleman raised her head as I approached. "Hi, Ngozi, right?" She smiled. "Mr. Holden told me about you. How can I help you?"

At Akarika Girls, I never would have approached a teacher, but here I was standing in front of Mrs. Coleman. "I . . . I have a question about the assignment."

"Hmmm, go ahead," said Mrs. Coleman.

My eyes darted from side to side. I wanted no one overhearing and making fun of me. I whispered. "I . . . . I was adopted, and I don't know who my biological parents are. So, who do I trace in my family history assignment?"

"Oh, that's easy," said Mrs. Coleman in her teaching voice. "It's up to you. Tracing the family tree of your adoptive parents is okay. By law, they are now your parents, and the adoption confers to you the legal rights a biological child of theirs would have. So, it's not a problem."

I nodded. "Thank you."

"As a side project, you can trace your biological parents' family tree too. Totally up to you. It might need digging into."

From what Mrs. Coleman said during the lecture, there were many websites and resources available to trace ancestors here in the US, but Nigeria would be close to impossible.

"Any problem?" asked Mrs. Coleman.

"My adoption was in Nigeria. What's your advice on the best way to approach it?"

"Start with your adoptive parents," said Mrs. Coleman. "Ask them questions and build up their tree. When you're done, then you can start the one for your biological parents, if you want to." She smiled and zipped up her bag. "That'll be the tricky one. Maybe your biological parents don't want to be found."

I nodded, but I didn't know where to start.

"But, remember," said Mrs. Coleman. "Before you start the search for your biological parents, think about it—why you want to know."

I left the classroom excited. A few seconds later, I realized I wasn't sure I was going the right way. I brought out the school map and tried to locate where I was. The library would be to my right. It wasn't that difficult to read. I stuffed the directions back in my bag, turned, and bumped into someone. Books clattered to the floor.

7

"I'm sorry, so sorry, it was my fault." I bent down and picked up the books.

"Watch where you're going," said the boy. He was on one knee, grabbing his books. He looked up, and for a second, our eyes lingered. My ears, neck, and face felt hot. I had picked up only one of his books. I handed it to him. He took the book, got up, and walked fast down the passage. I jumped to my feet and walked in the opposite direction he went. I hoped he wasn't mad at me. It was an accident. A few steps later I realized I was approaching the classroom I'd just left. I turned around and headed toward the library, careful not to bump into anyone again.

Jennifer came to the library and grabbed me. We went to the cafeteria, and I did whatever she did. She got a carton of milk and some chicken nuggets, and I did the same. I almost drenched myself trying to open the milk carton.

We sat on a table with some girls Jennifer knew. She introduced me, but nobody asked me how to pronounce my name this time. Most of the talk was about last weekend. Then the conversation moved to boys, which boy was cute and who did what. I thought about the boy I'd run into and wondered what his name was. Jennifer must have noticed my mind was drifting.

"What's your next class after lunch?" asked Jennifer.

I looked at my schedule. "Physical education."

Jennifer made a motion as if shooting a basket. "I can show you the rest of the school and then end up at the gym."

"Sounds good," I said. We left the cafeteria, and Jennifer pointed out the bathrooms, the labs, the classes, and the teachers' offices—most of the things the principal had shown me on the first day—and we ended up at the gym.

I'd brought shorts in my backpack but no T-shirt. I noticed other kids had a gym bag for their sneakers and gym stuff.

When we got there, two other classes were going on. The instructor had us warm-up. We ran laps around the court. It was demanding. The last time I ran this fast, I'd been running for my life in the bushes of Nigeria. I looked around me. I'd come a long way in a very short time.

My classmates dribbled and shot. I'd never been good at sports. I could run, I had the stamina, and that was it.

The trainer was very strict about the rules. His whistle went off every so often. One time, Jennifer passed the ball so I could take part. I ran with the ball toward the basket.

The coach went into overdrive with his whistle. "Traveling!" said the trainer and raised his hand.

I threw the ball to him.

"That was more like vacationing," said one of my classmates.

We practiced three-point shots and ran one more lap at the end of the period. I felt a dull pain on my thighs. I pushed the memory to the back of my mind. The final bell rang, and it was time to go.

"How are you getting home?" asked Jennifer.

"My mom will pick me up."

"Sometimes I walk, go by bus, or ride with my brother," said Jennifer. "I'll take the bus today. See you tomorrow, then."

There were two lines, one for students who rode the bus and the other for students who got picked up. Some students had their own cars, and they had designated parking spots.

"You made it through the first day. How was it?" asked Mom as we drove home.

"It was fine. The people were nice. This girl Jennifer Davis, my partner in the chemistry lab, she showed me around."

"That was very nice of her," said Mom.

"I didn't see Preeti in school, though."

"Oh, yes, her mom said she wasn't feeling well this morning. She stayed home."

When we got home, I dropped off my bag, washed my face, and ran downstairs.

"What do you want to eat?" asked Mom.

"No, what do you want?" I asked. "I'll make it for both of us."

Mom smiled. "There's some egusi soup in the fridge. You can make the garri. I'll heat it up."

On weekends Mom would make different soups and stew and put them in the freezer. So all we needed to do for lunch was make the garri or pounded yam. For dinners, sometimes we cooked from scratch depending on the day of the week. But there was always stew in the fridge and a backup in the freezer, so you could eat it with rice, yams, or potatoes.

"You survived your first day at school. How was it? Any new friends?" asked Dad when he came home from work later that night.

"It was all right," I said. "I made a few friends."

"I'll run upstairs and get out of these scrubs," said Dad and headed for the stairs.

Mom looked at me. "Do you want to make food for your dad?"

I nodded and wondered why people in America, instead of telling you to do something, pose it as a question.

"Ngozi, your dad prefers pounded yam. I'll show you how to make it."

I marveled at the yam flour. Instead of boiling yam and then pounding it in a mortar until it was all mashed, as we did at Auntie Halima's kitchen, Mom showed me how to make it like mashed potato.

"*Adaeze, dalu,*" said Dad as he washed his hands in the kitchen sink. "Do you know what that means?"

I dipped my head. "I know it's Igbo. *Dalu* means thanks. *Adaeze* is a girl's name. Thank you, *Adaeze*?"

Dad laughed. "Ngozi is an Igbo name, your parents are Igbo, yet you're fluent in English and Hausa, not Igbo."

"Stop teasing her," said Mom.

Dad laughed. "*Adaeze* is a girl's name. But it means 'the king's first daughter.' So, 'Princess, thank you.'"

I snapped my fingers. "I knew it!"

Dad started with his food. He dipped his fingers into the pounded yam and rolled the fufu in his palm, poking it at intervals with his fingers, as if they had taste buds and tasted the food before his mouth did. He dipped the fufu in the egusi soap and pushed the bolus into his mouth and swallowed in one loud gulp without chewing. My mouth flooded with saliva. Watching Dad would increase anyone's appetite.

"Ngozi has a family tree assignment from school," said Mom.

Dad swallowed another huge bolus. "Really?" He stuck

each finger into his mouth one after the other, licking them clean and then carving out another portion of fufu, which he molded into shape.

I wanted to attempt the assignment alone and ask for help when I got stuck.

"That's exciting!" said Dad. "I've always wanted to create a family tree but never had the time. When do we start?"

8

For a second, I didn't know what to say. I'd expected Dad to be mad that my teacher suggested making a family tree despite knowing I was adopted.

Dad pushed his plate to the side, walked over to the kitchen sink, and washed his hands. "When do we start?" he repeated. He dried his hands on the hand towel. "Do we need to do the sputum thing for DNA analysis?"

I frowned. "Emmm . . . I don't think so. Mrs. Coleman only talked about asking questions, unless you want to dig deep."

"You two can start off," said Mom. "I'll clear the dishes." She got up and took the dishes to the kitchen.

"I'll ask the questions, and you supply the answers."

"Okay," said Dad.

I ran upstairs and came down with my notebook and the handout from school. I started the tree with Dad's great-grandparents on his father's side because he could remember that far back. Dad came up with the answers as if he had been working on a family tree in his mind already.

"Let's see now, I think Uncle Fred died from cancer of the

bone or blood. I can't remember. I was a little boy then. But his wife died from heartbreak. Uncle Peter is still alive. Then there is . . ."

"This is excellent," I said. It went fast. Dad assured me it was accurate to the best of his knowledge. I'd learned the names of my uncles, aunts, and cousins and studied at the same time. Neat.

"Some names I can't remember," said Dad. "I'll call Nigeria in the morning and find out. It's already past midnight there."

We finished Dad's tree with a few empty slots to plug. It was now time for Mom's side of the family. She remembered from her grandparents down.

"How many sisters do you have, and what were their names?" I asked.

Mom's eyebrows furrowed. "I don't know for sure."

"What!"

"Hold on, I'll explain. My mother had three girls, Ijeoma, Ifeoma, and me. And three boys, Chike, Ikenna, and Uche. My father had three wives . . . some wives we knew about and some we never knew about until their kids showed up." Mom chuckled. "We'll call tomorrow. Or maybe just stick to my side of the family so that things don't get muddled."

Dad looked at Mom. "Do you think we should let them know now about Ngozi?"

"Hmm, I don't know," said Mom. "What do you think?" Mom threw the question right back.

My pulse raced. Mom and Dad hadn't told their families about me? Were they that disappointed in me? Dad must have seen the look on my face.

"It has nothing to do with you, Ngozi," said Dad. "After Nkechi got your text, she called the number, which was

Maryam's phone. At first, nobody answered. We were so worried.

"Maryam answered the next day and said they didn't know your whereabouts," said Mom. "but, that she thinks you might have been kidnapped at school. I thought she was joking. She was so nonchalant about it. Then I found out it was true from the papers. I blamed myself for not trying harder to adopt you after Matron passed. I didn't think I would be able to forgive myself. I felt I had let the other two women down, and you too."

"Which . . . which women?" I asked, my voice small.

Mom glanced at Dad and back at me. "You don't know? Nobody told you anything? Come. I thought you knew."

We walked to the living room. Mom sat on the couch and patted the space beside her. I sat down. My stomach felt hollow. It felt hot in the room. Dad sat on the couch armrest beside Mom.

"Let me start from the beginning," said Mom. I'd just graduated from medical school and was doing my internship. When the schedule came out, my first posting was in pediatrics, and they'd posted me to the neonatology emergency room." Mom smiled.

"You stood out. Neonates are babies aged from birth to four weeks. You were a year old. You clearly didn't belong there. So I asked Matron Bashiru."

"You knew my mom that well?" I asked.

"Yes." Mom pointed at Dad. "So did he. In fact, every house officer in my graduating class that did their house job at the teaching hospital must have come in contact with you."

Dad nodded. "That's true, over a twelve-month period, about thirty doctors or more would have passed through."

Mom exhaled. "Anyway, Matron said you'd been brought in from the motherless babies' home at Warawa with meningitis a year earlier. After they treated you and you recovered, the parents that had wanted to adopt you never showed to take you. The home didn't want you back either. They didn't believe you were cured and might cause an outbreak at the motherless babies' home. So you stayed on at the emergency room. You were such a beautiful baby."

Mom's voice broke, tears streamed down her cheeks.

"It's all right," said Dad and rubbed Mom's shoulders.

"When Nkechi finished her rotation," said Dad, "she worried about what would become of you? Not just her. Others were concerned, but everybody was getting on with their lives. Nobody did anything to find a solution. She, Matron, and Nurse Balogun struck a deal. Matron Bashiru would adopt you, and Nurse Balogun and Nkechi would become your godmothers and contribute to your upkeep."

"It worked as planned," said Mom in a whisper, until . . . First we lost Nurse Balogun in a car accident in Lagos, then your mother, Matron Bashiru. Matron and her brother were close, and that was why he treated you as his own daughter. Then we lost him too. I tried to bring you over to the States then, but you didn't want to come." Mom's body shook with sobs. "Then we got your text . . . and heard about the kidnapping. We took the next plane out to see what we could do."

Nobody spoke. Mom sniffled. My vision became blurry. Mom hugged me, and we sobbed together, with Dad joining in the group hug.

I laughed. "Now I know why I have Igbo, Hausa, and Yoruba names."

I went back to my room. The next step was to type the information into my computer. I turned on my laptop, and Dad's information popped up, new window tabs for Medscape, Dad's medical school alumni group on a social media website. I always had to close several windows before

I could use the laptop. Eyes glued to the screen, I opened a blank document and started to type. I transferred the information I'd collected from Mom and Dad to the report.

Writing up my adoptive parents' family trees made me realize that Matron was my tree. When I finished, I decided to create one for my biological parents. The blinking cursor urged me to write, but I had nothing, only tightness in my chest. Who in their right minds would abandon a baby? Who in their right minds would abandon me? Despite having two loving adoptive parents, somehow I felt alone.

I tried to remember Matron's face, but I couldn't. Shame washed over me. How could I have forgotten her? I went to the closet and dug out her picture and refreshed my mind.

The computer screen had shut off from inactivity, replaced by my reflection. My lips twitched and trembled. I fought hard not to cry.

9

The two girls waded through the white sand and reached the man in the uncompleted building.

He was in his late twenties. Bushy hair, scanty beard, and a dirty white singlet with holes. His shorts were equally tattered. His dark skin was dry with blotches of white over the back of his hands. Cement could do that to you.

A cigarette dangled from his lips. He grabbed it, took a long drag, and blew out smoke through his nose.

"Sannu, hello," he said and smiled, exposing a gap tooth. "Put your fruits down." He switched to Pidgin English.

The girls put their fruits down. "Which one do you want?" asked the girl with the banana tray.

I woke up before the man made his choice. I tried to go back to sleep and continue the dream where I'd left off. It didn't happen. Who were the people in the dream? What was going on? I knew it must have something to do with me, but how?

I spent what was left of the night thinking about what

Mom had said. I wondered why Matron never told me about the pact they had. Maybe she'd planned to and never got to it. Nobody ever expected to die in an automobile accident.

But Maryam knew I was adopted. Uncle Thomas must have told his wife, and she, her daughter, or Maryam eavesdropped. At least that had put an end to the curiosity of having such a unique name. Who were my biological parents?

The next morning, Mom dropped me off at school. The discussion the previous night had instilled confidence in me, some order among the chaos.

"Are you sure you'll be okay taking the bus back?" asked Mom.

Mom and Dad had already done more than enough for me. The least I could do was find my way back from school. I thought Mom would prefer to drive straight back from work, which she had done for many years before I came into their lives.

"It's straightforward. I'll ask for directions when I need them," I said.

Mom smiled. "Someone who asks for directions never gets lost. It's a popular Igbo saying of wisdom."

I got out of the car and entered the building. Tuesday was like Monday except for starting in some new classes.

"It's a class about learning how to write a story, like novels," explained Jennifer when I asked her what it was. It never occurred to me that writing was a skill that someone could learn. I always thought writing was one of those gifts you were born with.

"I hope I'll write a story one day," I said, all shy.

Jennifer gave me a thumbs-up. "Then you're in the right place."

Mrs. Basogne's creative writing class was an eye-opener.

She taught things I knew were components of a story, but I never realized that most stories I enjoyed followed the same plot structure. Act I, Act II, and Act III. She gave us an assignment to read *To Kill a Mockingbird*.

At lunch, I sat with Jennifer. Paul saw us and left his friends and joined us at our table.

"What do you think of Falls Lake High so far?" asked Paul. "Are there a lot of differences from your old school?"

I choked on the apple juice I was sipping and went into a coughing fit.

"Differences?" I asked and wiped my mouth. "It's like night and day. First, it was an all-girls school."

Paul leaned closer, a smile on his face. "Really?"

"Yes, no boys, and most of the students lived in the dormitories."

Paul had a disappointed look. "No boys at all?"

"No boys," I said. "And nobody looks like you."

"What do you mean, nobody looks like me?" asked Paul.

"There are no white people. You'd be in a sea of black faces, unless you consider Felicia, an albino in my school. We call her 'the unfortunate European'."

"Oh, that is cruel," said Paul." Was it an inner-city school?"

"Inner-city? No, Akarika is a village in Nigeria." I looked around. "The school population reminds me of here, but the opposite. I'm the only black person here. There, you would be the only white person."

Paul looked around. "You're right! I never thought of that. Do you feel hemmed in?"

"Ngozi!"

I whirled around, surprised someone was yelling my name. "Preeti!"

She walked toward us with a big smile on her face. She

looked elegant in a white top and a pair of jeans ripped at the knees.

"You two know each other?" asked Jennifer.

"Yes, our moms work together," said Preeti.

"I heard you were sick. Are you better?" I asked.

"Yes, sorry I wasn't there to help you on your first day."

"But I met Jennifer, and she's the best," I said.

Preeti pulled out a chair and sat down. "Did I miss anything yesterday?"

"Just the usual," said Jennifer.

"I had algebra earlier, and it's driving me crazy," said Preeti. "I don't know why they teach stuff you'll never use in real life."

Jennifer looked at her watch. "We have to go. History." She jumped to her feet and carried her tray.

I did the same. I placed my empty tray on the counter with the others. Preeti got up and followed us, mumbling something I couldn't get.

In Mrs. Coleman's class, as we waited for the lecture to start, Jennifer talked about her brother and his friends. How they wanted to have a party at their home when her parents went out of town.

"I told them about this new girl in school that is pretty and nice and doesn't seem interested in boys—"

Heat rushed to my cheeks. "I like boys, just that I have other things on my mind." I wanted to disappear.

"What else could be on your mind?" said Preeti, smiling.

"What were the boys in Nigeria like? Are they—" Jennifer stopped talking, and her eyes drifted to the door. I turned to look.

A tall boy with an athletic build, dressed in T-shirt and blue jeans with his hair in spikes, walked in. He looked like he was in a boy band. Jennifer and Preeti sat up straight as he approached. It was obvious they both wanted his attention.

"Hello, girls." His voice was deep. Close up, he was even more gorgeous.

"Hi, Alex," said Jennifer. "We didn't see you yesterday either."

Alex sighed. "I had a few errands to run. Who else wasn't in school?"

Jennifer pointed at Preeti.

Alex jerked his head toward Preeti. "Hi, pretty." He said it as if he referred to her beauty.

Jennifer's eyes narrowed, and she looked at Preeti, then Alex. Preeti opened her mouth to speak, but Alex beat her to it.

"Who's your friend?" Alex extended his hand toward me for a handshake.

For a moment, I forgot my name as his eyes bore into mine.

"Emm, Ngozi meet Alex Wade. Alex, Ngozi Obi," said Jennifer.

I tried to stare him down, but I was too shy. I looked away. "Pleased to meet you," I said. I found my voice.

Preeti wasn't happy. Just then the teacher walked in.

"Ah, Mr. Wade, you joined us today."

"I had an emergency yesterday," said Alex as he walked toward a seat.

Once everybody sat down, Mrs. Coleman started her lecture. I thought she would refer to Preeti's absence too, but she didn't.

She had gone on for about twenty minutes when she stopped talking. I looked at what she was looking at. Alex was whispering into his phone. *He's in deep trouble*, I thought. The teacher would take his phone and march him to the principal's office. That is, if we'd been in Akarika Girls.

"Put that phone away, Mr. Wade, or I will place you in detention," said Mrs. Coleman.

To my surprise, Alex put it away. I thought he had a plan to be disruptive, but maybe he had an emergency. As the lecturer continued, Alex put his phone under the table and stabbed at the screen with a finger. When the bell rang, Mrs. Coleman gave us another assignment and left.

Alex walked to where Jennifer and I were putting away our books. "What's the assignment?" asked Alex.

I told him. Jennifer finished packing her bags and hooked her hand around Alex's.

"I'm going on the bus today, are you coming?" I looked at Jennifer.

Jennifer looked at Alex. "No, Alex will drop me off."

"I'll walk with you to the bus line," said Preeti, walking up to us. "I'm taking the bus too."

We waited in line with the other kids, and at last, it was our turn. The bus made frequent stops, but I enjoyed the ride, looking at different neighborhoods, and how other students interacted with each other, telling jokes, pulling pranks on each other. The kids' behavior was no different from those of Nigerian schoolchildren.

"See you tomorrow," said Preeti as she got off the bus. "Don't forget or nod off. Your stop is the third one."

I got off at the third stop. Walking would have been faster.

Dad had shown me how to punch in the garage door code, but what if it didn't work? I would have to remain outside until Mom got home. I punched in the numbers, and the garage door hummed and lifted. I exhaled and went inside through the door that led into the house. A beep went off and a female mechanical voice said I had thirty seconds to disarm the home alarm. I punched in the right numbers and the flashing light on the alarm went off.

I went to the pantry, got cookies, and filled a cup with orange juice. I did my homework and watched a Nigerian movie. Then my eyes fell on the wall with a portrait of Mom and Dad beside the TV. But it was the portrait below that caught my eye, a picture of Mom, Dad, and me taken at the elementary school fair the week I came. They must have put it up last night after I went up to bed. My vision clouded. I was home.

10

On Thursday during chemistry, Paul rushed over to where Jennifer and I were doing an acid-base titration. He pulled off his safety goggles. "Guys, Preeti agreed to go with me to the dance." He let out a boyish giggle. "Who are you guys going with?"

I poked my cheek with my tongue. "What dance?"

"Paul Tarval! Back to your station!" said the chemistry teacher.

"Busted! See ya!" Paul walked away with a spring in his step.

"What's he talking about?" I asked.

Jennifer's shoulders slumped. "It's a dance organized by the culture club. We'd talked about it before you joined us."

"Oh, okay." I smiled. "You should go with Alex. You guys look good together."

Jennifer looked away. "He hasn't asked yet. What about you?" She fiddled with her goggles.

I chuckled. "I only just heard about it. I've never gone to any dance." I shoulder-bumped her and grinned. "Don't wait for him; ask him!"

"I don't know," said Jennifer.

I glanced at Jennifer and wished she would cheer up. It was only a dance.

After chemistry, Jennifer left for econ, and I went to the library to read up for my next class: biology.

The alarm on my phone went off with flashing lights. I shut it off. Time to go to creative writing already. I closed my book and stuffed it into my backpack. I zipped it halfway and took off, mad that I'd spent the last hour reading the same paragraph, my mind on Jennifer and Alex.

I headed toward the creative writing class. Halfway, I felt the weight of my backpack shift, and I heard the clatter of books as they hit the floor.

"Ahhh!" I gritted my teeth and bent to pick them up.

"Ouch, sorry," said a voice.

I'd bumped heads with a figure that had come to help. I looked up. "Alex!"

"Hi, Ngozi."

Those blue eyes looked right into mine. I wished Jennifer hadn't mentioned them; now I was drawn to them.

"Hello, Alex." Heat rushed to my cheeks.

He held out one of my books.

"Thanks," I said.

He got up as I did and handed me the rest of my books.

"Whenever I see you, you're with Jennifer. This is the first time I've seen you alone. I hope I'm not intruding on your personal time."

"I thought you came to help me pick up my books," I said with a smile.

Alex looked like he was contemplating something. "There's this dance next Friday, and I'd like to take you."

My nostrils flared. I had to come up with a solid excuse to say no. Jennifer was waiting for him to ask her.

"Yes! Well . . . I mean, no! I'm unavailable that day."

Alex looked like he'd been slapped. "Can't you be unavailable another day?"

Before he could protest, I continued. "You should ask Jennifer. You two look good together."

He stared at me as if I'd made the stupidest suggestion ever. Then he nodded.

Pulse racing, I stuffed the rest of my books in my backpack. "I have to run. See you."

At creative writing class, my mind was not there. I kept thinking about Alex and how he'd asked me to the dance. Only a week has passed by and I was already in a challenging situation with my new friends. *Ngozi, be careful. My friendship with Jennifer is more important than any boy.* Maybe Alex saw me like a new toy to play with. If they only knew. Would they still be my friends if they knew?

Alex was waiting outside the classroom door when Jennifer and I came out.

Jennifer beamed. "Hey. I was just about to look for you."

"I'm here to see you too," said Alex.

Did he come to ask her to the dance? I figured I'd better give them space. "I'll go ahead and join the bus line."

"No, wait," said Jennifer. She turned to Alex. "Why don't you pick me up for a drive later in the evening? There's—"

"What time?" asked Alex, nodding his head.

My phone, all of a sudden, felt like a stone in my pocket. I walked away to give them privacy and took the phone out. I felt left out. Pretending to be busy, I typed a text I would not send. When would I be hit by the boy bug and go boy crazy like Jennifer and the other girls in class?

Jennifer hurried after me. "Wait for me, Ngozi." She tapped me on the shoulder and smiled as if she had just won some kind of prize. "Isn't he cute? I'm going to ask him when he comes."

"You're a lost cause," I said, smiling and shaking my head, fascinated that she could go mad for a boy.

Friday morning was all talk about Alex from Jennifer. They would go to the dance together.

Our last class for the day was English, and for some reason, it went a little longer. Alex would give Jennifer a ride home. They had invited me, but I declined. Now I had to catch the bus.

Carrying my books in my hand, I dashed out of the class-room and ran straight into a boy.

"Watch where you're going," said the boy.

"Sorry, so sorry. I was rushing for the bus."

He helped me pick up my books and handed them over. "Just watch where you're going," repeated the boy.

This time his voice wasn't so harsh. Our eyes lingered, and I took off toward the bus line. The bus was pulling out of school as I got there, leaving in its wake the smell of diesel fumes. I watched it turn onto the road, the engine grunting as it picked up speed.

I felt like a stone had been dropped into the pit of my stomach. Should I run after the bus? That's what I would have done if I were still in Lamija. But was it allowed here? I let out a big sigh. If only that guy hadn't knocked down my books.

I reached into my pocket and pulled out my phone. Mom said to call her when I needed help. But she was busy and calling her would distract her from work. No, I would not call her. Maybe I should walk. The way I knew to our house was on a highway, and I couldn't remember seeing anybody walking there. Who knew whether I would break the law or put myself in danger if I walked?

"Hi," a voice said beside me. "You missed the bus?"

I spun around. It was the boy I'd run into a few minutes ago. He stared ahead where the bus had been. It was all his fault, but I didn't say that. "Yes."

He turned and faced me. "I could drive you home."

There was something familiar about him. His blue eyes bore into mine as if he'd cast a spell on me.

11

———

A prickly itch traveled from my scalp down my back. I fought an incredible urge to trail it and scratch. I moved my backpack from my left shoulder to my right shoulder, the movement giving me some needed relief. The last time I got into a car—or rather was forced onto a truck by a stranger—it didn't end well for me.

He must be a student here since I'd found him inside the building. I took a deep breath and exhaled. But this was America. I shouldn't let the past define me. Yet the driving force of our future comes from past experiences.

The boy patted his hair with his palm. "So, do you need a ride?" His lips curved in a crooked grin.

I looked at my cell phone and wondered what to do. Should I call Mom? She'd want to know why I missed the bus. Not that she would be mad. I didn't feel like bothering her.

"I'm a bonafide student here," said the boy. "You can ask anybody." He turned to look around, and his voice trailed off. Nobody was within reach. "I made you miss the bus. The least I can do is give you a ride home."

"I appreciate the offer. My house is not too far, and it's sunny and nice." I looked up. "I'll walk."

"Are you sure?" asked the boy.

I nodded.

"All right, sorry again. Maybe I'll run into you at school. No, wrong choice of words, but you know what I mean. More like see you at school." He gestured with his hands.

I laughed, and the boy drove off. I started to walk. There was something about his smile, as if there was something he knew, like a secret I didn't. *Ngozi, you're getting paranoid.* This is America and a nice neighborhood. That was a nice guy, you should have gone for the ride.

I hadn't done this much walking in a long time. In fact, the last time I traveled a considerable distance on foot was the night we left the terrorist hideout. *There you go again thinking about what you shouldn't be thinking about.* If I were in Lamija, a motorbike would have pulled up by now and offered to give me a ride at a price. I smiled. I wondered if it was against the law here for motorbike taxis to operate.

The sun wasn't harsh. It was pleasant, and I hadn't broken out in a sweat. A few minutes later, a blue Honda Accord passed and honked. A hand shot out of the window and waved at me. I waved back out of courtesy. Ahead of me, I saw kids I was sure were students from Falls Lake High. I walked closer to them. Safety in numbers.

I got home without incident even though it was a longer walk than I'd expected. I was tired and my legs and knees hurt. I'd walked longer distances before; why was I so tired?

I entered through the garage, dropped my backpack, turned on the TV, and went to the fridge. Time for some ice cream to cool me down. I collapsed into the couch. The refrigerator was one of those ones with two doors, the freezer on the left with an ice dispenser on the door and the fridge on the right. I took out the Snickers ice cream, which was just as I'd left it. I grabbed a spoon and threw myself on the couch.

"Thank God it's Friday," I whispered and smiled. *That was a handsome boy.* I hoped I'd run into him again at school. I stuffed my face with ice cream.

12

Saturdays seemed to have become a bonding day for Mom and me. Dad left us girls to get on with it. We agreed that if he came back early enough, we'd all go to the movies.

"Make a list of the things we need to get from the grocery store," said Mom.

"Okay." I opened the fridge and looked for things we had run out of. This was a familiar task. I did this at Lamija at Fatima's beckoning. *How was she doing?* I wondered. I would have called her every day, but guilt wouldn't let me. I felt like I'd abandoned her. Knowing her, she would say to focus on where I was. I pushed the thought away.

The milk was low. The crate of a dozen eggs was down to four. Orange juice was halfway. I added it to the list. In the freezer, there was no more ice cream, so I added it to the list. There were two packs of skinless chicken thighs; they could go fast.

"Mom, should I add more chicken to the list?"

"No, that's enough. Just add some mixed vegetables."

We got in the car and drove off. We drove down the road I

took while walking back from school. "The distance from school looks short when you're driving, but not that close when you walk it."

"Did you walk back from school?" asked Mom with some hesitation.

"Yes, I missed the bus yesterday, and I walked. It was—"

"No, Ngozi, you should have called me as we planned," said Mom.

"It wasn't much of a distance," I said. I felt the argumentative side of me rearing its head.

"That's beside the point. Anything could have happened," Mom spat. "You could have gotten lost or kidnapped or gotten in an accident."

I was quiet, this was the first time Mom had ever raised her voice. "I'm sorry. I didn't want to bother you at work. I know you're busy."

Mom smiled. "No, you won't be bothering me." Her voice had returned to normal. "Just call, okay? If I'm busy, we'll come up with a plan."

We rode on in silence. I didn't know what to feel.

Mom glanced at me. "Sorry, I yelled. It's just that I wouldn't forgive myself if anything happened to you."

I tried to come up with something to say to cover the awkward silence, but nothing came to mind.

"You know, when you get your driver's license, I'll leave all the grocery shopping to you."

"Me, drive?" I chuckled.

"One day you will. I think you can get a learner permit at sixteen. Let's wait until you get used to the way of life here in the US."

The thought that one day I would drive terrified me. I'd do my best not to encourage her. Mom drove into the parking lot and looked for a parking space.

"I always look for parking near the cart return," said Mom. "I hate having to walk a mile to return the cart after loading my stuff onto the car."

Mom led the way, and I pushed the cart. She knew where things where. The store was busy. It seemed as though weekends were not the best time to shop. Everybody was there. Parents ran after small children as they grabbed stuff from the shelves to stuff the cart.

Mom wanted to go to the mall to do more shopping, but because we had ice cream in the car, we went home to drop the groceries off.

Mom thumped her forehead with her palm. "We should have gone to the mall first and the grocery store last," said Mom.

The mall was even more jammed than the grocery store. There we didn't have a choice about where to park. Empty spots were quite some distance from the mall entrance. We parked and walked. I never liked window shopping; it made little sense longing for things I couldn't afford. Spare yourself that heartache and only shop when you need to get something. But Mom was a different animal; she enjoyed shopping.

"Look around. Find things you like and put them in the cart," said Mom as soon as we entered an expensive-looking shop.

"All right." I walked around, looking at the clothes. Then looking at people shopping.

"Do you need any help?" asked a voice behind me.

I turned to see a man wearing a black shirt with the logo of the store on it. "No, just looking around. Thank you." I smiled.

"Let me know if you need help."

"I don't think I will, but thank you." I continued to travel the aisles. Mom had added a few things to her cart. I walked over to her.

"See anything you like?" asked Mom.

I shook my head. "Just browsing."

"You know what, your job is to find yourself a pair of jeans and a blouse or T-shirt to go with it, then bring it. That will be my cue to stop shopping. I've already got a lot of things here I don't need. The sooner you bring something, the earlier we will leave."

I remembered Preeti's jeans with the horizontal tear and decided I should get jeans like those. As I searched the jeans section, from the corner of my eyes, I realized the store attendant was always around me. Was I becoming a guy magnet? Now that I needed help, he wouldn't come and ask. I found a pair of jeans similar to Preeti's. Excited, I looked up to find Mom, and the guy was still lurking around. Was he following me? I saw Mom and walked to her.

"Found something?" asked Mom.

I raised the pair of jeans.

She gave it a look. "It's ripped. Young people." She shook her head. "What about a blouse or a T-shirt?"

"I couldn't find any I liked," I said.

"Okay, let's go pay."

As we stood in line, I noticed the store guy that had been hovering around me. I leaned closer to Mom and whispered, "That man over there, he's been following me around the store since we came in."

Mom looked and nodded. "It's SWB?"

"SWB?"

"Shopping while black. Some people judge you by the color of your skin. He must have thought because you're black, you would steal something."

"Steal something?" I was confused.

"Sometimes you get that too when you're driving, more so if you have a nice car."

"DWB," I said.

Mom laughed. "You're catching on."

"I've gotten that on the plane too," said Mom. "One time someone was sick, and the attendants asked for a doctor. When I showed up, they wanted to see my credentials, but not for the white gentleman that came up too. It blows my mind. Why would someone say they are a doctor when they are not?"

I looked at the guy who had been following me. Apart from Preeti, my friends in school, even the cute boy, were all white. Did they harbor such sentiments?

"Come on, it's our turn," said Mom.

13

The only thing I missed in school on Monday was the boy who had offered me a ride on Friday. I thought I would see him, but it had been four weeks since that incident, and I hadn't seen him. It was as if he appeared, impressed me, and disappeared.

I'd gotten used to my routine in school and knew my way around. Jennifer, Preeti, Paul, Alex, and I were more like a gang now. They had their culture club dance a few Fridays before, and all assured me I'd missed nothing. We sat in the cafeteria during lunch and I looked around to see if he was there. I never told Jennifer or Preeti about him. I'm sure they would have laughed at me for having walked home instead of hopping into his car.

"We have gym after lunch," said Jennifer.

Jennifer was good at managing our schedules. For the past few weeks just thinking about any physical activity got me tired. "Why did they have to put it after lunch? Nobody should exercise after eating." I leaned toward Preeti, who was busy typing furiously on her phone. "What are you mad about?"

"My cousin is getting married in Pennsylvania over the weekend and sent a reminder," said Preeti. "I don't want to go. My dad's side of the family is all dentists and doctors. And their kids my age are following in their parents' footsteps. Then there's the matchmaking . . . oh."

"Matchmaking?" I asked.

"Not with my cousins but with other Indian families."

"But your mom's a doctor. You don't want to become a doctor too?" I asked.

Preeti laughed. "I'm a Jersey girl, and I'm not interested in becoming a doctor. Not now, anyway."

I shrugged. "So, tell your cousins you can't come."

"Right! But it's not up to me. My parents love to go for these things."

I punched my phone, and it lit up. "Jennifer, time to go. Creative writing," I said.

Jennifer was standing. "I was ready minutes ago."

Preeti stood up, still tapping at her phone. "I have biology. See you guys later."

We left the others. What I'd wanted to ask Preeti about was going out with a boy. What happened when you went on a date with a guy? I didn't know why I didn't want to ask Jennifer. She might have just said, "Come with us." That I didn't want to do.

"What's your plan after school?" asked Jennifer.

"Nothing. Do homework. Watch a movie or read." I shrugged. "Or both."

"I think there's a football game or practice later in the evening at the school field. You should come over."

"Who are you going with?"

"Can't say for sure. Sometimes I'm bored at home and go on my own. Other times, my brother or any of his friends would come with me."

"What time will you be there?"

"Like 6:30, 7:00, maybe."

Mom would be back by then. I didn't want to walk to the field and get in her bad book again. Not a good feeling. It was more likely she would suggest dropping me off.

"So, are you going to come?" asked Jennifer.

I wasn't sure, but I nodded. "I'll come."

14

Everybody loves Fridays, and Mom was no exception. I knew she would be pleased when I told her I wanted to go to school to hang out. "I know you don't want me walking, but I think I'll be fine."

"I'll drop you. That's no problem."

Mom looked around as we drove to school. As she eased into a parking spot by the football field, I looked around for any sign of Jennifer.

"You see her yet?" asked Mom.

"No, I'll go look in the seats. Maybe she's there."

"You know, maybe it's not that bad to walk," said Mom. "I think I overreacted. If you need a ride, call me."

I got out of the car and shut the door just as the window went down.

"Send me a text when you meet up with her, okay?"

I nodded. Mom drove off, and I walked toward the small gate that led into the field. Two teams, one in white and the other in blue, were playing. I'd glimpsed American football on television, but this was the first time I'd watched it live. It amused me that it was called football, and yet the players played the game with everything but their feet.

I approached the bleachers, looking for Jennifer. A lot of kids from school where there. There were some adults too, parents I guess, but no sign of Jennifer. Maybe she was on her way. I climbed the bleachers and took a seat. Most of the kids came in groups, and they were chatting or chasing each other around, having a good time. I felt all alone sitting there by myself.

"N-GOZI!" a voice yelled.

I whirled toward the sound. A stone's throw to my left, two girls and a boy were on the bleachers. One girl was waving at me with both hands. I raised my hand, unsure who it was. Was that Jennifer? I waved back and smiled. Yes, it was Jennifer.

"Come over!" said Jennifer.

Who was she with? Almost every eye glanced at me before finding something else to look at. My pulse beat faster. Everyone looking at me at the same time made me freeze.

But if I didn't go over, I would look snobbish. At that moment there was a game-making play on the field, and the audience responded with cheers.

That cheer melted my frozen limbs and provided me the cover I needed. I got up and walked as fast as I could to where Jennifer and her group were.

She jumped to her feet, giddy with excitement. "Ngozi, this is my brother, Ken, and . . . Mary Ann." She pointed at the boy, then the girl.

"Hello," said Mary Ann.

"Hey, Ngozi!" said Ken. "Did I get it right?" he asked, eyebrows raised toward the baseball cap on his head.

His eyes were on me, a sly smile on his face, and I recognized him as the boy I'd been covertly looking for, the boy who bumped into me in the hall.

He had the same pointed nose, blond hair, and green eyes as Jennifer; only his square jaw set them apart.

Ken took off his baseball cap and shook his hair. Heat rushed to my cheeks.

"You! You're the guy who bumped into me in school?"

He nodded and raised a hand. "Guilty as charged."

I didn't know whether to laugh or cry. At the same time, I felt embarrassed. Had Ken told Jennifer I'd refused a ride from him? I'd been searching for him and all the while he was Jennifer's brother.

"A thing of beauty is a joy forever," said Ken. "It's loveliness increases . . . it will never pass into nothingness. John Keats." Ken extended his hand.

My hand flew to my mouth. "Oh God." I laughed and shook hands with him.

"What!" exclaimed Mary Ann. She shook her head, her jet-black hair covering her face, and elbowed Ken in the ribs.

Somewhere in her heritage was an Asian ancestor, I thought.

"The poet materializes," said Jennifer in a mocking tone.

"Nice poem," I said.

Ken bowed his head and put his baseball cap back on, turned to his sister, and stuck out his tongue. They both laughed. It must have been their inside joke. I hoped it wasn't at my expense. I stole a look at Mary Ann, trying to gauge her reaction to her boyfriend reciting a poem to another girl.

"How was your walk?" asked Ken.

"What walk?" asked Jennifer, her eyes moving from me to Ken.

Ken smiled. "She missed the bus a few weeks ago, and I offered to give her a ride. She declined."

Jennifer's eyebrows shot up. "You guys have met before? How come you didn't tell me?" She looked at me with a mock expression that seemed to say, "What else are you hiding from me?"

"How long ago was this?" asked Mary Ann. There was an edge to her voice.

"A week after we broke up," said Ken.

There was silence as we all seemed to forget Ken's poem. His remark created a charge in the atmosphere. I kept my eyes glued on the field, not knowing the rules or what the objective of the game was, as my mind tried to figure out what exactly was happening here.

"Why don't we head out now?" asked Jennifer. "The game is boring, and I'm hungry."

"We're going to the Blue Canary. Do you want to come?" asked Ken. "It's not far, just around the corner. They have the best burgers and fries."

I remembered I'd seen the sign before and wondered what a blue canary would look like inside. I also knew the answer I gave would break the tension or make things worse.

"Sure," I said and contemplated whether to text Mom and tell her. I sent her a text to say I'd found Jennifer. "Have fun," she'd texted back.

We piled into Ken's blue Honda Accord, Mary Ann in the front passenger seat and Jennifer and me in the back.

Ken drove around for a few minutes in and out of streets as if he was trying to lose someone behind us. He stopped in front of a large white house.

"Nice meeting you," said Mary Ann, looking at me without trying to say my name. "Bye, Jennifer." She looked at Ken and said nothing.

Ken stared ahead as if unaware of her gaze. Mary Ann

opened the door, got out, and headed toward the main entrance of a large house.

Ken sighed and drove off.

15

"Mary Ann said she had an errand to run with her mom," said Jennifer. She threw open her palms. "If you two are broken up, why are you hanging out together?"

"She wanted to talk, but there was nothing to talk about." Ken turned to look at the back. "One of you has to come to the front. I'm not a chauffeur."

"Whatever!" said Jennifer and climbed to the front seat.

Ken repeated the same route that got us here, only in the opposite direction.

The Blue Canary was a bar and restaurant.

"Seating for how many?" asked the receptionist with a big smile. Behind her were portraits of sports teams of some of the schools in the area. I saw a picture of a football team with the caption "Falls Lake High Football Team 1990."

"Three," said Ken.

The receptionist grabbed a few large leather folders. "Follow me, please."

We walked past the bar section with its flat-screen TVs suspended from the ceiling, showing a game. Men and women sat on the high barstools, eyes glued to the TVs. In the restaurant area, some families with little kids sat in booths, eating or waiting for their orders.

"Here you go," said the receptionist. She pointed us to a booth and handed each of us one of the leather-bound over-sized menus.

Ken sat on one side while Jennifer and I sat together opposite him. I went through the menu several times, not sure what to order. I decided to get whatever Jennifer got, like I did in school. When Jennifer ordered, she spoke fast, and all I heard was "banana." I wouldn't order just a banana.

Ken said he would have a cheeseburger with pickles, fries, and a Coke.

"What would you like?" asked the waiter, looking at me.

"Burger with pickles, fries, and a Coke," I said in a low voice. The waitress repeated my order. I nodded.

"Anything else?"

"Oh, I'd like the burger well-done." Burgers reminded me of times in Nigeria when I'd stripped suya meat off the stick and placed them in the middle of fresh bread. The only thing it was missing was pepper.

"What's the weather like in Nigeria?" asked Ken.

I thought for a second. "It's always hot. Like it was here in August. And it could be wet or dry depending on whether it's the rainy season or dry season."

"What do you want to be when you grow up?"

A smile flashed across my face. "I am grown up."

"Touché," said Ken, smiling.

"She wants to be a doctor," said Jennifer. "Both her parents are doctors."

I nodded. "I hope so. I know it's tough. What about you?"

Ken adjusted himself in his seat. "Hmm, I want to have

my own band. If only her parents would let me have my way." He pointed at Jennifer.

I jerked my head up. "You want to be a musician?"

"Yes, but our parents think I should do something with a safety net. Go to college, study something that would get me a good job with a salary."

The food came, and we dug in. The pickles I set aside, too salty. I liked the fries. They reminded me of yam that was first boiled and then fried. I looked at the bun and wondered if I should remove the seeds on top of it.

"Why did you come to Falls High?" asked Ken.

"The high school?"

"Yeah," said Ken.

I shrugged. "I live here in Falls Lake and—"

"How old are you?" asked Ken.

Jennifer's forehead furrowed. "Time out, time out. Why all the questions?"

"No, that's fine, I'm sixteen." I was amused by how they went at each other. I didn't know why, but I felt free in their company.

This was the first time I'd hung out with people my age. I felt safe like I was around people who wanted me in their company. In Nigeria, it was Zainab I hung out with. I had zero friends outside of school. Apart from the boys in my class in primary school and in the neighborhood, I had little contact with boys at all. But now, I was wondering what Ken was like.

"I can name all the capital cities in Africa," said Ken. He picked up fries, dunked them in ketchup, and shoved them into his mouth. "Quiz me," he said with his mouth full.

"Why do you think I know them?" I asked as the names of a few capital cities popped into my mind. Nairobi, Accra, Tripoli.

"All right, mister running your mouth," said Jennifer with a smirk. "Why do you think she would know? Because she's from Africa . . . Nigeria?" She took a drink from her glass. "You don't even know the capital of New Jersey."

"I know the capital of New Jersey," said Ken. "Trenton."

I smiled. "I'll ask you one question. If you get it right, then I'll assume you know the rest."

Ken's eyes lit up like Christmas tree lights. He rubbed his hands together. "Bring it on!"

"Ouagadougou is the capital of which country?"

Ken stopped as if someone had slapped him and wiped the smile off his face. His eyes narrowed, and he leaned forward. "You made that word up."

I laughed out loud. "Nope."

Ken was thinking. "Hmm." He looked up at the ceiling, stared at the table, and smiled. "It's in West Africa, right?"

"Maybe," I said, laughing.

"Burkina Faso!"

"Fantastic!" I said.

Ken punched the air and smiled. "That was a calculated guess. What's your phone number? I have a few questions I want to ask you later?"

"Wow, Ken, that was smooth," said Jennifer.

My throat went dry. What would happen when Ken found out who I really was? Was I ready for this? And there was Jennifer. She was my friend. Most of all, what did he want from me?

Jennifer looked at my plate. "Are you done? We can ask for a box."

I nodded. "Let's do that." They finished eating. I put my leftovers in a box. I couldn't eat anymore after Ken asked for my number. They dropped me off at home at about 7:30 p.m. I was so excited. What were the odds that the boy I'd knocked into was Jennifer's brother? I remembered his poem and now knew why Mary Ann hadn't given him a knock on the head when he'd recite it to me. I felt good inside.

"Did you see your friends?" asked Mom when I walked in.

"Yes, I did. Jennifer was there with her brother and his friend."

"Do you want dinner?"

"No, we went to Blue Canary, and I got a burger."

"Oh, okay." Mom chuckled. "How's their food? I always pass it. I've never been in there."

"It's good."

"I'm glad you enjoyed yourself," said Mom. "I fried plantain for Dad's dinner when he gets back. There's more than enough. You can help yourself if you have room."

"I always have room for fried plantain," I said with a laugh. We sat together on the couch in front of the TV and watched *American Idol* while snacking on fried plantain.

Later I was about to doze off when a text from Ken came in.

Ken: *Blue Canary was fun, right? See you again tomorrow?*

Me: *I had a good time too.*

My finger hovered on the screen. My heart started to beat faster. What should I say to "see you tomorrow?" I wanted to see him tomorrow. But . . .

Ken: *Are you there?*

Me: *See you tomorrow then.*

16

The hyena was upon me. There was no place to hide. I'd collapsed on the ground, the stitch in my side unbearable. I wanted to move, but my legs refused to obey. I gasped; the odor of decay filled my lungs, suffocating me. The big beast's head brushed against my neck.

"*No!*" I woke up sweating. I listened to hear if Mom would come out of her room. I'd been thinking of Ken before I drifted off to sleep. You can't choose your dreams. I ended up dreaming about hyenas instead of the girls. At least with the hyenas, I knew how it ended.

After a minute, Mom didn't show up, and I relaxed. Maybe I didn't actually scream out loud this time, which was good. I thought of Ken and yesterday evening. As the sun rose, I drifted off to sleep.

Saturday was a beautiful day. The sun was out in all its glory. Dad was home. Mom had left; she was on call. I'd made oatmeal and akara for breakfast. Dad and I had finished eating, and I was clearing the breakfast table when Dad spoke.

"Don't tell Mom, but that was one of the best breakfasts I've had in a long time."

"Thank you," I said, laughing.

Dad picked up the remote and channel-surfed. On weekends, when he was home, he would spend a great deal of time watching European soccer.

"We should do something together, just you and me," said Dad. "The past few weeks, you and Mom have been hanging out while I worked. Pick one, lunch or dinner, since we've already had breakfast?"

It was tough making plans for the next meal when you'd just finished a large meal.

Dad was quiet. We would definitely struggle to find something to say, but I couldn't just say, "No, thank you." It had to be lunch so there would still be time to hang out with Ken. I didn't know where we were going to meet.

"Or do you have plans already?"

I wasn't sure how he would take it. I didn't want him to think I preferred other people's company to his. "A friend of mine from school wanted to hang out this afternoon—"

"That's fine," said Dad before I changed my mind. He made a quick sign of the cross and looked at me, eyes shining. "Hang out, have fun. Arsenal is playing against Manchester United! And somehow it slipped my mind. Can you believe that? Go ahead, have fun. Would you need money?"

"No, I have money from my allowance."

"Here, take more." He brought out his wallet and handed me some bills.

I took the money and shook my head. Men and soccer. Ken sent me a text. He was driving. Could I send him my address so he could swing by? Maybe we could go for a drive.

I didn't know what I would do with Ken. Perhaps it was just peer pressure because all my friends had someone. But deep down, I knew I was not ready. I sent him the address anyway. I could see the front of the house from my room and saw his blue Honda pull up, and I stepped outside to meet him.

"This is a nice house," said Ken when I went outside to meet him. "It's not that far from school too, so that day you didn't have far to walk," said Ken. "Do you want to get something to eat?"

"No, I'm not hungry. But if you want to eat, we could go."

We drove to Burger King, which was the closest fast food to my house.

"Do you have a favorite place you like to go to?" asked Ken. "Like the mall, movies, a park?"

"There's a park close to my house I like to go to. It's beautiful and quiet. I take walks there every now and then. We can go there. We drove back toward my house.

"Stop here," I said and pointed to a parking spot by the side of the road close to the footpath.

We walked along the tarred pathway. I didn't know what to say. Then a raccoon came out of the bushes and stared at us.

"A raccoon," said Ken. "He looks friendly."

"He's mine.

Ken halted and looked at me. "What do you mean? You have a raccoon as a pet? They're wild animals. Raccoons are nocturnal. If they're out during the day, they're usually rabid. But he seems friendly enough."

"The first time I discovered pond up ahead, a few days after I arrived from Nigeria, I saw the raccoon for the first time. I was walking and eating a sandwich. I stumbled, and the sandwich fell. The Bandit here came, grabbed it, and ran away."

"The Bandit? It has a name?" asked Ken.

I laughed. "Before then, I'd seen nothing like it before. The black color around its eyes reminded me of burglars in cartoons."

"Oh, nice."

"The next day I brought food, and he showed up again." We continued to walk to the pond. "What do you think?" I looked at Ken to see his reaction.

"Nice! This looks like a postcard." Ken tossed the rest of his chicken nuggets to the side, and the raccoon rushed them. "This will be excellent to sketch."

"You draw too?"

"I try," said Ken.

"An artist through and through. We sat on the bench looking at the pond. A few walkers, joggers, and bikers went by. "So, what is it you do that your parents would rather you don't?"

"I sing in a band, but my parents want me to be thinking of college, a career, after high school. But what I want to do is write music and sing. If I ever went to college, I have no idea what I'd study."

"I never talked about career paths with my parents," I said. We agreed, without describing it in detail, that I would follow in their footsteps." Not everybody saw things the way I did. "Can't you do both?"

Ken stared ahead. "As a child, my parents taught me to follow my passion. I could be whatever I wanted if I put my mind to it. I did that. Learned the guitar, the piano. Now I'm being told to follow my passion with caution. Quite confusing, isn't it?"

"What do your parents do?" I asked.

"Jenifer never told you?" Ken feigned surprise. "Some friend, eh. Don't ask, don't tell."

"No, it's that . . ." My voice trailed off. I had no reason. It never came up.

"Just kidding. Dad is a lawyer, Mom is a bank manager. It's just us two kids. You don't have any siblings, right?"

I shook my head. I didn't know what else to say. Funny enough, Preeti and Jennifer never asked me much about my life in Nigeria. I didn't want to volunteer information about my previous life— about Auntie Halima and Sambisa . . .

Ken stood up. "I like your pond; it's a nice hideout. Where did Bandit go? Off looking for more food, I guess." Ken looked at his cell phone. "I have to run."

We walked back and passed a few more joggers on the way. Bandit was gone. Had this outing gone well? Why was he leaving so soon? I tapped my phone, and it lit up. We had spent almost two hours out there. Well, I guess it was fun while it lasted. This would probably be the last time I saw him.

17

"Can I see you tomorrow?"

I stood against Ken's car. He leaned danger-ously close and my pulse beat faster. Even though I liked him, a danger flag went up and the urge to run reared its ugly head.

"Sure, we can work out when tomorrow," I said. I shifted away and made to walk to my house.

"No, you will not walk," said Ken. "I have to make sure you get home in one piece."

I protested. "I can see my house from here."

Ken took a deep breath. "God forbid anything happened to you, and the police question me . . . 'So you left your date in the park and went home with no concern for her safety?'" said Ken in a deep voice, mimicking an officer.

"All right, you win." I got in the car, and we drove the short distance to my house. I got out and walked to the garage. Only when I stepped in did Ken's car move. Mom's car was there.

"You're back," said Mom when I walked into the kitchen.

"Hi, Mom. Hi, Dad."

Mom smiled and reached into the cabinet. "Dad told me you went out with a friend."

Mom looked tired. Her shift must have been eventful. "Yes, Ken from yesterday came by, and we walked to the pond."

"Ken?" Mom tilted her head. "Ken, Ken, Ken," she mumbled as if she was trying to jog her memory. "Hmm. Beautiful weather for a stroll. I'm glad you're coming out of your shell. I was like that too as a teenager. I liked staying home and doing things on my own."

"You look tired. Did you have a busy day?"

Mom rolled her eyes. "You can say that again." She took a bowl and filled it with roasted peanuts. "Dad is not in a good mood. His team lost. Let me see if this will cheer him up."

"Do you need help with anything?" I asked.

"Nope. We're good," said Mom.

I went upstairs and took a shower. I checked if I had any homework due on Monday that I should work on. Sunday might be busy.

Was I lying to myself? Was I one of those people who said they were not interested in dating but were only waiting for the right person to show up? But who even said Ken was the right person? I didn't know him. If he weren't Jennifer's brother, we wouldn't be where we are now. Zainab had friends, but it was all about what she got from them. I felt a tightness in my chest thinking of her.

I picked up my copy of *To Kill a Mockingbird* and read several pages. Nothing made sense. I was going through the motions, reading the words, but they were not registering.

Should I text Jennifer? I wondered as I put the book down. The thought alone sounded creepy. Asking her about her brother. What about texting Preeti? She was probably in a foul mode in Pennsylvania.

My phone buzzed. I looked, and it was an incoming text from Maryam. Now and then she would text to find out how I was doing. I knew she was just keeping in touch, playing me along for when she wanted to come to America.

I always texted her back, but at first, I would ignore her. After a day or two, I would calm down and reply with something nice, like 'Sorry for getting back to you late. Schoolwork is killing me. Extend my regards to everybody'.

For a second, I was tempted to call Maryam and ask her if there were any new developments about the girls taken from Akarika. I remembered the call Gambo had received that last day. A cold chill traveled down my spine. The person who wanted me dead was still out there. It was a good thing I left Nigeria when I did. If it hadn't been for Maryam, I would be dead by now. My heart softened. I would send her a reply.

I decided to take the same approach with Ken. Let's see what happened tomorrow.

18

———

Mom was on call the whole weekend. Dad was home watching the English League wearing his second-best team's jersey. There was no question of him wanting to take me out anywhere today. This was a soccer Sunday for him.

I watched a Nollywood movie about a man who found out his fiancée was in love with his older brother. He gave her his blessing because he was so much in love with her and cared about her happiness. He went into the priesthood after that. Personally, I thought he should be put in a psychiatric hospital. Man or woman, no person is worth throwing your life away. I'd ask Preeti to watch it and tell me her opinion of the young man.

I took a nap, watched another movie, and then napped more. Each time I woke up or turned my volume down, the sound of the spectators drifted up from the TV downstairs.

It was afternoon, at 2:15 p.m., and I hadn't heard from Ken, so I sent him a text and he called me back.

"I'll be at your place in fifteen minutes. We'll be having a picnic."

"Picnic?"

"Yes, see you soon." The phone went dead.

"Picnic?" I repeated to myself. I was wearing jeans and a T-shirt. I changed my top to a multicolored dashiki top.

Downstairs, Dad didn't look happy. I didn't need a genius to tell me that the history of yesterday was being repeated. I let him be. I got a yellow sticky note and wrote, "To whom it may concern." I stuck it on the refrigerator to let them know I'd be at the pond with my friend. They should send a text or call me if they needed me.

I stepped out once I got Ken's text that he was outside. He drove ahead once he realized I was walking the short distance to the park. As I approached, he got out of his car and brought out a huge box.

"What's that?" I looked at him and looked at the box.

"It's a surprise. Could you please help bring the little basket in the backseat?"

Ken had draped a piece of cloth over it with different-shaped loaves of bread drawn on it. Was that food he had in there? I was comfortable around him, like an old friend. As if we'd met after a long separation and picked up where we'd left off. "What about Jennifer?"

"She's fine. She's hanging out with Paul but sends her regards."

We continued down the pathway, the earthy freshwater smell getting sharper as we got closer.

"All right, here will do." Ken put down the box and looked at the sky.

"Are you taking pictures?"

"Close," said Ken. He opened the box and brought out an easel with white sketch paper clipped onto it. He extended the telescopic legs out and stood it up.

"You're going to draw the landscape?" I asked.

Ken gave me an amused look. "You are too smart for your own good. I'll draw both you and the landscape."

"Really?"

Ken continued to set up. "Yes. Look at some of my work."

He handed me a sketch pad. I opened it and was impressed by what I saw. Amazing pencil drawings of nature, houses, and people filled page after page until I got somewhere in the middle. I clenched my teeth. A burning sensation traveled from my chest to my stomach. "Is that Mary Ann?"

Ken glanced at the drawing. "Yes." His eyes lingered on my face. "But yours will be a lot better."

"Why do you keep staring at me?"

"I'm taking a picture of your pretty face in my mind's eye, committing your face to memory so I'll never forget it."

Heat rushed to my cheeks. Had Ken called me pretty?

He brought out a small container filled with different pencils. "Sit on this rock with your back to the pond and Ken da Vinci will go to work," he said, imitating an Italian accent.

I sat on the rock he had pointed at and felt at ease. A desire to spread joy and make everyone feel good engulfed me. My eyes were on Ken, eager to follow his instructions.

"Now look at me as if you want to see my soul with the ghost of a smile in your eyes."

"Ghost of a smile?" I said the words slowly, emphasizing each word one by one.

"Yes! A smile that is there, or maybe not," continued Ken in his Italian accent.

I couldn't help it, but I gave him a big smile.

"No! No! No! Little smile. Little smile."

I went into a fit of laughter gulped in air to quiet myself.

Once I calmed down, Ken started. The scratch of pencil on paper, birds calling out to each other, and the faraway sound of a plane above were our only companions.

"Fantastic," said Ken, changing pencils now and then.

There was no other place to look. Ken had given me permission to check him out. It was uncanny the way he and Jennifer looked alike. Ken had nice full lips that changed depending on the stroke of his pencil. He would bite them, pucker them, and curve them, and I wondered what it would feel like if he kissed me with those lips. I became suddenly aware of what I was thinking, and heat rushed to my cheeks. I dipped my head.

"Chin up. We're almost done."

I looked up, but I couldn't meet his eyes. Did he know what I was thinking?

Ken made a few exaggerated strokes and threw his hands up in the air. "Done!"

I smiled. "About time." My joints popped as I got up off the rock and shook my hands and legs to get rid of the dull pain from staying too long in the same position.

"Sorry, I didn't mean to take that long."

"Can I see?"

Ken waved me over. "Sure."

I was speechless. I folded my hands in a ball and pressed them against my lips. I felt butterflies in my stomach.

"You like?" asked Ken.

"Wow!" I lowered my hands, fingers fanned out. "It's beautiful." It was a close-up of me with some detail of the background bushes and pond. It showed my face and my braids cascading down. He had signed his name at the bottom.

"You can keep it."

I looked up and into his eyes. Nobody had ever done anything like this for me before. "Thank you." Our eyes met, and we stared at each other. I felt like an electric current was passing between us. Many fights were going on inside me as our faces seemed to move toward each other.

Ken pulled away. "The work is done. It's now time for our picnic. Could you please put the basket of food over there?" Ken busied himself putting the sketchbook and other drawing paraphernalia away.

I took the basket to one of the picnic tables. Ken opened it. He had packed a few cold sandwiches and two bottles of orange juice.

"You have many talents," I said and bit into a tuna sandwich. "You sing, you draw . . ."

"My singing is even better than my drawing."

"I must hear you sing," I said.

"One day you will, soon."

We made small talk and sat eating in silence, enjoying the sounds of dusk as it approached. Fireflies lit up now and then. Crickets chirped, frogs croaked. The sound of wildlife and the freshwater smell of the pond reminded me of another body of water I had bathed in several months ago. I shivered.

"Are you cold?" asked Ken.

"No . . . not . . . not really," I stammered.

"Your lips are trembling, and you have goosebumps all over."

"No. I felt a cold breeze."

He rubbed my shoulders to warm me up, and my body went tense right away. He moved his hand away fast.

"Are you sure you're all right?"

I nodded. "It's getting dark. I think we should go," I said.

I carried the basket and Ken brought the box with his art

stuff. We walked back along the tarred bike pathway with bushes on each side. I rode with him back to the house.

"Thank you for letting me sketch you," said Ken.

"That was the best day of my life. Thank you."

"See you at school?"

I nodded.

19

---

om held the sketch and raised it with both hands. "Wow, this is beautiful. And he made it in just these few hours you were out?"

"Ben, come and see Ngozi's sketch. It is amazing."

"Hi, Ngozi," said Dad with a big smile on his face. "We finally won!" I thought it would be the worst weekend of my life. "Whoa, this is nice. Signed *Ken*?"

Mom looked up. "Your Ken?"

My nose flared. "No . . . yes! The same Ken. But . . . not *my* Ken."

"We have to meet this Ken," said Mom. "Spending the whole weekend with my daughter and then drawing her."

"Yes, that would be nice," said Dad. "Good drawing. Tell him to keep it up. He walked back to the couch and flopped in front of the TV.

"I need to get organized for school tomorrow," I said and started toward the stairs.

"We should get that framed," said Mom. "There's a frame shop in the mall. During the weekend, we shall go."

"Okay, Mom." I ran up the stairs. I wanted to getaway. I'd already arranged my things for school. The discussion was hovering around Ken and made me uncomfortable. I didn't want the talk to drift to Ken again. I checked my phone. Nothing. Maybe I should text him. No, not yet.

I walked over to the fish tank and looked at Faith. I wasn't sure if I'd fed her today, so I gave her a smaller pinch of food than I usually would.

The aquarium glass was cloudy. Cleaning the fish tank was one of those things that came as a shock. It's all cute to have a fish, but maintaining a goldfish is hard work. But I was glad I had Faith to talk to. A whiff from the tank reminded me of the pond and Ken.

I rechecked my phone. Nothing. *I'll text him.* I started to type.

ME: *Are you home yet?*

I waited, then got ready for bed. I brushed my teeth and changed into my pajamas. My phone beeped. Incoming text message.

Ken: *At home. Finished unloading the box. How are you?*

Me: *Good. Thanks again for the drawing. My parents love it.*

Ken: *I'm glad.*

The dot dot dot on my screen showed he was still typing. It stayed there for a while, and I guessed he was typing and deleting. I wondered what he was trying to say so carefully.

Ken: *I'll let you sleep. Have a good night.*

Me: *OK.*

I lay awake, lost. There was this surging emotion in me where I wanted Ken to take me in his arms and look at me the way he did at the pond—as if I meant something. As if I mattered. I must tell him about my past. That I was damaged goods. Before he found out on his own and then it would all be over before it even started.

Or maybe I should just stop hanging out with him. Throw myself into schoolwork, and somehow all this would fizzle out. I pondered this problem for a while until I drifted off to sleep.

20

"What have you been doing with my brother?" asked Jennifer during chemistry lab on Monday morning.

"What?" I asked.

"He spent the whole weekend with you and all you have to say is 'what?'"

"Well, nothing from the ordinary. He came to my house. I showed him the neighborhood. That was on Friday."

"I've never even been to your house," said Jennifer.

"He invited himself," I said. "He didn't come in."

"You've never been to my house either," said Jennifer. "I guess we should rectify that soon. So what else happened?"

"Nothing. On Sunday we went back to the park again."

"Park?"

"Yes. Close to my house, there is a footpath, a bicycle path that leads to a pond and park. They have picnic tables and benches. People can sit out and enjoy the—"

"Ngozi and Jennifer, please focus on your work!" said the teacher. "The chemistry lab is not a place to get distracted."

I faced my work. My plan was to never get on any of my

teachers' bad books. It always amazed me how students interacted with teachers here, sometimes as if they were buddies, blurring the line between teacher and student. I concentrated on the experiment and ignored Jennifer. At last, the bell rang, and we removed our safety goggles and lab coats and headed for the door.

"I'm impressed," said Jennifer. "You dislike upsetting your teachers."

"Hello!" said Preeti walking up to us. "Who upset who?"

Jennifer pointed at me. "Ngozi here spent the whole weekend with my brother." Jennifer seemed to do a little dance.

"Get out of here!" said Preeti. "They hooked up? Scandalous!"

"No, no, no," I said, shaking my head. "We only went for a walk. He made a sketch of me, and that was it."

"I visit Pennsylvania for a weekend, and things explode here."

We continued down the corridor. I let out a sigh of relief. Thank God, they didn't get to the part of asking me about my feelings. It's funny how your thinking changes based on the people or person you hang out with.

Zainab dated and never pushed me to follow her footsteps. But here with Preeti and Jennifer around me, I was seeing boys as a possibility. Maybe this was the age for that, who knows.

"I'll run to the bathroom," said Jennifer.

"Wait!" Preeti put her hands out to stop Jennifer. "What about Mary Ann?"

There was a pause. I felt like a match had been struck inside me, and I was waiting for it to ignite. An itch shot across my left armpit.

"What about her?" asked Jennifer with a shrug. "I need to pee."

Preeti raised her eyebrows, making her big round eyes even bigger. "Isn't she dating Ken?"

"They broke up," said Jennifer. "I know that for sure. Why do people break up, anyway?"

"There are millions of reasons," said Preeti. She jerked her head to face me. "Ngozi, that means Ken is free, you're in the clear. The boy is yours."

Jennifer took off. "Guys, wait for me," she called to us over her shoulder.

Now I had Preeti all to myself. What should I ask her? "How were your cousins?"

Preeti rolled her eyes. "Just as I predicted. Too competitive. But they brought some of their friends with them. One was really cute."

"What about Paul?"

"Oh God, Ngozi." Preeti fanned herself. "I've known Paul since seventh grade, and suddenly he thinks I am cute. We have to wait and see on that one. In the meantime, I can look around."

I saw my opening. "What do I do with Ken?"

"Do?"

"I mean we enjoy each other's company. But it's not like we are boyfriend and girlfriend."

"Just give it time. You guys just met and you hit it off. He broke up with his girlfriend not long ago. Who knows what's going on inside his head."

"He hasn't texted me since last night. Do I text him?"

"Absolutely not. Wait for Ken to text," said Preeti.

The bathroom door opened, and Jennifer rushed out. Her head whirled from left to right. She saw us and walked over. "Let's go."

Throughout the lectures, I checked my phone under the desk to see if Ken had sent anything, but nothing. The last period before lunch was annoying. Mr. Kent, the science teacher, asked me a question. It seemed like he had called on me a few times before I answered, and some students were giggling.

Mr. Kent eyed me over his glasses. "Please keep your mind in the class. Now, what's the longest bone in the body?"

I thought for a moment. "Femur."

"Good. Now tell us the largest organ in the body?"

"The liver," I said.

"Anyone?" asked Mr. Kent, looking around the class.

"Brain, stomach, heart," a few students chorused.

"No, the skin," said Mr. Kent.

Thinking about it later, it made sense. It covered the whole body. I just never knew it was an organ.

At lunch, I looked around, hoping to see Ken. Come to think of it, I'd never seen him actually in school, even during lunch. Or maybe I never noticed. By the time the final bell went and it was time to leave, I was tired and just wanted to get home. I joined the line of students heading toward the exit, going to bus lines.

My phone beeped. Incoming text.

Ken: *Would you like to hang out tonight?*

My lips stretched out in a smile. I was about to say yes when I remembered what Preeti had said. I clutched the phone to my chest and shuffled toward the exit. I would reply when I got home.

21

Other students do it when they want no one to talk to them, so I did it. I plugged in my earphones. Buses pulled up, students climbed in, and they left, belching dark smoke in their wake. It seemed like a long wait. I shifted my weight from one leg to the other. My joints were killing me. I usually only felt pain when I walked a great deal, but now it was there from standing.

In Nigeria, I was always on the move and never noticed it. Here things were more organized. People stood and waited for their turn, no jumping the queue, and I did that a lot.

My bus came, and I climbed on and sat in a window seat. A loud shrill sound made me jump. Everybody seemed unconcerned, then I realized I had my earphones on. A loud noise interrupted my thoughts. *What the…?* I looked at my phone

Ken: *This is what I've been thinking all day. [Link.]*

It was a YouTube link. I clicked on it, and the first thing I heard was the sound of a string instrument. I froze. I knew that song, and I'd seen this music video so many times. I closed my eyes and put my head back. My heart thumped so loud I thought the boy sitting behind me could hear. The lyrics to "African Queen" by 2Face started.

After the song finished the first time, I hit replay. The song had a new meaning for me. This time I opened my eyes and looked out of the window at the people, houses, and cars that drifted past. I felt like I was in a music video and Ken was singing all those words to me. Should I send him a text and say he was my American King? I shook my head. Not a good idea. It also sounded silly to me. I remembered Preeti's warning that he might be on a rebound.

What if he was on a rebound? He broke up with his girl-friend and jumped into another relationship. He might make up with his ex-girlfriend, and that would leave me stranded. That was one experience I didn't want to have.

The bus stopped every now and then, and people got out. Any other day, I would have wanted the bus to move as fast as possible. But today, I wanted the ride to last forever, never stopping as I listened to "African Queen" over and over again.

The bus stopped at the nearest crossroad to my street, and I got off, 2Face still playing in my ear. I passed our pond, which was what I called it ever since Ken and I visited it. I walked passed it and continued home. *Was it all right to reply to him now?* I wondered. Even if I did, what was I going to say? I punched in my combination at the garage, and it opened.

"Oh, Mom's home," I said out loud. Today must be her day off. I opened the door that led from the house to the garage.

"Ngozi, is that you?" asked Mom.

"Yes, good afternoon."

"I heard the garage opening. How was school?"

"Good." I walked over to Mom and sat on the couch beside her.

"I'm home today. Just bored. I was so bored that I checked out the news in Nigeria. It's all politics and the upcoming elections."

"It's always about who has the most money," I said. "Politicians buy votes, and the incumbent always wins."

"But this might be different. The current president has had a lot of negative publicity from his handling of Boko Haram and the kidnapped young girls from their schools. Maybe he might let the election be free and fair, and that would put him down as one of the greatest presidents. African leaders, it seems, find it difficult to hand over power without a struggle."

My mind drifted to the day I'd tried to e-mail Mom from the business center in Lamija. A political rally had been going on outside the establishment. I had run away from the rally, only to get home and get into more trouble. Auntie Halima's sister, Beatrice, had given me the first taste of what was to come. I pushed the thought to the back of my mind where other sad memories resided.

"Ngozi?"

I jerked as I realized Mom had been talking to me. "Sorry, what did you say?"

"A penny for your thoughts?"

"Nothing important. Just thinking about a political rally I'd seen in Nigeria."

Mom's eyebrows shot up. "Oh, you follow Nigerian politics?"

I shook my head. "No, it was the day I decided to go back to school. I've replayed it so many times in my memory to see what I could have done differently."

There was a pause. "I'm sorry. I didn't mean to . . ."

Mom's voice trailed off. It's frustrating when you don't want to think of something and all you do is think of the thing.

"Where was I?" Mom clapped her hands together. "Yes, I will make food. Do you want me to make garri for you? I should pamper you, you know," said Mom. She jumped up from the couch and headed to the kitchen.

"I'm not that hungry. I'll eat a little. Let me put my bag away." I dashed to my room, and the smell of the fish tank almost knocked me over. I left the door open, letting most of the smell out. The fish tank really needed to be washed. Was it safe inhaling that foul odor from the tank all the time?

"Food is ready!" said Mom.

"Coming!"

"You can bring the food to the living room."

Mom and I sat together watching an episode of *The Real* with Tamera Mowry-Housley, comic Loni Love, Adrienne Bailon, Jeannie Mai, and Tamar Braxton. In this episode, they were talking about relationships. We ate and listened to the different analysis of relationships.

Mom turned to me. "How's Ken?"

Some of my food must have gone down the wrong pipe because I coughed and gagged and tears stung my eyes.

Mom clapped me on the back. "Say something!"

"Something," I croaked, coughing and clearing my throat.

"Drink water, you'll be fine." She handed me a glass.

"I'm all right now." I fixed my tear-filled eyes on the TV. I dared not move. Maybe she would forget about Ken. There was an awkward silence between us.

Mom exhaled. "Ngozi, we have to see this boy. Invite him over for lunch or dinner over the weekend."

22

———

I literally ran up to my room rubbing my palms together, excited and embarrassed at the same time. Was I acting like a kid? This was all new to me. My cousin Maryam hung out with boys, and Auntie Halima never talked about boys with her. I thought that was the way it should be. Parents didn't interfere. Or maybe I was sensitive because deep down I cared. Did Mom ask me to invite Ken because she sensed I had feelings for him?

My head felt like a bag of popcorn tossed into the microwave. I needed to distract myself. The task came to me at once. I went to the garage and got my fish-cleaning bucket, filled another bucket with tap water, and retrieved my old small glass bowl aquarium. Back in my room, I watched Faith swim around in the murky water with no care in the world, no boy fish or parent to deal with.

I scooped up some of the aquarium water with a cup and placed it in the glass bowl. Then I fished out Faith with a net and put her in the glass bowl. I sprinkled food on top, and right away Faith was at home.

I picked up my gloves and stopped. Once I had them on, I

preferred to keep them on until I finished cleaning. I picked up my phone, tapped on the message icon and typed.

Me: *Hi, this is a weeknight. What about Friday?*

Ken: Friday? It's far. What about tomorrow?

Me: *Still a weekday.*

Ken: *Friday is a weekday too.*

Me: *End of the week.*

Ken: *Lol, you win.*

ME: *My parents also want to meet the person that sketched my image.*

All I could see were dots, no words. What was he doing?

Ken: *We'll talk about that on Friday.*

Me: *See you Friday. I'll text. Bye.*

Ken: *Bye.*

I PUT MY GLOVES ON AND STARTED TO SCRUB THE aquarium. I removed the old water pump filter. Its smell reminded me of the pond, mixed in with urine. A greenish slime coated the surface of the filter. I threw it into a plastic bag I had for that and slid in the new one, which I had presoaked. I rinsed off the glass with clean water and washed the multicolored stones. They smelled just as bad as the filter. I hoped Faith would appreciate my effort in cleaning her abode.

It took the better part of an hour before the aquarium was clean and the buckets, brushes, and nets were put away. The difference when I put Faith back in was like looking through a smudged eyeglass, wiping it, and looking through it again. Her color was brilliant. I took a shower and collapsed on my bed.

Tuesday dragged into Wednesday. Uneventful, and no texts from Ken. I checked on the hour. Just like before, I never ran across Ken in school. Thursday morning rolled in, and the only thing on my mind was seeing Ken on Friday.

Jennifer's eyebrows narrowed. "Did you sleep at all?" You look like you studied all night. Wait, do we have a quiz?" She brought out her folder and flipped through her schedule.

"No, I couldn't sleep." I didn't want to ask Jennifer if Ken was in school. I hoped he would send a text that morning. In algebra, I kept on checking my phone to see if he had sent a text. As we left class after algebra, I couldn't hold it anymore. "Jennifer, is Ken in school today?"

"Yes, we rode in together. Why?"

"How come we never run into him in school? Like at the cafeteria."

"Different lunch periods, remember?" said Jennifer.

I felt like disappearing. That was a stupid question. It never occurred to me.

"I don't see you around with Paul that much."

"Please, we only went to the dance together, that was it. There's nothing special between us. Most of the time he's hanging out with Ken, practicing in their band in our garage."

My eyebrows shot up. "Paul and Ken are in a band together? I didn't know that."

"The garage at my house is soundproof. Yet they manage to disturb the neighborhood.

It is said that when you're expecting someone or something, everyday noise sounds like who or what you're waiting for. I must have checked my phone a million times because every squeak from a chair or desk seemed like an incoming text.

"He's avoiding you," said Preeti. We walked side by side toward the bus line. "Why else would he not text you? He's wanted to see you all week, and now it's time to see you, he won't even send a text. You might have to text him."

I looked at my phone. Nothing.

"Wait, he knows you're going to invite him to come to the house and see your mom?"

I hesitated. "Yes . . . my mom out of the blue said she wanted to meet him."

"Maybe. Relationships are considered serious when parents know about them." Preeti stopped, looked at me, and blinked repeatedly. "Or maybe he got back with Mary Ann."

I felt like a knife had been plunged into my heart and twisted. I downplayed it by telling myself there was nothing serious between Ken and me.

"Just joking," said Preeti. "You should have seen your face." Preeti made a sad face. "But no matter what you do, don't text him."

Nobody was home when I got there. I fed Faith, watched her swim around, and wondered if I should just call him. By the time Mom and Dad came back, Ken hadn't called or texted.

23

Three hyenas played tag team behind me.

"Get her!" Gambo screamed. He was covered in blood. Both ears, nose, and an eye were missing. He dragged his left leg along with the trap that bit into it.

"Don't hurt her," said a weak voice.

I looked behind me; it was Danladi with blood flowing through a wound in his head. I was confused. He had damaged me, then saved my life.

I continued to run through the bushes of Sambisa. The hyenas always close but never catching me.

I woke up panting, soaked in sweat. This time I didn't scream, thank God. As much as I tried to push thoughts about Ken to the back of my mind, they refused to move and took center stage. I couldn't help but wonder what the dream meant. Hyenas, Gambo, and Danladi, all in the same night. Was something terrible about to happen? A shiver ran through me, and I covered myself with a blanket.

Once the sun was up, I would disregard Preeti's advice

and call Ken. I picked up a book from my shelf and tried to read. All I did was flip through the pages, waiting for sunrise.

I jerked awake by six with the book on my chest. At least it helped me sleep. My plan for the day was to be happy, no matter what happened. I picked up my phone, and my heart beat faster. A missed call from Ken. The phone beeped, I had a voice mail. It was the phone ringing that woke me. I tapped the voice mail icon.

"Hi, Ngozi, I'm so sorry about yesterday. Please call me as soon as you get this."

I touched Ken's name on the screen. He answered on the first ring.

"Hi, you got my voice mail, right? Sorry about yesterday. I went for this singing thing in South Jersey and coming back was a nightmare, and my phone was dead. I had no charger. The traffic—oh. I want to make it up to you. What about a movie tonight, my treat?"

I was glad he called. What type of holdup was that? He could have just sent me a text. Okay, no charger.

"Hello, are you there?"

I exhaled. "Yes, I'm here. Let me ask Mom—"

"Can I see them tomorrow?"

Suddenly, I was wide-awake. "Are you sure? You don't have to."

"Yes, I'm sure," said Ken.

"Weekends are Dad's soccer day, we can go see a movie in the evening," I said.

"Have to go. My mom wants me to help her move stuff. So 7:00 tomorrow night, okay?

"Okay." The line went dead.

Mom and Dad were good with Ken coming on Sunday, and also with me going to see a movie with him that evening.

"Try to get back by ten," Mom had said when I asked her.

Ken came around at 6:30 p.m., and we drove to the AMC theater in the mall. We circled the parking lot close to the theater entrance a few times looking for a parking space. No luck.

Ken scanned the parking lot. "Why can't people stay home?" he mumbled as he tapped the steering wheel with his finger.

I smiled. "We are one of the people you're referring to."

Ken tried another section of the mall, but everything was occupied or had someone with his blinker on waiting for a car to exit so they could park there. Finding parking was a daunting task.

"That's it," said Ken. "We'll just have a little romantic walk."

We found parking outside the mall, beside a children's playground. I looked at the swings, and happy memories of me as a kid on a swing came to mind. I smiled as we started the long trek back to the mall.

Ken looked at his watch. "Two movies will start in the next twenty minutes. Eat first or after the movie?"

I'd been to the theater a few times with my parents, so I knew food-wise there were other options we could explore. "Maybe buy some food and take it in with us. What I need is water, though. That long walk made me thirsty."

"Let's get in line then," said Ken. "The line is always long, then you have to wait for your order. The only thing they make that you can get fast is popcorn."

I got bottled water and Ken got a huge bucket of popcorn. "Are you going to finish that?"

Ken waved his hand. "Piece of cake, but you'll help me? I hope you like butter on it."

"I like 'see food,'" I said.

Ken looked at me for a moment, then smiled. "Ah, you

eat any food you see. You're not a picky eater. My kind of person."

His eyes bore into mine, and I felt butterflies in my stomach. Ken took the bucket, and we walked over to the butter stand. I looked at him and tried to read his mind. What did he really want from me? What would he do when he found out what I'd been through? I remembered the African saying, "It's easy to be upbeat when the going is good." I didn't want to spoil this for him and for me. He mustn't know, not yet anyway.

"What?" said Ken with a laugh and looked away.

He had turned and caught me staring at him. It amazed me how his ears and cheeks flushed red.

"Nothing. I was just watching what you were doing."

The movie Ken chose was *The Good Lie*. As soon as it started, I felt chills all over. It brought back a lot of memories. At one point the siblings were in the bush and Theo saw enemy soldiers approaching. All I saw was Faith, Lami, and myself crouched together in the hole and Ronke sacrificing herself so we could live. Tears trickled down my cheeks.

Ken tried to put his arm over my shoulders. I raised my hand as my whole body stiffened.

"That was a heartbreaking moment," said Ken in a quiet voice. "Sorry, I was only trying to comfort you."

Why had he chosen this movie? Did he know? I couldn't take it anymore. The sufferings. The deaths. How children's lives get turned upside down by no fault of their own.

I leaned closer to Ken. "I can't watch anymore. I'll wait for you in the lobby."

"No. Let's go."

I went to the bathroom and splashed cold water on my face. I felt so guilty. I couldn't forget that Faith would still be alive if I hadn't convinced her that escape was an option.

Tears continued to stream down my face. I almost wished Mom hadn't come to my aid. She should have just left me to perish in police custody.

Ken was pacing by the ladies' bathroom door when I came out. "I'm sorry. I thought it was just a movie about Africa . . . I didn't know it would bring up . . ." Ken's voice trailed off.

"I'm fine. It was just too much. I guess when I was in Nigeria, I was insensitive to these things. But being away from it all and taking a step back, I see the real picture." I looked around at other movies that were showing. "We could watch *Spider-Man*."

Ken shook his head. "No, it's not about me." Ken held the popcorn bucket in one hand, wiped his hands on his jeans, and took my hand. He looked at me with a pained stare. "What do you want?" His voice choked with emotion.

This time I did not cringe from his touch. "What do I want?" I thought for a moment, then I giggled. "Come!" I pulled Ken's hand and we ran through the lobby laughing. People stared at us, making way for us to pass.

24

"Yes! Push harder!" I screamed.

Ken grunted and shoved me as hard as he could.

"Yes!" The wind screamed past my ears, and my body jerked as the chain on the swing reached its limit and fell back. Memories of my childhood in Nigeria when Matron and Uncle Thomas were alive flashed through my mind.

"Should I push you some more?" asked Ken.

Ken had been pushing me higher and higher for the past few minutes. I looked over my shoulder and saw him step back to a safe distance as gravity pulled me back on the swing. "You should get on the other swing. This is fun!"

"I'm happier watching you being happy."

Tired, I stopped kicking out and let the swing slow down. "I'll try the slide now." Before the swing stopped, I jumped off and landed on my feet. I was a little girl again, happy. Without breaking stride, I ran to the slide like a kid at an all-you-can-eat chocolate store. Does that even exist? I climbed up and slid down. And did it three more times before I was winded and the novelty was gone.

Ken stood by the side watching me with interest.

"When I was younger," I said, gasping, "I could spend an entire day just swinging, sliding, and going on the merry-go-round and the one that goes up and down with a kid on each end . . . the seesaw."

"Teeter-totter?" said Ken.

"I think so. We called it a seesaw." Panting, I sat on a bench, and Ken sat beside me, still holding the popcorn bucket. I eyed the popcorn.

"Emmm, I have wipes in the car, if you want to wipe your hands."

I dusted off my hands and smiled. "The God that protects little kids is here in this playground." I scooped up a handful of popcorn and shoved it into my mouth. Ken did the same, and we sat there on the playground bench munching popcorn, surrounded by encroaching darkness and the sounds of cars passing by.

"Wow, we finished it," said Ken, running his hand inside the empty bucket. "I guess all that swinging worked up an appetite, eh?"

Now I was embarrassed. "I'm sorry, I got carried away."

"No, there's nothing to be sorry about. You don't know how much I enjoyed just watching you being you." Another awkward silence. Ken looked up. "Look at that. I've never seen so many stars in the sky . . ." He paused and now I watched his childlike wonderment. "I see a shooting star," he squealed.

"Where?"

Ken pointed. "Over there."

I looked up. It was all the same. "What exactly am I looking for?"

"One of those dots that move."

"Okay, I think I see one. It is moving fast and blinking too."

Ken laughed. "That's a plane."

"Oh."

"You know," said Ken, "when you make a wish upon a shooting star, it comes true."

It was my turn to laugh. "As a kid, they also said when you drink water from the first rain after the dry season and make a wish, it would come true."

"Yeah? I never heard of that. Did you try it?"

"Yes, I did. Every year after my Uncle Thomas died . . . until lightning struck a tree close by."

Ken laughed, and I laughed with him.

"Thinking back, it was funny," I said. "Little me running around in the rain and hightailing it when lightning struck close by."

"What did you wish for?"

The smile faded from my face. I thought about it. Why not? "You know, I'm adopted."

Ken nodded and looked at his hands. "Jennifer told me. Preeti told her."

I nodded. "That makes sense. This is my fourth adoption. After my uncle died, my adoptive mother's brother, I wished I knew who my biological parents were, and they would come and get me."

Ken was quiet. I heard him swallow. "We . . . we can try to find them."

I whirled to look at him. "How?"

25

We both stared at each other. In my mind I pleaded with Ken to show me what I'd always wanted to know. I hoped he knew the way.

"Let's get going, it's getting late," said Ken. He picked up the empty bucket of popcorn and dumped it in the playground garbage container.

I sat in the car and my hand trembled when I reached for the seat belt. The weather had cooled as it got darker. Despite the chill, my palms were sweaty. I rubbed them on my jeans. Ken engaged the gear and drove. He turned and looked at me.

"We can order a DNA kit and do a DNA analysis—"

"That only tells you the person's ethnicity. At least that's what Mrs. Coleman said in her class."

Ken's eyes darted from me to the road. "Ngozi, listen. That's true, it tells you the individual's ethnicity and . . . and that helps narrow down the possibilities."

I felt a tightening in my chest and continued to rub my palms on my jeans. The last ray of hope slipped out of my fingers. A laugh bubbled in my stomach and burst out before

I could stop it. "But Nigeria has no such database to analyze." My disappointment seeped through my voice.

"There must be a way," said Ken, his voice a whisper.

Light drifted in from the street lights, and I saw Ken's jaw tighten. "I have a strong feeling about this. I read that Nigeria has three major tribes. At least with DNA analysis, we can narrow it down."

"You've been reading about Nigeria?" My voice softened.

"A little."

I shook my head. "There are too many people."

"Think about it!" said Ken, eyes wide. "Some Americans, no matter where their ancestors came from, have narrowed down their ancestry to the part of the world they came from. Science and technology have come a long way on DNA analysis, and the accuracy is excellent. If we order a test, we can at least know which ethnic group you belong to."

I looked at him and wanted to be as excited as he was. But I already knew the answer. I lowered my head. "I'm Hausa."

"Oh, I didn't know," said Ken. He exhaled. "But DNA analysis . . ." Ken's voice trailed off.

As we drove toward Falls Lake in silence, what Ken said ran through my mind. In class, Mrs. Coleman had shown us her own DNA analysis. She had a mixture of Native American, English, and Gambian ancestors. But, when I looked at her, all I saw was the Gambian part. Maybe, it might work. I didn't want this night to end on a sad note. I stared at Ken and after some time he turned toward me.

A grin tugged at the corners of his lips. "What?"

I exhaled. "Thanks for the movie."

"But you didn't even watch it."

"I saw a little, and it led us to the playground. I had the time of my life."

Ken's grin widened, and then he laughed. "I've never seen anyone have so much fun on a swing before."

I smiled. "Is the mall always that full?"

"No. Maybe during the holidays, like Christmas Eve, yes. Maybe a concert or a huge celebrity party was going on. I almost forgot, Jennifer and I are having a party at our place. Mom is going to a convention in Boston and Dad is tagging along."

"You'll have a party while they're gone? Won't they be angry?"

"They won't know about it, and you're invited."

I shook my head. "I won't give you an answer until you come to my house."

"That is blackmail!" said Ken, throwing his hands up.

"Why not whitemail?" I said.

Ken thought for a moment. "Good question. I don't know. When I find out, you'll be the first to know."

Ken pulled over in front of my house. "See you tomorrow?" I asked and opened the door.

"Yes."

I started to get out of the car.

"Ngozi, wait!"

I turned. "Yes?"

Ken looked into my eyes. His lips moved. "Will be at your house tomorrow. Ngozi . . . I also wanted to . . ."

I turned my head. "Wanted to . . . ?"

"You know what? Don't worry. It's not important," said Ken with the wave of his hand.

"Okay, have a good night, and thanks so much." I headed for the garage, chewing on my lower lip. What was he going to say? I could only assume it was something nice. Maybe he'd say it tomorrow. That night I dreamed of Ronke, Lami, and Faith. Ronke sacrificing herself to save us, and Lami leaving Faith and me on our own. I dreamed of the first hyena attack, and I remembered my scream that had scared the hyena off.

In the morning, there was a text from Ken thanking me for agreeing to come out with him. He attached a few links that led to articles about people finding loved ones and even the police solving long-dormant cases via DNA.

Ken: *Should I order the kit?*

26

———————

I didn't send a reply to Ken's question. *We'll talk about it later*, was my thought on it. My legs, arms, and every muscle in my being was sore and hurt once I got out of bed. I chuckled. It was a pleasant feeling, muscles I hadn't used in so many years. I would love to revisit the playground.

Mom and I went for the first mass. We took care of the Sunday service. The rest of the morning progressed as usual. Dad worshiped on his shrine of the English League. Mom went back to their room. Now and then I could hear her talking on the phone.

I fed Faith and Googled what to expect when a boy visits. All I found was the book *What to Expect When You're Expecting*. Somebody should write what to expect when you're expecting a boy to visit your home. I laughed out loud. All I wanted was for the visit to start and end without conflict.

As the time got closer to noon, all my senses were heightened. Every sound in the house, no matter how faint, sounded like the doorbell. I would get up and rush downstairs, only to find it was a false alarm.

Just before the clock struck noon, Mom rushed into my room all dressed.

"Ngozi, sorry, I have to go to the hospital. There's an emergency." She touched my cheeks. "You and Dad should be okay."

I felt like someone had punched me in the stomach. Dad and I combined had limited talking points. Mom must have seen the doubt on my face.

"I'll be back as soon as I can," she said and headed for the door. "Bring out the stew from the fridge and defrost it so he'll have something to eat."

Mom's feet pounded down the stairs. Moments later, I felt the slight vibration as the garage opened and the faint sound of her car engine came life. Within minutes, Mom was gone.

What was I going to do? Should I call Jennifer or Preeti and ask them to come over? It would be awkward for Jennifer; after all, Ken was her brother. For Preeti, I wasn't sure what she would say. *Do you want me to come and hold him down for you?* Might be her response. Maybe I should ask Paul. I cocked my head and listened. Were those voices I heard downstairs?

"Foolish boy!" It was Dad. "Who said you could do that? No! Not in my living room."

With a sinking feeling in my stomach, I yanked my door open and sailed downstairs, taking the stairs two at a time.

"What is it?" I asked as I scanned the living room. Dad didn't look at me. His eyes were glued to the TV, and he was all alone.

"Don't miss that corner kick!" Dad pointed at the TV. "Don't miss that corner kick!" Dad walked toward the TV and crouched as if he would take the kick himself.

On the screen, the player took a few steps back, strolled casually toward the ball, and took the kick. The ball sailed

over the top of the crossbar. The crowd roared its disappointment.

"Anu offiah!" Dad screamed in Ibo, grabbed his head
with both hands, and spun around. He saw me and stopped.
He stood up straight and hissed. "That wild animal couldn't
aim for the post. I was expecting one of his legendary banana
shots." I raised an eyebrow.

"Banana shots?"

"Yes! The shots that curve in the air like a banana!" Dad
demonstrated with his hands.

"But he did. Just that it went too high."

"Well, you can say that." Dad turned back and faced the
TV, hands on his hips.

I exhaled. "I thought you were scolding someone."

Dad shook his head. "My team is taking a beating." He
squinted as the camera focused on the player that had missed
the shot. "If I were the coach, he'd get the beating of his life
when the game was over." Dad walked back to the couch and
sat down.

On TV the players were busy passing the ball around. I
wasn't sure what to do with myself. Ken must be on his way.
I was about to head back upstairs when the doorbell rang. I
nearly jumped out of my skin.

"Yes, yes!" said Dad. He leaned forward. "Pass the ball!
This is not a dance."

I tried not to panic and walked to the door even though
my legs wanted to run to it. I opened the door.

Ken smiled. "Hi, I'm here."

We stood there for a few moments with Ken still smiling.
"Oh, come on in," I said.

"Take the shot, take it!" shouted Dad. "Oh!" Both dad and
spectators on TV lamented.

"Dad, this is my friend Ken. Ken, my dad, Dr. Obi." I'd

already told Ken about the difference in custom where Nigerian parents would find it disrespectful if their kid's friends or people way younger than them called them by their first name. It was Uncle, Auntie, Mama, Papa, even though there's no blood relationship. My stomach was tied in knots. What would happen? The first friend I brought home was a boy and I wished Mom was here.

"Good afternoon, Dr. Obi," said Ken.

"My friend, there's nothing good about this afternoon," said Dad, his eyes glued to the TV.

Ken took a few steps toward the television and focused on the game. "Yes, yes," said Ken.

The player for Dad's team stole the ball from their own end of the field and skillfully dribbled his way to a few feet away from the goalie of the opposing team.

"Take the shot!" screamed Dad.

"Go for it!" said Ken.

The man seemed to hear them and in an elegant display of showmanship sent the goalie diving to the left side of the goal while the ball went into the right side.

Dad's hands shot into the air. "Goal! Good man!"

"Yeah!" Ken pumped a fist in the air.

Funny enough, the player that had scored was the same one dad had called a wild animal a few minutes earlier. The spectators went wild.

"I thought we would lose," said Ken a tinge of red on his cheeks.

"Who are you?" asked Dad, noticing Ken for the first time.

"I'm . . . I'm Ken, Dr. Obi." Ken's eyes glanced from Dad to me.

"Oh, Ngozi's Ken? The artist?"

Ken nodded.

"Sorry, I didn't see you come in," said Dad. "You understand soccer?"

"Yes, Arsenal is my team—"

Dad cut him off. "Name the players?"

Ken rattled out name after name, and I could see the skepticism on Dad's face change to admiration.

"Good, you're really a fan. Ngozi, get my new friend a beer."

"No, sir!" blurted Ken.

"Oh," said Dad. "Get him whatever he drinks. Soda, apple juice?"

"Pepsi would be nice, if you have any," said Ken.

I went to the kitchen as Dad and Ken continued to talk soccer. By the time I came back with a bottle of Pepsi, Ken and Dad were sitting on the couch watching the game.

"Dad, should I get lunch ready?"

Dad looked at Ken. "You'll stay for lunch, right?"

"Yes, sir."

"Call me Doc," said Dad.

I set the table for three and went back to the kitchen to heat the soup and make the fufu. In my excitement, I'd forgotten to defrost the stew. And there was no rice. I would have to boil some and defrost the stew.

"Is the food ready?" asked Dad.

"Almost," I said. By the time food was ready their team had finished playing and another match was about to start.

"Good timing," said Dad. "I'm famished."

We went to the dining table. "We have rice and stew with vegetables, and okra soup with fufu."

"I'll start with fufu," said Dad and helped himself.

"I'll try fufu too," said Ken.

"Young man, it's spicy," said Dad.

"I'll manage," replied Ken and scooped out some fufu

and okra soup. He watched Dad walk over to the sink and wash his hands.

"I'll eat with my hands too," said Ken.

Ken washed his hands, sat down, and watched Dad. I'd taken some food, but I was too on edge to eat. I pushed my food around with my fork. I saw Ken watching Dad from the corner of his eye as Dad expertly rolled the bolus of fufu in his palm.

Ken took some fufu and rolled it with both palms as if he was in kindergarten playing with Play-Doh. When it was nice and round, he poked a hole in the middle.

He used his spoon to fill the hole with soup and shoved it into his mouth. I pushed a large portion of fufu into my mouth to stop me from laughing.

"You like it?" asked Dad.

Ken nodded as he chewed and continued the demanding task of rolling the fufu, poking a hole, and filling it with soup before eating it.

"How come you like soccer?" asked Dad.

"My mother used to take my sister to soccer camp when we were younger," said Ken. "I played basketball and our schedules used to clash, so I enrolled in soccer too. I watched the European League and became a fan."

Dad nodded. "Interesting."

We finished lunch, and I cleared the table. I was surprised that Ken ate all the fufu he took. As we sat in the living room, I heard the garage door open; Mom was back. I closed my eyes and let out a deep breath. I felt a release of tension.

"Hello!" said Mom. She dropped her keys and handbag on the kitchen island and headed toward the living room. "You guys ate already?"

"Welcome, sweetie," said Dad. "Yes, we did."

Mom had a big smile on her lips. Her eyes darted around. "Where . . . where's Kenechukwu?"

Ken hesitated, stood up, and extended his hand. "Good evening, Dr. Obi, I'm Ken."

Mom's smile faded as her eyes widened. She rubbed her chin with one hand, and hesitantly shook Ken's hand with the other. "You're Ken? Short for . . . ?"

"Mackenzie," said Ken.

"Mackenzie?" I blurted. "I didn't know that."

Ken turned to me and laughed. "That's why I prefer Ken."

"Oh, I always thought you were Nigerian. You're . . ." Mom's voice trailed off.

om looked at me, and I averted my eyes and dipped my chin, unable to meet her gaze. I didn't know what to say, or how to handle this.

"There's a Mackenzie I know," said Dad. "Brilliant chap." Dad turned to Mom. "Sweetie, you should have seen this guy mold pounded yam and put it away with okra soup. Anyone that can do that and loves soccer is a Nigerian in my book."

"Oh, that's not what I meant," said Mom. She extended her hand. Her smile returned as she shook hands with Ken again. "Welcome. So you liked pounded yam?"

"Yes," said Ken. "It's just like mashed potato. Reminds me of Thanksgiving. The okra soup was delicious."

Mom let go of Ken's hand. "I'm hungry too. It was a busy call." She headed back to the kitchen.

I joined Mom in the kitchen.

"He's white," said Mom in a whisper.

"He's always been white," I said.

Mom paused and looked at me. "Cheeky," she said out loud. "I'll go up and change."

I went back to the living room and hoped Ken hadn't

noticed. He and Dad were engrossed in another discussion about soccer. A few minutes later, Ken said he would be leaving.

"No way!" said Dad. "You can't leave. You haven't drawn my portrait yet!"

Ken's eyes widened, and his lips parted in a grin.

"Only joking," said Dad. "It was nice watching soccer with a fan. Thanks for coming."

"Leaving already?" asked Mom as she walked into the living room.

"Yes," said Ken.

"Hope to see more of you," said Mom.

I walked Ken to his car. He said he enjoyed the food and would be happy to come again if I invited him for lunch. We didn't talk about what Mom had said. Maybe he hadn't even noticed.

With Dad done with the TV for the day, he retired to their room. I removed the empty bottle of Pepsi and went up to my room. A few minutes later, there was a knock and Mom's head popped in. She walked in and shut the door.

"What was the emergency at work?"

Mom waved her hand dismissively. "We handled it. The main problem is what happened with Ken." Mom sat beside me on the bed. Head down, she twiddled her fingers.

I tried to make it less awkward. "I never knew his full name was Mackenzie either."

Mom nodded and looked up. "What happened there wasn't nice, especially coming from me. My action was subconscious. I have nothing against white people. In my head, I thought Ken was a Nigerian American, according to Dad."

Mom paused. What was she going to say, that I should stop seeing Ken?

"Many years ago, before Ben and I became a thing, I had a boyfriend . . . My behavior today was exactly what my boyfriend's father did to me back then. In Nigeria, it's tribal because everyone is black. The disagreement comes down to which tribe are you from. Which religion. Apart from a few bad mangoes, we mostly get along."

Mom paused for a moment as if she was contemplating what to say.

"Many years ago, I was in love with a man who I felt was not into me as I was into him. He was three years older than me, and he was doing his internship at the teaching hospital I was a student at. There were rumors that he ran around with nurses, other students, and just about anything in skirts. I ignored all those signs and pretended they were not true. One night, there was a party. He was on call, so he could not go. So, I went to the library to study."

I liked the story so far. I said nothing but waited for the Ken connection.

Mom looked at me and sighed. "I don't know if it's a good idea to share this with you." She looked at me, a Mona Lisa–like smile on her lips. She glanced down to her hands and fiddled with her wedding ring.

"Anyway, after an hour, I was tired of studying and went to see my boyfriend in the children's emergency room, where he was on call. I walked in, and the place was empty."

"No sick kids?" I asked interrupting the story.

"Well, sometimes you have a lull, and you think, oh, it's a good night." Mom laughed. "Suddenly there'll be an avalanche of sick kids as if they were outside somewhere waiting for you to think how lucky you were. So, I walk into the doctors' call room and there . . . I found him in bed with one of the nurses on duty."

Mom paused, there was no more sign of Mona Lisa. She

smoothed out an invisible wrinkle on her dress, clasped her hands together over her thigh, and continued.

"I couldn't pretend the rumors were not true anymore. I wasn't thinking. Only revenge was on my mind. I went back to my room, got dressed, and went to the party."

"He didn't come after you?" I asked.

Mom shook her head. "I planned to have my way with the first guy I fancied at the party. It wasn't hard. There were a lot of medical students and a few interns there. Most had had a little too much to drink. I drank some punch that was loaded with sugar so I wouldn't taste the alcohol until it said hello with a buzz. Uninhibited because of the alcohol, I talked to one cute, drunk guy. His speech was slurred; he was hammered."

Mom giggled, then her smile faded, as if she remembered she was talking to me.

"Now, that was a wasted soul," Mom said. "We danced, or rather he dragged himself around the floor for a while, and I asked him if he could walk me to my car."

28

Mom exhaled. "I'm very ashamed to say I got my revenge. Instead of making me feel better, I added an additional load of guilt and regret." There were tears in Mom's eyes.

"You don't have to continue . . ."

"I have to get this off my chest. I've never told anybody before. It will be therapy for me."

Mom's face looked like she was reliving the agony of that day.

"My boyfriend apologized. He said he would have come after me, but sick kids showed up. He begged for forgiveness and assured me it would not happen again. I took him back, and I believe he kept his word. Four weeks later, my period didn't come. I ignored it; my periods were erratic. But after the sixth week, I checked and my HCG was high. HCG is human chorionic gonadotropic hormone. I was pregnant."

I gasped. My hands flew to my lips.

"I faced a dilemma . . . I was ashamed . . . what do I do?" Mom sighed. "The pregnancy must continue."

I pursed my lips "So, you planned to keep the baby?"

"Yes, my boyfriend told his father that he wanted us to get married." Mom smiled and shook her head. "His father was a piece of work—very controlling—and he worshiped at the altar of tribalism. My boyfriend was a Muslim from the north and I was a Christian from the south. His father would never let him marry outside his tribe."

Mom looked at me. Now I knew for sure where she was going with the story.

Mom's voice broke. "In America it's racism, in Africa it's tribalism. I'm so sorry how I reacted when I saw Ken. I feel so bad, like a fraud."

"So, what did you do?" I asked.

"My boyfriend's dad had a change of heart. He said he would take care of all the expenses and would let us get married once the baby was born."

"What about your parents, grandpa, and grandma? How did they take it?" I asked. Mom's story was unfolding like a Nollywood movie.

"They must have been disappointed, but they didn't show it. That helped me get through those nine months. I was an unwed girl in medical school and tongues wagged. 'Irresponsible! What type of doctor is she going to become?' people said. Anyway, as my EDD approached—"

"What's EDD?" I asked.

"Oh, expected date of delivery. My boyfriend's dad had arranged a doctor for me. We already knew the baby was big, and the placenta's insertion in my uterine wall was abnormal so there might be complications. The doctor had recommended Cesarean section, CS, but I refused. Foolish! As a medical student, I knew C-section was the best option, but I wanted a natural process. I'd seen women belittled by other women because they opted for surgery. That was stupid of me —it's water under the bridge now. To cut a long story short, my uterus ruptured as I attempted vaginal delivery. I bled a lot. The doctor had to perform a hysterectomy to stop the bleeding."

I didn't know what that meant, but it didn't sound good.

Mom paused and looked at me. "Hysterectomy is the removal of the womb. They removed my womb to stop the bleeding and save my life."

Mom nodded and smiled. The kind of smile you resorted to when the only other option was to cry.

"I was transfused and sedated for two days. When I woke up, the first thing I asked for was for my baby. They had already buried her." A sob burst out of Mom's mouth and wave after wave wracked her body.

"Oh no!" I clasped my hand over my mouth. "I'm so sorry."

A big tear trickled down Mom's cheek, and she stopped sobbing.

There were tears in my eyes. I didn't know what to say to her.

"It wasn't easy." Mom's voice broke. She wiped her eyes. "But life went on. Once I recovered and came back to school. I broke up with my boyfriend. He finished his house job and left. I found God and put all my trust in Him. I went to mass every day. I took a while to date again. My last experience clouded my judgment. Ben didn't have a chance, and I nearly passed on him. He knew I cared for him and vice versa. I told him I would never have any children, but he persisted. I couldn't trust any man; however, Ben stuck around. I love that man so much, and the rest, like they say, is history."

29

My respect for my parents grew after I heard Mom's story. Some Nigerian men without sons married a second, sometimes a third, wife to get a male child, yet Dad knew he would not have any kids at all and still married Mom. That was true love.

Ken didn't ask me about Mom, nor did I mention it. We agreed to text each other during the day but only hang out on weekends.

In school on Monday, I was back to my usual routine, strolling to classes with Preeti and Jennifer. In my science class, the teacher was fond of calling students at random to answer questions, and because of that I always had to study extra hard the day before each class to prepare for the topic.

The week rolled by fast, and Friday was upon us again. Ken said he would pick me up and take me to another playground.

"Is your dad watching soccer this weekend again?" asked Ken as we drove toward a park close to Falls Lake.

I shrugged. "He watches every weekend. Unless he's on call or there's a wedding or party."

"That's nice," said Ken and drank from a bottle of water he had. "And they don't bother you?"

"Bother me how?" I asked.

"Like when we're playing music in the house, I always feel guilty that my parents would be happier if I was doing something else."

"Well, I do what's expected of me most of the time," I said.

"That's exactly the problem," said Ken. "Can't they let me be to make music and live my life the way I want to?"

I looked out of the window as we drove away from Falls Lake and continued toward unfamiliar territory.

"I think I know what you mean. You have this constant turmoil of feeling guilty when you're being creative or doing something you like divides your attention. You can't give what you like your best, and you end up feeling guilty, unfulfilled, and angry."

We drove on in silence for a few blocks.

Ken broke the silence. He took his eyes off the road for a second and looked at me. "How did you come up with that?"

I hesitated. Ken was my best friend. Even his sister Jennifer knew less about me than Ken did. "I used to be like that when I lived with my Auntie in Nigeria. I wasn't happy and always felt there was something better, somewhere. I tried to find it but never did."

"Okay, go on," said Ken.

"In your case, you are who you are. You like to make music and draw, but your parents have more experience than you when it comes to making a living. They've been there, done that. They've seen things and maybe know people who strived to become singers, actors, and writers but never made it. I think they don't want you to end up with nothing after putting in so much."

Ken stopped the car in a parking lot. To our left was a playground, but unlike the one we went to the previous week, this one was full of kids.

"So what do I do?" asked Ken.

I bit my lip. "You shouldn't just disregard your parents' advice. It would be terrible if you get to be their age and realize that the advice they gave you many years before was right, but you disregarded it for the follies of youth. Listen to them and talk to them and find out how their advice can fit into your plans. Do whatever you guys agree on to the best of your abilities, then do your own stuff in your spare time. Since it's something you enjoy, you could put energy into it without it being a chore."

We sat in the car for a few more minutes watching the kids.

Ken exhaled. "You know, just the thought of doing what my parents want instead of fighting them already feels like I've achieved a lot."

"Do you have memories of your parents taking you to the park when you were a kid?" I asked.

Ken nodded. "Why do you ask?"

"Just looking at all the parents here, I wonder if there are other things I missed as a child."

Ken looked at me for what seemed like a long time. "Come on." His voice was heavy with emotion. Let's go for a walk. Maybe by the time we get back, there'll be room in the playground for us. We must catch up on all you missed."

This park was a lot bigger than the one at Falls Lake. It had a lake, large enough for people to paddle boats on. Two or three people stood by the shores with a line in the water and fishing rod in hand.

Ken and I went for a long walk, often stepping aside for bikers, joggers, and the occasional rollerblader to get through.

By the time we came back, one swing was free. I got on it and swung. For some unknown reason, I couldn't capture the fun of the last time. Was it because this wasn't a surprise? Or because the novelty had worn off?

Ken looked at the tire suspended by chains on the branches of a tree and pointed. "Do you want to try the tire swing? It's fun. I'll swing you around."

"Why not?" I got in from under the tire and hoisted myself up. I held on to the chains.

"It can get intense." Ken placed his palms on the tire. "Are you ready?

I nodded.

"Hold on tight. It will spin like crazy." Ken gave the tire a push, and each time it came back to him, he would push harder at an angle that made the tire spin.

"Weee!" I screamed as air rushed past my ears and I was spinning. I shut my eyes, and I felt like the bottom disappeared. I was flying.

"Let me know when you feel dizzy," said Ken and kept on pushing at an angle.

I felt dizzy, and I told Ken to stop. Once the tire slowed down, Ken grabbed it and held on until it stopped.

I looked up at the branches of the tall trees surrounding the park. "Everything is still spinning!"

"It's going to stop in a minute," said Ken with a laugh. "Did you feel the rush?"

"Yes," I said as things slowed down. "How am I going to get down? I feel so tired."

Ken stood behind me. "I'll bring you down. I'll wrap my hands around your waist, you lean back and let go of the chain, okay?"

As soon as Ken's hands touched me, it felt like I went limp and fell back. His breath was hot against my neck as he guided me down. It still surprised me I didn't feel like backing away from him when we touched. Maybe I was getting used to him.

Ken grunted. "I'm dragging you out now. Let go of the chain."

I let go. Ken gasped and struggled to support both of us. He lost his footing, and we crashed to the ground. I giggled uncontrollably.

Ken was laughing too. "What's funny?"

As I struggled to get up, still giggling, my face was a few inches from his. We stared at each other, breathing hard. Were we going to kiss? The thought alone made me tingle all over. It was like a magnet pulling on a paper clip closer and closer. Ken's eyes widened. His face turned ghost white.

30

My smile faded. "What is it?"

"Nose bleed!" Ken patted his jacket, brought out a pack of pocket tissue, and gave me some. "Does anywhere hurt?"

"No." I took the tissue and touched my nose, it came back red. Only then did I smell the rustic odor of blood.

"I read somewhere that spinning fast can do that to you," said Ken. "I'm so sorry. Pinch your nose and tilt your head back."

I felt and tasted the trickle down my throat as I held my head in that position. I brought the tissue to my lips and spat into it. Minutes later when I lowered my head, the bleeding had stopped.

"It's all my fault," said Ken. He took the wet tissue from me and handed me fresh ones. "I shouldn't have spun you so fast. Any pains?"

"Just my neck from tilting back." I looked around, the few people still in the park did not bother with us.

We got in the car, and I pulled down the sun visor to look in the mirror. There was some dried blood. I didn't think I should tell my parents. "Can I swish out my mouth with your water?"

Ken handed me the bottle. "Sure."

I opened the door and spat the water out, then took a long drink from the bottle. "The swing tire was fun, though."

"Well, we shouldn't be doing that again," said Ken.

I soaked a tissue with water and wiped dried blood from my nose.

Ken started the car and drove us out of the parking lot. "I have something for you."

"What? Where?"

"It's in the backseat. It came in the mail."

I reached behind the seat and grabbed the brown bag in the back. I brought it out. It was a DNA kit.

"I told you I would not rest until I did everything I could to make your wish come true."

"What wish?"

"Remember the day we went to the movie and you said you would like to know who your biological parents are?"

I nodded. "Oh. But we also talked about Nigeria not having a DNA database to compare it against."

Ken was quiet for a while. "Okay, let's just do it for fun."

"Based on what I know from Mrs. Coleman's class, it would be a waste of time and money."

"I've already paid for it, we might as well use it," said Ken.

When we stopped in front of my house, Ken brought out the kit, read the instructions, and passed a tube to me.

Ken pointed at a black line on the tube. "It says you should fill it up to that mark with saliva."

I spat into the tube. "I hope the bleeding won't skew the test."

"Who knows, there's nothing we can do about it now,"

said Ken. He sealed the tube and put it back in the box. "I'll mail it out first thing tomorrow."

I got out of the car. "Thanks for the nosebleed."

Ken lowered his head, shoulders slumped.

I leaned back in and patted him on the shoulder. "Only joking. See you next weekend?"

He recovered fast and smiled.

I walked away, tipped my head back, and looked into the sky, a warmth radiating throughout my body.

Over the next few weeks, I noticed Ken was pulling back, rarely letting us hang out alone. Most of the time he brought Jennifer or Paul along.

Jennifer, not Ken, invited me to their house. It was walking distance from my home. I was surprised to learn they were a blended family. Their parents had married ten years earlier. Ken had a different biological mother and Jennifer a different biological dad. But both parents adopted them.

October rolled in, and the weather fluctuated from cold mornings to warm afternoons to chilly evenings. And I'd thought harmattan season in Nigeria was cold! After two months in school, I felt at home with the school pace and interacting with other students.

"Halloween is coming, and we're thinking of having a party," said Jennifer as we walked out of Biology II.

I didn't want to ask a stupid question, but if I didn't, I'd never know. "Okay, so what exactly happens on Halloween day?"

Jennifer chuckled. "On the thirty-first of every October, people dress up in costumes and go around saying 'trick or treat'."

"So where does the party come in?" I asked.

Jennifer exhaled. "Oh, it's the same party we've been planning to have all the while. Mom is finally dragging Dad to Boston the Saturday after Halloween. It's going to be fun. We'll just have a few friends over for snacks and drinks."

"Sounds great," I said. "The few parties I've gone to were birthdays, wedding after parties, mostly whole family affairs."

"What? You've never been to, like, a party for someone our age?"

"Nope."

Jennifer did a little dance. "Just show up on Saturday evening for your first party in the USA. What costume are you going to wear for trick-or-treating? I will be a witch!"

"That's demonic. My Mom explained the whole Halloween thing and trick or treat to me. I'll stay home and eat candy. And she bought a lot!"

"In that case, we'll start trick-or-treating from your house," said Jennifer. "Don't eat all the candy before we get there. It's a lot of fun. We drive around in two or three cars all dressed up and visit different streets. We only take one candy each to leave some for others. Are you sure you don't want to come?"

"I like to observe first, then participate later. Maybe next year's Halloween."

Jennifer went on and on about how great trick-or-treating would be. And their party would be something else too. I couldn't wait.

31

"**I** want these," said the man. "Peel them." Hissing sounds escaped from his gap-tooth as he spoke.

The man selected four oranges from the tray and handed them to the orange girl.

The man's eyes met those of the orange girl, and she looked away. She saw the danger. The hunger. She sensed there might be trouble.

"I want bananas," said another voice.

The orange girl jumped, almost cut herself. A newcomer emerged. He too was shabby and dirty, dressed in similar attire as the man with the gap tooth. He selected a bunch of yellow ripe bananas.

"Do you have groundnuts?" asked the newcomer in Pidgin English. "How much?"

"No groundnuts," replied the banana girl. She told him the price of the bananas.

Mr. Gap Tooth kept his eyes on the orange girl and looked up with an amused grin as his friend haggled for the price of bananas. At last, they agreed.

The newcomer held the banana bunch close to him. "I

don't like the price, but I'll pay. Come, I have the money inside." He walked toward an opening with a piece of cloth draped across it in place of an actual door.

The girl looked at her friend peeling an orange. "Give me a minute, I'll be right back."

I woke up gasping for air, my chest tight. I was covered in sweat, my throat dry. I went to the bathroom and drank water from the tap. Nothing about the dream made me comfortable, yet it kept coming back. There was no going back to sleep, I lay on the bed staring at the ceiling as darkness turned into day.

Again, I kept the dream to myself. It was my problem alone.

Saturday morning was unseasonably warm, so I decided to walk over to Jennifer's house to see if she needed help with the party preparation.

Ken was outside in front of the garage shooting hoops. He must have been out for a while; his sweat-soaked T-shirt clung to his body. Ken's face broke out in a smile once he saw me.

"Hi, Ngozi. Pleasant surprise." Sweat trickled down his forehead. He bounced the ball once, leaped into the air, and took a shot at the basket. The ball sailed in.

"How often do you do this?" I asked.

"Apart from practice in school, only when the weather is as warm as this morning. I wish it had been this warm yesterday for Halloween."

For a few seconds, there was nothing to say. We stared at each other.

Ken's eyes lit up. "Hey, I need to go to Thomas Edison's museum at West Orange. I could use some company. Do you want to come? Please say yes? I'm writing this paper about the invention of the light bulb. I thought I might as well visit his workshop."

I hesitated. "Okay . . . when? . . . And who is Thomas Edison?"

Ken grinned. "When? As soon as I take a shower. Who was Edison? The guy that invented the electric bulb. He was a prolific inventor. I've been there before. I'll give you a quick tour when we get there."

This was a chance to hang out with Ken alone for the first time in a while. "All right, I'll check on Jennifer, see if she needs help. If she doesn't, I'll go with you." I pulled my eyes away from his sweaty, toned body and went inside. I found Jennifer still asleep in her room.

"There isn't much to do," said Jennifer, groggy. "Punch, music, people. All of that would take less than thirty minutes to set up. Music is the easiest part. My dad bought a new audio system with a Bluetooth app so we can control the music with our cell phones. Isn't that cool?" Jennifer yawned. She looked like she wanted to get back to sleep. "How was Halloween night for you after we left?"

"The first time the bell rang, and I opened the door, two little girls yelled, 'Trick or treat.' I said, 'Trick,' and they just stared at me."

Jennifer slapped her forehead and laughed. "No."

"A woman with them said, 'No tricks, we want treats,' so I gave them some chocolate. I'm going with Ken to West Orange—"

Jennifer groaned. "The museum? Ken admires Tesla, yet he's always going to the Edison museum. We were up late. Can you do me a favor?"

"Sure."

Jennifer exhaled. "Could you call me in four hours to make sure I am awake?"

I promised I would and left. Ken and I drove to West Orange, and I'd expected to see a museum like you see on TV. It turned out to be Edison's factory, preserved as it was when he worked there starting in 1887. It looked like the inventor had just stepped out and would be back soon. On more than one occasion, I thought I saw a gray-haired old man in a lab coat whistling as he bustled around.

Ken led the way to the section of the museum with the different iterations of the electric bulb, and he took notes.

"You like movies, right?" asked Ken.

I nodded.

The films for the first motion pictures were produced here. I'll show you," said Ken.

"He invented motion pictures too?"

"Well, the forerunner, called a Kinetoscope, a peep show–like viewing device. They placed them in hotel lobbies and amusement parks back in the day." Ken made an air quote. "Those movies were made in a kinetograph studio, which Edison constructed right here. I will show you in a minute. He finished the construction in 1893."

"Right here? That's more than a hundred years ago." I didn't know why I got excited, because everything here plus the building was all more than a hundred years old."

"He nicknamed it the Black Maria," said Ken.

We exited the main building and headed toward a flight of stairs. I climbed behind Ken and wracked my brain. The name was familiar, Black Maria, but from where? We reached the top of the flight of steps, and I stopped. My chest felt so tight I struggled for air. The memories of that day at the police station flashed through my mind. I remembered the prisoner shouting obscenities at me from the back of the truck.

"Presenting the Black . . . Are you okay?"

I turned around as if to walk down the stairs.

"What's wrong?" asked Ken.

I held the railing, inhaled, and lowered myself to the step and sat down. It cleared my head. "I'll sit here."

"Exhausted? Sorry, I wasn't thinking," said Ken. He sat down beside me on the stairs.

"Just tired," I said. I couldn't tell him why the black metal fabrication made me react the way I did.

Ken looked at the several floors of the museum opposite us. "It's quite a lot of walking. When you're inside, you don't realize it."

"Why don't you explore?" I said. "I promise I won't go anywhere."

"Sure, you don't mind?"

"Go ahead, I don't mind."

Ken got to his feet. "All right, I'll tell you all about it."

Ken walked in and explored the Black Maria. He didn't take long, and we left after he was done. The drive home was silent most of the way. I must have dozed off because when I opened my eyes, we were in Falls Lake.

"Get some rest," said Ken. "I don't want you to miss the party."

"I will. I guess all that walking about made me tired." I promised I'd be at the party in a few hours. I sent Jennifer a text. She replied right away. She was awake, and the party was on.

32

As I walked toward Jennifer's house, at about half a block away, I could hear the thump, thump, thump of loud music. Cars lined both sides of the road.

Inside, the house was full. I walked around looking for Jennifer. There were kids in the living room playing video games on the big-screen TV, in the dining room, in the kitchen—everywhere. It was a house party!

There were some kids I'd never seen before; some of them were smoking inside the house, and I wondered if that wouldn't get Jennifer and Ken in trouble with their parents. I struggled through the sea of people looking for a familiar face. Then I saw Paul dancing with Preeti. Paul waved at me and I waved back. Preeti was dancing with her back to Paul. I tapped her on the shoulder.

Preeti spun around. "Hey, Ngozi!" she screamed. Preeti's face glistened with sweat.

I realized how hot it was inside and took off my jacket.

"Show me some moves!" said Preeti and moved her shoulders from side to side to the beat of the music, her long black hair gyrating.

I cupped my left ear to hear. "Where's Jennifer?"

"Jennifer?" Preeti continued to dance to the music and pointed toward the door that led outside.

"Thanks!" I made a sign I was coming back, gave Paul a thumbs-up, and walked toward the sliding door that led to the back.

I itched all over, too many unfamiliar people. I ran my hand through my hair and took quick breaths. It didn't help. There were just too many people. Each thump of the bass music seemed directed at me. I saw the open patio door and walked toward it. I stepped outside, and the fresh air was a welcome relief. I walked toward the railing of the deck and looked at the yard. There were people there too.

"Hi, Ngozi!"

I turned. It was Jennifer! "Hey, I've been looking for you!" We hugged. "What a party!"

"Yeah," said Jennifer and looked around. "There're kids here I don't even know!" she said. Her eyes sparkled. Her hands flailed in every direction. "Have you tried the punch?"

"No."

"It's toxic! Try it!" She laughed.

Mom's story about the punch at her party came to my mind. "No, thank you, I'll just have a Coke."

"Okay." She gulped from the cup she was holding. "I'll go get you one."

Jennifer turned and bumped into a guy who was standing right behind her. "Oh, I forgot to introduce you. This is Brian. Brian, meet Ngozi, my best friend from school."

It was then that I noticed the blond guy with a Jay Leno jaw standing beside Jennifer. We shook hands and I wished Leno would go with Jennifer to get my drink. I wasn't in the mood for small talk.

"Wait for me," said Brian, running after Jennifer.

Thank God. He must have read my mind.

I stood there and looked around. The itch in my armpit and scalp had stopped. This was my first house party. I remembered the few birthday parties I had gone to in Lamija. There would be cabin biscuits, chin-chin (thick fried biscuit batter), Fanta, Coke, and a professional photographer. There was usually a cake plastered with white icing. I'd never known icing came in other colors until recently. All I wanted to eat was the icing. I didn't care much for the cake. I nodded to the music.

I felt awkward standing there as people milled around me. Then Jennifer and Brian reappeared with a can of Coke and two brownies.

"This is gorgeous!" Jennifer said and pointed to the brownie. "Look around, feel at home. I need to talk to Brian. We'll be over there. Come get me if you need anything." She pointed in the general direction ahead of her. They walked away.

I stood where they'd left me and took a bite of the brownie. It was moist and sweet, just the way I liked it. The first brownie disappeared fast, and I started on the second. That too went down quickly, and I washed them down with a long drink from the can. I wouldn't mind another brownie; they were delicious.

The brownies made me feel warm and fuzzy, relaxed. I surveyed my surroundings for any familiar faces. Maybe I should drag Preeti out and listen to her talk. Then I saw Ken sitting on the stairs that led to the backyard.

I walked over to him. "Ken."

He looked up and just stared.

Those eyes. My nose flared up. I had this fluttery feeling in my stomach. I smiled.

"Wow," said Ken in a low voice. "You look nice. Glad you made it! Come and join me."

He made room for me.

"I'll take your jacket," said Ken, a broad smile planted on his face. "You look gorgeous."

I handed him my jacket and sat one step down from him, forgetting about the brownie. He had a plastic cup with a drink in it. My guess was it contained the punch. From the corner of my eye, I saw someone familiar coming toward us. The person hesitated, stopped, and went to the railing of the deck. I turned to get a good look.

"Was that Mary Ann?" I asked.

33

Ken leaned back and stretched his legs out in exaggerated casualness. "Oh yes, she came."

"Why?" My pulse raced. "Emmm, sorry, I didn't mean for it to come out like that. But I thought you guys were done." My body moved with each beat of my heart.

Ken exhaled and looked away. He brought out a folded piece of paper from his pocket and tapped it on his hand. "It's a long story. She thought we should give it another chance. I had to remind her it's been months already, and there's you."

My lips quivered. My stomach muscles tightened. I had to brace myself. Whatever I would hear wouldn't go down well.

Ken waved a hand. "I told her I had moved on, and the reasons we broke up hadn't changed. She was applying to a different school, and she wanted the freedom to see other people. She can't have her cake and eat it too."

My whole body trembled.

"You're shaking," said Ken. He opened my jacket and draped it over my shoulders.

When I tried to talk, my teeth chattered. I nodded and pulled my jacket closer. The weather was also getting nippy.

Ken ran his fingers through his hair. He looked down, and when he looked up, he had this crooked grin on his face. "Do you want to go inside and see my trophy collection? It's not that I want to show off, just something I'm proud of and I'd like to share with you."

I knew where this was going, to get me somewhere private and tell me it was over. All I wanted to do was go home. We might as well get it over and done with. "That's fine, let's go."

We got up and walked into the house, into the deafening music. We evaded boys and girls dancing in the living room and those who sat on the stairs talking. I felt like I would meltdown. I needed somewhere private on my own. The bathroom. I tugged at Ken's hand.

Ken turned. His eyebrows shot up.

The music was too loud, and I didn't have it in me to shout. "Bathroom." I pointed toward the bathroom.

Ken nodded. "Bathroom?"

I nodded and headed in that direction. As we approached, the door opened, and a girl came out. Good timing.

"Will be out here," said Ken.

I shut the door and looked at myself in the mirror. "Don't cry, don't cry," I whispered. But the tears came anyway. I splashed water on my face and reached into my jacket pocket for my Kleenex pack. I felt the folded paper, the one Ken had been holding. He didn't have the guts to say it to my face. I unfolded the paper, an envelope addressed to me. With trembling hands, I opened it.

34

———

I jumped. Someone had banged on the door.

"Ngozi, are you done?"

I cocked my head. "Jennifer?"

"Yes, it's me. Come on out. You have to see this."

I shoved the envelope back into my pocket, and brushed imaginary lint off my face with my palms. I tried out a fake smile on the mirror, then opened the door.

Jennifer grabbed my hand, her eyes sparkling. "Come, Ken and his band are about to sing."

"Sing?"

"Yes!" She dragged me toward the center of their living room where Paul and Ken stood with mics in hand. A guitar hung on Ken's shoulder; a drum set was in front of Paul.

"Check one-two," said Ken. "This is a song I wrote a few weeks ago. I thought I'd share it today." Strumming the guitar with practiced ease, Ken sang while Paul worked the drums.

"Now that you've stolen my heart
   Each time I see you the deeper I fall

I know you feel the same, just give us a chance

WE COME FROM DIFFERENT BACKGROUNDS
    But our core is the same
    True love can overcome any obstacle
    Our love will grow if given a chance

OH, BABY BABY, IT'S A LOVE THING
    Of all the girls in the world
    It's you that has captured my heart
    You bring out the best in me
    I want to share my life with you."

"WOW," I WHISPERED. I CLUTCHED MY HANDS TOGETHER IN front of my chest. I couldn't believe my ears. Ken had such a lovely voice, and it seemed like I was his only audience. I had this intense desire in me to share with everyone that I felt the same for Ken.

Jennifer bumped me on the shoulder. "He's good at this, right?" She jumped, clapped her hands, and whooped.

I glanced around the living room. All eyes were on Ken and Paul. I caught a glimpse of Mary Ann. What if Ken was singing for her? I stiffened.

Both Ken and Paul went wild on their instruments, and the crowd exploded. Ken lowered his voice and sang with emotion, giving it his best, like he was trying to win the heart of the person he loved.

"Who's the girl?" a voice shouted.

Ken smiled and continued to sing. He scanned the room and, like a panther, took slow steps into the crowd. He was like a celebrity. Girls reached out to touch his hand. Guys fist-bumped him. His eyes focused on me and at that moment, my inside froze.

"He's making a move!" another voice shouted.

"He's coming for me!" yelled a female voice.

It was apparent what Ken sought, but I didn't believe it. People dashed out of his way, creating a part straight to me. Ken sauntered toward me, belting the chorus.

"Oh, baby baby, it's a love thing
Of all the girls in the world
It's you that has captured my heart
You bring out the best in me
I want to share my life with you."

KEN STOPPED IN FRONT OF ME. HIS EYES BORE INTO MINE AS he finished the lyrics. He placed a hand on my shoulder. My pulse raced. I didn't know where to look. My knees felt like jelly.

Ken leaned closer. As he finished the song, his lips brushed my cheeks and a jolt of electricity passed through.

"Whoop! Whoop!" said a female.

People applauded. Ken held my hand as he bowed. People patted him on the back, congratulating him on a job well done. The party music started up again.

"I have this dance," said Ken.

I'd never danced with a boy before. What was I going to do? I'd never danced with anybody before, and I didn't know how. There was no way I could extricate myself. I doubted my legs would support me if I tried to move away. Ken held me tight, and I forgot everything as our hearts melted together. Right there and then, nothing mattered but Ken's arms around me.

"Ngozi, I wrote that for you," said Ken. "Do you like it?"

I could only nod. I didn't trust myself to speak. We held each other until the song was over.

"Come on, let's get some air." He led me toward the porch. As we headed for the door, my eyes met Mary Ann's again. Her brief look of amazement turned into an icy stare.

"Oh, that was much-needed air," said Ken when we got outside. He drew me closer. "Ngozi."

"Yes." I moved closer as if I was being pulled to him by a magnetic force. Our lips met. It felt like divine rapture, something that was meant to happen.

"I love you," said Ken.

"I love you too," I said. So, this was what it felt like to be in love. I gripped Ken and wished the moment would last forever. My mind was millions of miles away when I heard Mary Ann laugh.

"Well, well, well," she said in a voice that spewed poison and dread.

I spun around, and there she was with a victorious smile on her face.

Ken pulled back and inhaled sharply. His face turned pale. "Mary Ann, don't!"

35

I looked at Ken. "What's going on?" He looked away and lowered his head.

Mary Ann waved a dollar bill in front of Ken. "You won!" Her voice was bubbly, face relaxed. "You did it."

"Mary Ann, stop!" said Ken.

Mary Ann glanced at me. "What's going on, you ask?" She waved the dollar toward Paul who was approaching us. "Ken here had a bet with Paul for a dollar that he would kiss Beyoncé here." She pointed the money at me. "And he did."

"Mary Ann. I . . . I told you we're over," said Ken with a stammer. "Why are you doing this?"

My pulse raced. People were gathering. I didn't like attention. My armpit, scalp, all over my body itched. I didn't know where to scratch.

Mary Ann clutched her chest in mock surprise. "Oh, my God, you look startled. Didn't Ken tell you?" She feigned surprise and looked at Paul. "He didn't tell her," she mocked

"He kissed her?" asked Paul, looking at Mary Ann.

"Yep."

"Yeah, Ken, we had a bet, and it seems you won," said Paul.

"I don't know what type of friend you are," said Ken. "But I told you—"

"You won!" Paul raised his hands in the air. "I don't believe you actually pulled it off. Ngozi kept everyone at a distance. She had this wall that seemed insurmountable."

Ken stepped toward Paul and whacked him in the face. Paul fell back, and when he looked up his nose was bleeding.

"We are through," said Paul. "You hear me? We are through!"

I wanted to run away as fast as I could. So, all the while we'd been hanging out, Ken had been pretending. Goose pimples appeared all over me, and I pulled my coat tighter around me. The only safe place now was at home. Head lowered, I walked with heavy steps toward the exit of their compound. I'd been a fool to think that he liked me for me. If I hadn't seen the whole thing unfold before my eyes, I wouldn't have believed it. I thought he cared. Tears welled in my eyes. Thank God I didn't open up to him.

"Ngozi!" Ken was running toward me. I walked faster.

"Please . . . stop." Ken reached me and grabbed my hand.

"No, Ken. Let me go!" He whirled me around.

"I'm so sorry," said Ken. "I tried to tell you about the bet with Paul, but I was so ashamed of it." Ken sounded as if he wanted to cry. He looked at me with a pained stare. "I wrote you a letter explaining it all, but I didn't have the nerve to give it to you. I put it in your pocket." Ken raised his hand to show me it was empty. "Can I?"

Before I could answer, he dug his hand into my right pocket. His face grew vacant. His hand came out empty.

"I put it there," said Ken. His voice cracked.

I'd stuffed it into my other pocket when Jennifer banged on the toilet door. Hands trembling, I reached in to get it.

A shaky laughter burst out of Ken's lips. "That's it, please read it."

Dear Ngozi,

I'm so ashamed of myself. Paul and I made a stupid bet. I overheard Paul and a guy in his class talking about a new girl in his class, pretty, does not stay around to talk to boys, and keeps to herself.

I had no dog in the fight. Paul dared me, and I foolishly accepted. I knew I would lose the bet even before it started, then I bumped into you in school.

As I got to know you, I learned how wonderful and sweet you are. You are different from other girls, independent, and I enjoy being around you. I like watching you emerge from your shell as you explore your new environment.

Who could not fall in love with you? Your genuine innocence and inquisitive nature. I was awake most nights thinking someone might tell you about the bet. Each time I wanted to tell you, I felt you wouldn't understand and I would lose you forever.

I put it off, again and again. But I knew I couldn't delay any longer, so I wrote you this letter.

I love you, Ngozi, and would never do anything to hurt you.

LOVE ALWAYS,
   Ken Davis

WHEN I LOOKED UP, KEN'S EYES WERE ON ME. *WHAT DO I do?* I wondered as I exhaled to relieve the burning in my lungs. *When did his feelings for me change?* I wanted to ask. But instead, an uncontrollable whimper escaped my lips. My knees felt weak, and I wanted to sit down. Clutching the letter in one hand, I wrapped my hands around Ken's neck, buried my face in his shoulders, and sobbed.

"Ngozi, I'm so sorry, so sorry," Ken mumbled over and over again.

We stayed like that for a while until the cold prompted me. My lips trembled all over.

"I can take you home," said Ken.

"No, you were going to show me your trophies, remember?"

Ken dropped his head to his chest. "That seems like ages ago."

I turned and pulled him toward the house.

Ken refused to move. My eyebrows shot up. "What?"

Ken's eyes glistened with tears. "I'm sorry, Ngozi." His voice was a whisper.

"I know," I said in a low voice. Then I raised my voice. "Now stop apologizing and let's go see your trophies, show off."

Ken laughed and let me drag him by the hand toward the house.

Once inside, Ken led the way to the stairs, dodging teens as we walked up.

"This is probably the last time we're having a party at home."

I felt the same. The cigarette smoke alone would linger for days. Plus things that people broke or stole. We walked to a door a few steps from the staircase. Ken opened the door and stammered.

"What the . . ." He waved his hand in the air to disperse the smoke. He squinted, and his mouth dropped open.

"Hmmm." Ken shut the door, changed his mind, and pushed it all the way open.

"Everything all right?" I asked, my mind racing.

"Guys, you can't do that in here!" Ken yelled.

I looked over Ken's shoulder and could see the smoky room, as if someone was burning incense. I recognized the smell, a pungent, earthy skunk-like smell. It was a smell I associated with impending doom.

"What! Are you guys smoking pot in my room? You shouldn't be upstairs in the first place. Get out of here!"

I couldn't believe my eyes. A boy and a girl, both naked to the waist, sat on the floor in some kind of yoga pose. Between them was an ashtray with a smoking joint. I shook my head. Was he about to take advantage of the naked girl?

The girl looked up, eyes glassy. "You can come and join us." Her speech was slurred. She took a drag from the joint, raised her head, and blew smoke toward Ken and me.

The boy turned to face us. "Sorry," he said in a squeaky voice. He was less stoned. He scrambled to his feet, grabbed their T-shirts from the floor, and tossed one to the girl. She was not interested in covering up. The guy pulled her T-shirt over her head, helped her to her feet, and they both staggered toward the door.

"I hope you didn't borrow anything from my room," Ken scolded as they shuffled past.

For the next few minutes, he opened drawers, one after the other, to make sure nothing was missing.

My stomach tightened and I felt nauseous.

"Jesus," muttered Ken. He pulled the blinds and slid open a window. "Can you believe they were making out in my room?"

Fresh air drifted into the room. I didn't know what to say to that. Ahead of me, against the wall, was a shelf dedicated to trophies and memorabilia. There were several framed pictures of Ken and his teammates over the years in different sports: basketball, football, and lacrosse.

I walked over to get a closer look. For an instant, I thought something was in my way, and I tried to sidestep it. I lost my balance but caught myself on time.

"Are you okay?" asked Ken.

I nodded. "I'm fine."

"It must be the joint," said Ken.

I looked at the floor; there was no obstruction. Then I felt the room sway.

"This trophy we got when I was in third grade," said Ken. He pointed at a golden basketball with gold and electric-blue color at the base."

My pulse raced. What was going on? The room seemed to dance in front of my eyes.

"This was from fifth grade," continued Ken. "We came second; the team that came first beat us like a drum."

My head felt heavy. The room spun. I leaned against a chest of drawers to stop the place from spinning. My knees wobbled and then could not support me. I slid down to the floor.

Ken had his back turned. He gestured toward his trophy shrine, still talking, but no words reached me. *Get up from the floor*, I screamed at myself. I placed my palm on the floor and recoiled, I'd touched something wet. My eyes stared at Ken's sweaty basketball T-shirt in horror. I wiped my hands on my jeans, and the smell hit my nostrils.

A shiver ran down my spine as the smell of marijuana and the musky male odor of Ken's basketball clothes brought up memories I'd buried. In the blink of an eye, I was transported back to that night in the Sambisa forest with Danladi.

"Ken," I whimpered.

Ken turned around, looked down, and his eyes widened. He dropped to the floor. "Are you all right?"

I sat on the floor, my legs drawn against my chest. I rocked back and forth with my hands against my ears. "Please don't hurt me. Please don't hurt me."

38

K en's face was inches from mine. "What's wrong?" His voice wavered. He took my hand, and it trembled. I wasn't sure who was shaking more, him or me.

My mouth quivered as I continued to plead, "Please don't hurt me!" again and again.

"Ngozi, I'm not doing anything to you," said Ken in a low voice. He lowered my hand, got up, and rushed to the door.

The sound of music got louder, and I knew he had opened the door.

"JENNIFER! JENNIFER!" yelled Ken.

The music was just too loud for anyone to hear anything.

Ken came back into the room and kneeled beside me. He ran his hand down the back of his head and neck. "Ngozi, you'll be fine. Just relax."

I looked at him and thought that he needed to relax. Ken swiped a finger across his forehead, wiping off beads of sweat, which he rubbed on his jeans. He paused for a moment, reached into his pocket, and pulled out his cell phone. Ken swiped and tapped on the screen a few times, and the music cut off, the silence was deafening. Ken yelled his sister's name again.

"I did nothing to the music!" Jennifer yelled back.

"I need help! Come to my room!" shouted Ken.

I heard the pounding of feet on the stairs, way too many feet. It sounded like an earthquake. But I'd never been in an earthquake. How would I know what one sounded like? I giggled.

A moment later Jennifer dashed into the room. I could see one, two, three Jennifers. "Jennifer, I didn't know you were a triplet," I tried to say, but it came out as babble. The three Jennifers brought their hands to their chests, their eyes as big as tennis balls.

The three Jennifers knelt beside me and put their arms around me. For a moment, I felt I was in a room lit by candle-light. A man was smiling at me and offering me something in his hands. *Wee-wee*, he had said. The man's hand reached for me. I shut my eyes as tight as I could. I felt his hands wrap around my body. I struggled to get out of his grasp. I tried to get away, but he gripped me.

Jennifer held me and squeezed me. "What happened?"

I felt reassured. I stopped trembling.

"It's okay." It was now a familiar voice.

I opened my eyes. Jennifer was still there holding me. Her voice calm and strong.

"You'll be fine," she whispered.

"Is he gone?" I asked, looking Jennifer in the face.

Jennifer looked around, eyes narrowed. She looked at her brother. Her face flashed with anger. "What did you do to her?"

"Nothing," said Ken. He had a helpless look on his face. "We came up here to see my trophies and surprised a boy and girl smoking pot. Before I knew it, Ngozi was on the floor, chanting, 'Please don't hurt me,' and rocking back and forth."

"Pot? Smoking pot!" said Jennifer. Then her eyes widened. "Oh my God! The brownies? Her hands flew to her mouth. "Brian said he baked the brownies with a pot mix! Who knows what else he put in them?"

I heard shuffling feet and looked up. Heads peered in through the door.

"I think we should send everybody home. The party was getting too loud, anyway. We don't want the neighbors calling the cops."

Ken came over, gave me a pat and squeezed my shoulder.

"I'll make sure everybody clears out." He walked toward the door. "Okay, people, the party's over, time to go!" He left the room and shut the door behind him.

"How do you feel?" Jennifer asked.

I nodded.

"Do you want me to take you home?" asked Jennifer.

I nodded again. Jennifer helped me up from the floor. I felt cold, soaked in sweat.

Leno and Jennifer dropped me off at home.

"Do you want me to come in with you?" asked Jennifer. Her voice lowered to a whisper. "And explain to your parents—"

"No, don't worry, I think I can handle it."

They drove off as I entered the house. I would have gone in through the garage, but I knew Mom and Dad were home and would be in the living room watching TV. What would they say or do when I told them what had happened? Maybe say I couldn't go to any more parties. I rang the bell, then remembering I had a key, I unlocked the door with my key just as I heard footsteps approaching.

39

"Ngozi, is that you?" Mom's voice came from the living room as I shut the door.

I cleared my throat. "Yes."

I heard her footsteps stop and shuffle away. I must tell them what happened tonight and what happened in Sambisa. After I arrived in the US, Mom had taken me to the pediatrician for a checkup. The doctor was going to ask personal questions and asked me whether I wanted Mom to stay. I was going to say yes, but Mom excused herself.

"Hey, Ngozi," said Dad, his eyes not leaving the TV. "You came back early. When I was your age, I would stay until the end of the party and help clean up. The leftovers, that is."

"When was that?" asked Mom shooting him a look.

I walked in. Mom turned, took one look at me, and sprang to her feet. Her eyebrows narrowed.

"What happened?" asked Mom, neck tilted as she walked toward me.

Dad looked, picked up the remote control, and turned down the volume.

Mom led me toward the couch. "Come sit down." Her voice was steady. Her jaw muscles clenched and unclenched.

I told them everything that happened at the party, except the letter from Ken and Mary Ann trying to make a fool of me in public. They listened without interrupting me. Ken's room became Jennifer's.

"Did . . . anybody, emmm . . . try . . . to lay a finger on you?" asked Dad.

"Did anyone touch you?" asked Mom.

I shook my head. "No."

I glanced from Mom to Dad and saw the relief in their faces.

Shaky laughter escaped Dad's throat. "You said the kids in Jennifer's room were smoking marijuana. How do you know what it smells like?"

"My friend Zainab in Lamija brought it to my attention whenever she smelled it." I looked down at my hands. "It was offered the night we were . . . forced to sleep with the terrorists. I'd pushed everything about that night to the back of my mind, but that smell in the room, it brought everything back."

"Oh God," said Mom in a low voice. "Where's Zainab now?"

"I don't know. The last time I saw her was the night the terrorists came." I told them everything that happened, beginning with that night, in between sobs, about Faith, the twins, the hyenas, everything.

Mom wrapped her hands around my shoulders and rocked back and forth. After a moment of silence, Mom and Dad talked amongst themselves, asking me questions now and then.

"Ngozi," Dad started, "we'll make an appointment with the specialist, and she'll take it from there."

Mom heaved a sigh of relief. "I'm glad you trust us

enough to share," said Mom. "At least now you know what to avoid at parties. Spiked punch is expected, but brownies?"

"Things like this do happen," said Dad with a laugh. "Back in the day, at parties I went to, there was *wee-wee* in everything. If food was served, you'd see the leaves in the rice, and you'd get high from eating that."

Dad caught Mom's stern look, and the smile left his face.

"Anyway, Ngozi," said Mom. "This is a serious matter. You might think we're dealing with it lightly, but we're not. We understand what you're going through, but it's not our area of expertise."

Dad laughed. "Funny, right? You have two doctors as parents, yet they can't help you."

Mom elbowed Dad. "But if everything remains calm, first thing Monday morning, we'll take you to the hospital to see a specialist."

Sunday was uneventful. Jennifer and Ken called to check on me. I told them I was fine. Jennifer said she would have come over, but their parents came back in the early hours of the morning, and their mom had discovered a party straggler asleep in their Jacuzzi. For now, she and Ken were grounded.

40

Dad's colleague saw me first thing Monday morning. *Could I become mad from this?* That was my thought when Mom said we would see a psychiatrist. The other thing that came to my mind was the naked, dirty man that controlled traffic in Lamija market junction and had his breakfast, lunch, and dinner at a rubbish heap. Some people said he was mad and needed a psychiatric consult. Others said someone had cast a spell on him and a *Babalawo* would fix him.

The psychiatrist took my history and did a quick physical exam. "I'll send Ngozi to the phlebotomist to have her blood drawn, and urine taken for a toxicology screen and blood work." She looked at her watch. "I hope there's someone there now. It's early. I'll get back to you with the results as soon as I get them. Do you have questions?"

Mom shook her head.

The psychiatrist wrote on a piece of paper. "We'll also have her see the psychologist. I've worked with Dr. Walters before. She's superb." The psychiatrist handed the paper to Mom.

"Thanks very much," said Mom. "I appreciate your seeing us on such short notice."

We had gone in early, and from what I saw, both the doctor and psychologist had squeezed me in before starting their schedules for the day.

Dr. Monica Walters asked more questions than the psychiatrist. As she spoke, she touched the gold cross pendant on her necklace. I told her of my ordeal at the party, the nightmares and the kidnapping in Nigeria. At no point did her face betray any emotion—disgust, surprise, or empathy. I wondered if there was a course taught in medical school on how to control facial muscles.

Mom leaned closer to Dr. Walters after the question-and-answer session. "Do you have a preliminary diagnosis?" Her voice was low.

Dr. Walters placed her pen on her notes. "Ngozi has been through some experiences that could become a stressor in most individuals in the long run. But we'll learn more as we delve deeper. Something along the lines of an adverse-event-induced condition like PTSD."

Mom nodded.

"What's PTSD?" I asked, the image of the madman still in my mind. I glanced from Mom to Dr. Walters.

"PTSD, post-traumatic stress disorder," said Dr. Walters. "It's a medical condition where an individual relives a traumatic experience when exposed to circumstances or experiences similar to the initial traumatic incident."

I nodded.

Dr. Walters swiped her shoulder-length black hair streaked with gray out of her face. "Patients with PTSD could be in the presence of someone or something that caused them harm or trauma and feel like they were right there experiencing it again. Things you remember about the experience could also put your mind right back in that situation."

Mom nodded, but her mind seemed far away.

"I will need Ngozi to come in for more sessions," said Dr. Walters.

We discussed with her different types of therapy approaches, and we settled on cognitive-behavioral therapy.

"Part of the therapy will include you keeping a 'thought journal' in which you will write down what you're thinking, and we'll discuss that. You'll be discussing your childhood with me. The idea is to find closure to those childhood experiences and leave past things in the past." Dr. Walters smiled. "Do you have questions so far?"

I shook my head. "No."

"I like questions. You can interrupt me at any time." Dr. Walters's gaze moved from me to Mom and back. "We'll set up an appointment to see you again in two weeks. We'll start with one session a week, and we can move it to two or three times a week as needed. But if anything changes in between visits, contact me, okay?"

Mom dropped me off at home and went back to work. Dr. Walters had given me a lot of reading material, and I dug in. Every sign and symptom described in the book seemed to be peculiar. Those that I didn't have magically appeared. The articles also alluded to the possibility of triggers or signs hidden in my subconscious.

Among the paperwork was the invoice for the therapy sessions and what each subsequent visit would cost. I converted the amount to naira and almost had a heart attack. I knew Mom and Dad were okay financially, but I must be making a major dent in their bank account. Did I really need to go in for these sessions?

I was sure they never planned on spending so much on me

when they adopted me from Nigeria. Suddenly I felt like I was becoming a burden to Mom and Dad.

While at the clinics, Ken had sent me a few texts, asking how I was doing. *I'll text him later in the day*, I thought.

As the day progressed, I felt like an impostor, like I didn't belong. I was taking advantage of these lovely people.

41

———

Back in school on Tuesday, I felt like all eyes were on me. The girl who freaked out at the party. People looked then lost interest; there was nothing to see.

"Sorry I brought your party to an end," I said as Jennifer and I walked to our next class.

"No. I'm the one that owes you an apology," said Jennifer. "I gave you the brownies, and I'm so sorry. I didn't . . . well, I knew it had pot, but I had no idea you would react the way you did."

I shrugged. "Don't worry about it. It's not your fault. Until yesterday when the doctor described that something triggered my reaction, I did not understand what a trigger was."

Jennifer exhaled. "The party ended at the right time. It was about to get out of hand." She stopped walking and looked at me. "So, how are you? I was so terrified that night."

I punched her lightly in the arm. "You handled the situation like a pro."

A flush crept across Jennifer's cheeks. "It was nothing, just things I learned from babysitting."

I exhaled. "We went to the doctor yesterday . . . now I have to see a therapist every week."

Jennifer nodded and gave me a look that said, "Go on, what else did they say?"

I'd never told her anything about my experiences in Nigeria, but she must have guessed something happened. It wasn't something I wanted to share yet, even though now I could say she was my best friend. I remembered what Fatima used to say when Maryam said she trusted her best friend with her innermost secrets. "Your best friend has a best friend who isn't you," Fatima would say. "She shares your secrets with her, and soon your secret becomes an open secret. The best-kept secrets are the ones you keep to yourself."

"Ngozi?"

"Sorry," I said. "Just thinking. I hope I didn't freak Ken out too much either. He must be traumatized." I looked down at the floor as I walked. I felt so ashamed.

"Don't worry about Ken," said Jennifer. "He's fine." Jennifer hesitated. "So . . . they think it was all because of some bad experience you had in Nigeria?"

I nodded but volunteered no information. Jennifer wasn't her usual confident self either. Their parents must have let them have it.

"Ken thinks it was the smell of all the pot in his room that set you off."

"Maybe," I said and sighed.

"Brian overdid the brownie," said Jennifer.

"How did you guys meet?" I asked.

"Oh, he's an old friend. I invited him over for body count. I didn't know so many people would show up. I doubt I'll invite him to any more parties. That is, if we survive this ordeal. We won't be having any parties soon. See you later," said Jennifer.

I continued to my class. Everything seemed sad. I wasn't in a happy place at all. I'd overheard things said a few times when I passed in the corridors.

"A bad trip," one guy had called it. "Happened to me last year."

The rest of the week sped past with no new incidents, and the talk about the party died down.

Friday' came and I went to school, as usual, then went home. Ken and Jennifer stayed home and were not allowed to receive visitors either. I couldn't understand why grounded children remained grounded when there was no physical restraint. When I was a kid, the only thing that could stop me was the cane. Matron and Uncle Thomas never used the rod on me, but Auntie Halima would flog me but not her own children. Maybe if she had grounded me instead of whipping me as a kid, it would scare me too.

I tried to read a novel, but couldn't get past a few pages. A walk would do me better instead, and I set out for the pond. I would usually see people doing one thing or the other, but this time around there was nobody. Was it always like this, or had I only noticed it because of how I felt inside? I thought of calling Preeti; she must be having fun with her sister. My phone buzzed, an incoming text. I looked at the screen and let out a shaky laugh. I felt a release of tension.

Ken: *Everything all right? You didn't return my text.*

Me: *I was going to. You beat me to it.*

Ken: *Liar* . . .

My phone rang. It was Ken calling on FaceTime. I let it ring. Sometimes it was easier to talk by text than to speak in real time over the phone. When I text, I can think before I write. A man and a woman rode up on their bikes, interrupting my thoughts. I got off the bike path and sat on a bench.

Ken: *I just called you.*

Me: *I know. You are not supposed to visit anyone or have someone visit you. You were about to cheat.*

The blinking dots just stayed there. Was Ken typing or typing and deleting?

Me: *Are you there?*

Ken: *That was a good one. I had to literally roflmao.*

Me: *Roll on the floor and laughing my ass off?*

Ken: *Yep!*

Me: *Ha ha ha. Would love to have seen that,*

Ken: *Miss you. Jenny said you went to the doctor. You didn't tell me.*

Me: *Yes. We'll start a weekly session.*

Ken: *I'm always here for you. Can't wait for this to be over. I have to go. Mom calling. I have to be nice. (Emoji blowing a kiss).*

Me: *(Emoji blowing a kiss.)*

42

The girl peeled the oranges and stood up. She'd peeled them with a razor, a work of art in its own sense.

"How much?" asked the gap-toothed man as he picked up one of the peeled oranges. He bit off one end, sucked the piece in his mouth dry, and spat it out.

The orange oozed liquid from the gash he created. With the flick of his tongue, he licked the juice and covered the slash with his mouth, squeezing and sucking until the orange was dry. His eyes never left the girl's face.

The girl told him the cost, wringing her hands together. Like a cornered rat, her eyes darted from the man's face to the door her friend had walked through and the opening through which they had entered the uncompleted building.

"Come, the money is inside," said the man. He jerked his head toward the curtained door.

The orange girl heard the other girl giggling and concluded there was no danger there.

The man picked up another orange. "I have work to do.

*Come and take your money." He headed toward the
curtained-off door.*

The orange seller hesitated and followed.

I SAT UP IN BED, PANTING. I WANTED SO TO GET TO THE END
of this dream, but I dreaded the outcome. It was now
tormenting me. The nightmare linked me to the girls,
but how?

I turned on my cell phone. It was 3:00 a.m., still pitch
dark outside. Should I tell Mom about these nightmares I'd
been having? I knew it was the best thing to do, but something deep inside told me not to. I didn't want them to feel
like they brought trouble into their lives by adopting me.

Like with previous dreams, I couldn't go back to sleep. I
counted from one hundred to zero twice. Sleep still eluded
me, and I started from two hundred back to zero. Tired, but
still awake, I increased my starting point to three hundred. As
the first rays of daylight showed up far away on the horizon, I
drifted off to sleep.

In the morning, Mom had come into the room and told me
they were leaving for a wedding. As soon as she left, I went
back to sleep. When I woke up, it was just a few minutes shy
of noon.

I took a long hot shower while I thought about the dream
and the little girls. Had I ever been in such a situation? What I
remembered during the party in Ken's room was in the past,
and so must be this dream. Should I write it down, as Dr.
Walters said, or let sleeping dogs lie?

Once out of the shower, I pulled out the drawer for my
underwear and noticed I was out of sanitary pads. My period
was around the corner. It was sunny and inviting outside, so I
decided to walk to the grocery store to buy pads.

I ate honey-roasted oat cereal for brunch and stepped outside, planning to head for the store. It wasn't as warm as it appeared. I had a black fleece jacket on and I zipped it up all the way. However, the more I walked, the warmer I got. I relaxed, the two girls forgotten. Leaves littered the walkway, shed from trees as they followed the laws of nature.

Once in the store, I located what I needed and waited in line at the register when my eyes caught a newspaper headline: "Adopted Child Returned to Birth Parents in Russia."

I stared at the headline in disbelief. I read it again and again to make sure I got the meaning.

The pounding in my ears drowned out the hustle and bustle around me. Why had the adoptive parents sent the child back? What had the child done? Was there anybody waiting to take the child back when he got to Russia? These questions rushed through my mind as I stared at the headline.

"Are you ready to check out?" asked a voice.

I looked up. A cashier was talking to me.

"Did you find everything you were looking for?"

"Sorry," I said and flashed a nervous smile.

She rang me up. I cast a glance at the newspaper one more time on my way out and a shiver went through me. I felt like people going about their business were watching me. That they could see through me. See I was adopted, tainted, more trouble than I was worth.

I looked around; nobody paid me any attention. Shaking like a leaf, I left the store and walked back home. Could Mom and Dad send me back to Nigeria?

I didn't think they would, but if they did, I guess I would go back to Auntie Halima. A chuckle escaped my lips. Auntie Halima wouldn't want me back. I didn't want to admit it, but I felt I had moved on. It's funny how absence and distance make you forget. What about the police? What about the people who wanted me dead? I shuddered. I couldn't go back.

The grocery store was about a fifteen-minute walk from home. As I walked down the wide clean sidewalks, past huge mansions with well-manicured lawns, I could see Falls Lake not too far away. The body of water the town got its name from. A few weeks ago, people having fun had filled its shores, alive with the sights and sounds of summer. Now it lay barren and abandoned, as desolate as I felt inside.

43

───────

Mom glanced at me. "Is anything wrong?"

I shook my head. "No, a little apprehensive about going to see the therapist—"

"No, not about that. That's normal whenever you see a doctor." Mom paused. "You're not eating. Are you not happy? Are you worried?" Mom looked at the light, which had turned green, and drove on.

I couldn't tell her about my fears, about the Russian kid in the headlines who got sent back because the adoptive parents couldn't deal with his tantrums. Even if she and Dad were thinking of doing that, they wouldn't tell me. I didn't know what to do. "No, I wasn't hungry."

"Remember, we are here for you. You can tell us anything. If you don't feel comfortable talking to us, Dr. Walters is there to help too."

I nodded.

"Oh, I forgot to call your school." Mom's phone was on a magnetic stand on the dashboard, and she turned it on. "Siri, call Falls Lake High."

I watched, listened, and marveled at the technology as

my school's automated answering service picked up, and Mom followed the direction to report an absence without speaking to anyone. I wished my life was that uncomplicated.

We arrived at the hospital for my 9:00 a.m. session with Dr. Walters. Mom walked with me to the section of the hospital where the psychologist's office was.

"How are you today, Ngozi?" asked Dr. Walters, a big smile on her face.

"Fine," I said and tried to smile.

"I have a copy of the results from toxicology." Dr. Walters leafed through the pages of a folder she had with her.

A million thoughts rushed through my mind. My heart beat faster. *If they found something out of the normal, would it get Jennifer and Brian in trouble? If negative, what next?* I wondered.

"Toxicology checked out fine, but with some residues of cannabinoids, which we already expected from the . . . hmmm . . . brownies you ate," said Dr. Walters.

I exhaled. "Good."

"So today we'll talk and sort this out.

"Dr. Obi, I want you to tell me about the home front." She glanced at me and back at Mom's arched eyebrows. "You and your husband adopted Ngozi, right?"

"Yes." Mom exhaled. "I was her godmother until we adopted her."

"Something changed?" asked Dr. Walters. "Sorry, I'm just trying to get 'the big picture' of the family dynamics." She made air quotes.

"I understand," said Mom. "She lived in Nigeria before the adoption. I didn't hear from her, and her guardian couldn't account for her whereabouts. So, I traveled to Nigeria to find out what happened."

"She left home telling no one?" asked Dr. Walters and took notes on her folder.

I glanced from one woman to the other. They talked as if I wasn't there.

Mom wrung her fingers. "Kind of. She went back to school and terrorists kidnapped all the girls in the school."

Dr. Walters head shot up. "She . . . she was one of the girls? Kidnapped? Terrorists? The 'bring back our girls' . . ." Her voice trailed off.

Mom nodded.

Doctors' poker faces had always amazed me, and so far I'd been impressed with Dr. Walters's unreadable face, so it surprised me when she let her guard down.

"Wow," whispered Dr. Walters as she adjusted herself in her seat.

Dr. Walters's eyes and mine met for a moment. There was a gleam in her eyes and this subtle grin on her lips that suggested admiration and encouragement. She tapped her pen on her notebook, and her face assumed the expressionless mask.

"Anything you'd like to talk about?" asked Dr. Walters, looking in my direction.

"Nothing really," I said and pursed my lips.

"Have you been sleeping throughout the night?" asked Dr. Walters.

"No."

"Why not?"

"I've . . . I've been having these dreams . . ." I shifted in my chair, looked at my palms. When I looked up, my eyes met the doctor's eyes, and I looked away.

"Dr. Obi, this might take a little longer, maybe you should go get a cup of coffee."

For a moment, Mom just sat there, eyebrows arched up.

She looked surprised or maybe hurt that I hadn't told her about the dreams.

"Sure," said Mom. "I think I have a few things to check at the office." She then turned and smiled. "Send me a text when you're ready, okay?"

I nodded.

"All right, Ngozi, for me to help you, you must help me. I need you to tell me everything you can remember about the dreams you've been having. It's vital. The dreams might give us a clue about what the issues are. Once we have that, then I can apply the tools at our disposal to handle it."

I nodded.

"Is there a particular time of the night they occur?"

"I'll say between midnight and 2:00 a.m." I told her the dream up to when I woke up drenched in sweat, just before the orange girl went with the man to get her money.

"What happened after that?"

"That's where it stopped," I said.

"Do you have the same dreams all the time?"

"No, sometimes I have hyenas coming after me in my dream."

"Hyenas? Like the animals?"

"Yes. I encountered hyenas twice in the bush. The first time with Faith . . ." I felt an aching in my chest. My voice broke, my shoulders heaved, and tears came. I told Dr. Walters about the escape from the truck, all that had happened, and ended with how I was to blame for Faith's death.

"Never blame yourself," said Dr. Walters. "The man with the knife was accountable, not you." She placed a box of tissue beside me.

I wiped my eyes and blew my nose. After a few minutes, I calmed down.

"Ngozi, I think that's enough for today. We must squeeze in two more sessions per week. You can text your mom to come get you."

Mom came, and we talked with the secretary to fill in the rest of the new scheduling. With all that talking, I felt a lot better, as if something had lifted a massive weight off my shoulders.

"Ngozi, I know you've been through a lot," said Mom on the way home. "There isn't much we can do about what has already happened. Ben and I are here for you, we are a family, and together we will overcome whatever life throws at us."

Later that night, Dad also reassured me that they were there for me. Back in my room, I cried. I'd never felt so loved.

44

I t had been four weeks since my first session with Dr. Walters. I still had the dream about the girls, but it replayed what I'd already dreamed of before. I slept through the night and stopped waking up sweating. It amazed me that just talking to someone who is not there to judge you takes a lot of weight off your shoulders.

The increased therapy sessions, talking about Faith, helped me reconnect with the loving and sweet girl I knew her as, and not her last days. Deep down I still believed if I had left her alone, she would still be alive today. But I'd accepted that what was done was done. I had to live with it.

Now and then I would dream about the hyenas and would wake up after Gambo screamed in my ears to help him. It wasn't as gut-wrenching as the dream with the girls. Maybe because Gambo got what he deserved.

Who were the two girls? If one was me, who was the other? What was it trying to tell me? Dr. Walters said she'd reduce our sessions back to once a week after my next visit since I was doing relatively well.

Ken and Jennifer were finally released from being

grounded. Ken and I maintained our habit of hanging out on weekends and using the school week to catch up on studying and other school activities.

We did a variety of things together: played basketball together, went to the movies, fast-food restaurants, and the mall. Sometimes it was just the two of us who went, or Jennifer would come along.

The hustle and bustle of Thanksgiving provided a needed distraction for me. Dad described Thanksgiving as church harvest, like we have in Nigeria.

"The same concept," Dad had said. "Everybody thanks God for the bumper harvest they got, and the surplus is auctioned off at the bazaar that follows. Here in America, it has a theme—family—and turkey."

"If Thanksgiving is like this," I'd said to Dad. "What will Christmas look like?"

"I think Thanksgiving is bigger than Christmas," said Dad. "Kids have the most fun during Christmas. Santa always shows up."

With Thanksgiving done, the cold weather brought with it the countdown to Christmas. The anticipation of Christmas was as electrifying in Falls Lake as it was in Nigeria. Most people would travel to their villages a few days before, and the cities would be empty while highways would be congested.

In Lamija, I would look forward to a new dress to wear on Christmas Day and some books as gifts. The main event was the food on the twenty-fifth. Lambs, goats, chickens, and cows would be slaughtered, and a feast would go on at most homes.

"I'm going to a farm to buy a Christmas tree," said Dad as we ate breakfast on the first Saturday morning in December. "Do you want to come?"

"Christmas tree?" I asked. "Why a farm? Why not at the mall?"

"We get a live tree," said Mom. "We should all go. Make it a family affair."

So we all bundled up and set out. At the farm, Mom said she would stay in the car. Dad and I got out, and only when we'd been out for about a minute did I envy Mom's decision. There was no snow, but it was so cold. And the wind didn't help matters. My teeth were chattering. There were a few other families, making a great show of inspecting the trees before selecting one. We did the same.

"What are they looking for?" I whispered to Dad. "The trees all look the same apart from height."

Dad threw back his head and laughed. "I've always wondered the same thing. Pick one!"

"Where do the trees come from?" I asked the farmhand as he sliced off a little of the stump and put the tree through a machine that covered it with what looked like fishing nets.

"We have a farm in Canada," said the farmhand. "Each year we cut down some and replant the same number."

At home, Mom brought out a box of Christmas lights and Christmas decorations, and I helped her decorate the tree and the living room.

"Next Christmas, you'll be in charge of the decorations," said Mom. "You have an eye for what goes with what and what goes where."

When we drove around and I saw the decorations on people's homes, I wondered how much they spent on electricity. One evening, I was in the car with Ken and Jennifer, and I laughed.

"What's so funny?"

"If the power company in Nigeria oversaw electricity

here, people would go mad. There wouldn't be electricity to illuminate all their hard work."

I got a lot of gifts for Christmas, including clothes and an e-book reader loaded with classic books. For New Year's Eve, we went to a ski resort in Sussex County, New Jersey.

As we got closer to the resort, I saw snow. I was so excited, it embarrassed me. It was my first time seeing snow, and I wanted to build a snowman, ride on a sleigh, and ski all at once. After about ten minutes, I could barely feel my fingers, despite wearing thick warm gloves. I remained indoors to thaw myself, and followed up hot chocolate.

We went to the restaurant for the all-you-can-eat New Year's Eve countdown party. It was the best vacation of my life.

After the New Year celebration, it was back to school again. The first week went fast, as if we never left. I threw myself into my schoolwork and activities. I got serious with basketball and spent more time at the court, or maybe it was an excuse to see Ken.

Before, I could practice with the group for the full period without getting tired. But these days, I would be struggling to breath after a few minutes.

This Monday I was distracted all day. The previous night I'd dreamed about the two girls, and for the first time, I saw the end of the dream.

I had an appointment with Dr. Walters after school, and I'd been battling with myself over whether to tell her and my parents.

"Ngozi, no daydreaming!" yelled the coach.

I jumped, startled out of my thoughts.

"You're paired with Preddy!" said the coach.

Preeti rolled her eyes. "It's Preeti." As she walked away, she mumbled under her breath. "The 't' is not a 'd' coach."

Preeti and I practiced chest passes. A battle was going on in my head. Dr. Walters might tell Mom, since they were both doctors. *They can share information, right?* I thought.

"Ngozi, focus!" said Preeti.

I looked up to see the ball coming toward me. I raised my hand. The ball slipped out of my grasp and slammed into my face. It was painful. I'd been hit before on the face with a ball, but this time, blood flowed.

45

Preeti's hands flew to her mouth. "Oh my God, what did I do?"

The coach blew his whistle, and the game stopped. He rushed over.

"Ball to the face?" asked the Coach.

I nodded.

"Sorry. You'll be fine," said the coach. "Pinch your nose and lean forward." He looked over his shoulders. "Someone, grab some Kleenex or paper towels! Breath from your mouth, Ngozi."

Someone thrust some paper towels into my hand. I tasted blood and dabbed it with the paper towel.

"Nosebleed?" It was the assistant gym teacher.

"Yes, ball to the face," said the coach. "I'll take Ngozi to the nurse. Continue with the game."

At the nurse's station, the nurse gave me an ice pack and showed me how to place it on the bridge of my nose.

"I think it was just trauma," said the nurse. "But I'll notify your parents. They might want to have the pediatrician examine you."

Mom would take me for a therapy session later in the afternoon. I'd still tell her when I got home. It was only then that I noticed Preeti and Jennifer. They had come with us.

"I'm really sorry," whispered Preeti. She looked like she would cry. "I thought you would catch it."

"It's not your fault," I said. My voice sounded nasal as I spoke through pinched nostrils. "I have basket fingers today; everything passes through."

Jennifer looked mortified. The bleeding stopped, and the nurse asked me if I wanted her to call my parents to come and get me, or if I felt well enough to stay in school. I felt fine apart from a minor throbbing on my face. I opted to stay. We went back to the locker room and changed.

After school, as I walked to the bus line with Preeti beside me, she felt she had to be around me to atone for hitting me in the face. As we stood in line, Ken showed up.

"Hi," said Ken.

I smiled. "Hello. What are you doing here?"

"Let's see." Ken touched my chin and made a show of examining my nose. "Everything looks fine. I heard you took one for the team at PE."

Ken's head turned to Preeti who looked like she would disappear if she had a magic wand.

I slapped his hand away. "I'm fine."

Ken wrinkled his eyebrows. "Seriously, are you all right?" His voice was soft.

I nodded and felt butterflies in my stomach.

"I was worried. Come on, I'll give you a ride home," said Ken. "You know, to make sure you get home safe and sound. Where's Jenny?"

"She forgot something in her locker. She'll be here—"

"Hey!" Jennifer ran toward us with her backpack strapped behind her.

We all went to the parking lot and got into Ken's car. Driving out of the parking lot took a little while. Maybe I should have gone with the bus, which had precedence over who left the parking lot first. The buses pulled up, filled up with students, and drove off.

The gym teacher who also doubled as a traffic guy after school stopped the cars each time a bus was ready to go. I hoped I wouldn't be late for the appointment.

When I opened the garage, Mom's car was there.

"Hello," said Mom when I walked into the kitchen. She sat on the couch, still dressed in what she wore to work, watching *The View* on TV. "How was school?"

"Nothing new." I took a bottle of water from the fridge. "I went to the school nurse today."

Mom paused the show. "What happened?" Mom sat up on the couch.

"Nosebleed. The ball hit me in the face during gym."

Mom slouched back. "Do you feel pain? Come."

I walked toward Mom. "Just a dull ache where the ball hit my face."

Mom nodded and got up. She looked at my nose and pressed a finger around it. "It's not swollen, good. Do you feel like your nose is stuffed? Congested?"

"No. No pain."

"Looks good, took a little beating. Let me know if anything changes. Do you want to eat? Change? Before we leave?"

"I'm not hungry. I'll change and we can go."

Mom walked me to the office and said to text her when I was ready.

"Hello, Ngozi," said Dr. Walters.

"Hi." I looked down at my hands.

"Is there anything you want to share with me today?"

My mind raced. Do I tell her? I'm sure she could sense there was something?

"There's something on your mind," said Dr. Walters. "Do you want to share?"

I pursed my lips and nodded. "The dream with the girls came back."

I'd expected Dr. Walters to react, lean forward, get excited, but she remained poised.

"Do you want to share it with me?"

I nodded. "Last night I saw the two girls again in my dream. The orange girl followed the man through the door. Inside the room, on the floor, were plastic bags with food in them and a kerosene stove. It seemed like the men lived there while they worked. The man pointed to the floor at a large cardboard box that had been opened and spread out. A small black and blue raffia mat lay on the cardboard. He told the girl to lie down there. The girl refused. The man rushed her and threw her onto the mat. She tried to fight back, but he was strong."

My eyes brimmed with tears.

"Do you want to stop?"

I shook my head, and a tear rolled down my cheek. She handed me a tissue and placed the box beside me. I sniffed and dabbed my eyes with the Kleenex. "Later I saw both girls. The girl with the bananas was all right but looked sad, the other was crying, hurting, and limping.

"Were you one of the girls?"

I stopped talking. My lips, my chin, my whole body trembled and a cold shiver traveled down my spine.

Tears rolled off my chin down onto my hands on my lap. I looked at Dr. Walters and nodded. "I was the orange girl!" More tears came.

Dr. Walters leaned forward as if she was about to get up, then stopped. Pursed her lips, leaned back and watched me.

I stopped shaking and took a deep breath. My whole being felt light as if I could leap into the air and fly away like a bird.

"I . . . I think . . ." Dr. Walters cleared her throat. "To cope, your mind hid this painful experience in your subconscious."

I blew my nose. "I feel a lot better." I shook my head. "For a long time, I always felt like there was something that happened, and it involved Zainab, but I couldn't remember."

"Zainab?" asked Dr. Walters.

"She . . . she was my best friend." I realized I used the past tense. "I think my friend led me to them." My voice was a whisper. It all came back. Zainab had asked me to help her hawk some oranges from her mom's kiosk. It sounded exciting, but it was a setup. She knew those men.

"Did you tell anyone?"

I looked down and shook my head. "No, it was something I wanted to forget." I lied to myself that it never happened. And I believed it until it haunted my dreams."

"Where's she now?"

"I don't know. The last time I saw Zainab was the night the terrorists came." I cried again.

"Was it Boko Haram? The terrorist group that abducted girls in Nigeria not too long ago."

"I don't know what they called themselves, but they are similar," I said through tears.

"You were one of the girls?" asked Dr. Walters with a look of astonishment on her face, already knowing the answer.

I nodded again. Maybe she hadn't believed us the first

time Mom told her. Or maybe she wanted me to say it again, to hear it again in my own voice.

Dr. Walters gave me another Kleenex.

"The night I escaped, they offered us all the opportunity to leave, but some girls refused to be separated from their new husbands."

"The men they were forced to marry?" asked Dr. Walters.

"Yes."

"God," whispered Dr. Walters. "Sometimes kidnapped or hostage victims develop affection or trust for their captors. It's called Stockholm syndrome." She shook her head. "How did you escape?"

"I jumped off the truck." I'd told her this before.

"Did they look for you?"

"Yes, but my friends and I ran."

"The one who led you astray?" asked Dr. Walters.

"No, these were Faith and the twins." I told her the story again. When I finished, bursts of laughter escaped from my throat. I did not understand how much all this had weighed down on me.

Dr. Walters's eyes narrowed, and she sprang to her feet. "Your nose is bleeding." She pulled out more tissue, put it to my nose, and told me to lean forward.

I learned the different causes of nose-bleeding. The commonest was trauma, especially in young people. The ball to the face could have accounted for my bleeding. But what I didn't know was that nose picking was also trauma. And it was the commonest cause of nosebleeds in schoolchildren.

"You pick a tough booger off the roof of your nose," said Dr. Walters. "A while later it bleeds. You don't even link the two events."

46

———————

I had closure from realizing that Zainab had set me up so many years ago, but why did she do that? I was a kid. We both were kids. Was she intimidated into doing that? But the dreams did not end. The final incident replayed in my dreams: the fear.

I preferred school days, when I didn't have to hang out with Ken. I felt people could see through me and did not want anything to do with me.

"Move it, slowpoke. Why are you shuffling?" said Jennifer.

It was Friday, and Jennifer and I were walking in the schoolyard. Ken had to stay back for an after-school music activity. Since the last time I saw Dr. Walters, I'd been feeling down. I'd replaced the relief from finding out who the girls were with constant worry that Ken would find out I had such secrets.

Headaches, runny noses, and flu-like symptoms were also another problem. Dad heard me sniffling and gave me some cold medicine and ibuprofen for the fever. My appetite had been down too.

My knees and my elbows ached. The dull pain in my thigh where Gambo had punched me returned like a long-forgotten enemy. Every muscle fiber in my body ached with each movement. The situation seemed to be getting worse.

I read on the Internet that the way I felt could be a sign of depression, but I didn't think I was sad. Worried, yes, but not depressed. It had been a stressful week at school too. I wanted to unwind and have fun.

"I feel like eating something cold," I said. "What about some ice cream?" I looked at Jennifer to see if she would go for it.

"The weather's not cold enough for you?" asked Jennifer.

"It's just a craving. We can—"

Jennifer laughed. "Just kidding, let's go for it!"

We got on the bus and got off at the second stop, which was closer to a coffee shop that also sold ice cream. "How are we going to get home?" I asked Jennifer.

"I was just thinking the same thing," said Jennifer, and brought out her cell phone. She typed then stopped. "I think it's better you do it."

"Do what?"

Jennifer groaned. "Text Ken to come to pick us up after his class. He might not show if I send it."

I nodded. "That makes sense." We walked into the store as I sent the text.

"It's so cold. I'll get hot chocolate too," said Jennifer.

I ordered plain vanilla in a cup. Jennifer ordered a large Oreo sundae and a small hot chocolate. I dug in, savoring every spoon of the creamy, delicious ice cream. Jennifer, sitting across from me, held her hot chocolate with both hands and took sips.

"Has Ken replied yet?"

I looked at my phone. "Not yet."

"They put their phones away when they're practicing so they don't get interrupted. So, he'll see it when he's ready to go." Jennifer put her hot chocolate down and brought her sundae closer.

"Warmed up enough already?"

"Couldn't resist," said Jenifer and chased a large chunk of Oreo with her spoon. "Why did they make the scooping part of the spoon so narrow?"

I smiled. "Mine is a regular teaspoon." I looked down to scoop ice cream up with my spoon. My vanilla ice cream had a drop of bright red in it, as if somebody had dropped scarlet coloring into it.

"What?" I said, confused.

Jennifer looked up. "You're bleeding!" It was the same look she had on her face when Preeti had hit me with the basketball.

Blood trickled down my nose.

"Here!" Jennifer handed me some napkins.

Some customers had shocked looks on their faces. I'm sure they thought Jennifer and I were monkeying around and I got hurt.

I pinched my nose with the napkin and tilted my head downward. Moments later the salty metallic taste of blood filled my mouth. It reminded me of the iron syrup I had as a little kid.

"What happened?" I heard someone with a deep voice ask.

"Oh, nosebleed," said another voice. "You know, kids."

A guy in a red apron walked toward us, first-aid kit in hand. "Are you okay?"

"Does she look okay?" It was the man with a deep voice again. "Stop asking stupid questions and call an ambulance."

I spat blood into the napkin. "I'm okay," I said.

The red apron guy's face looked pained. "Is there . . . anybody we can call, or should I call an ambulance?" stammered the apron guy.

"I'll call my mother," I said.

My head still tilted downward, I held the napkin on my lips with my left hand, stood up and fished for my phone in my pocket.

"Let me do it," said Jennifer and took the phone from me.

"It's ringing." She handed me the phone.

"Hello, Mom?"

"What are you eating?"

"Blood."

"What?"

I could see her face in my mind's eyes. Eyebrows narrowed. I told her what was going on.

"The coffee shop close to your school by the grocery store?"

"Yes."

"I'll swing by and pick you guys up. I was already on my way home. You and Jennifer, right?"

"Yes. See you." Mom hung up.

"She's coming to get us?" asked Jennifer.

I picked up more tissue and spat into it and lowered my chin to examine my top for blood drops. No drops and no new spots after a few seconds. There were little spots when I wiped my nose. *Remnants*, I thought.

"I . . . I think it's stopped," said Jennifer. She looked like she would cry.

Mom came about eight minutes later, and we got in the car. She glanced up my nose.

"Were you picking your nose?" asked Mom, lifting my head up from the chin with a few fingers.

"No!" I jerked my head away. I was getting annoyed with

these nosebleeds.

"You said this was the second time?"

"Yes, the first time I took a ball in the face during basketball practice. Then at Dr. Walters's office."

"That could explain it," said Mom.

We dropped Jennifer off at her house and then went home. We sat on the couch in the living room, and Mom reexamined my nostrils.

She exposed my lower eyelid by pushing down on the skin under my eye. "You look a little pale." She poked her fingers under my chin, around my neck, down to my shoulders.

"Ngozi, I will check the lymph nodes in your armpit, okay? I'll slip my hand under your T-shirt. Raise your right hand for me."

She poked around my armpit. It tickled me. Then she did the same for my left. All the time her face was expressionless.

"How have you been feeling?"

"All right," I said. Concern crept into my mind. What did she find? Was I sick?

"What about weakness? Have you noticed any difficulty in doing things you're used to doing every day?"

"Not really."

"Any pain in your muscles when you walk?" asked Mom.

"Talking of pain, yes . . . my elbows and knees hurt when I walk . . . and I get tired easily during basketball practice. Thinking of it, my legs have always hurt. I noticed it about a year ago, but it always happened after I'd walked a long distance or ran."

"When did you notice it?"

"When I played basketball after the break . . . like two weeks ago. I thought I was just rusty from having not played in a while."

Mom nodded and thought for a second. "Maybe, come with me. I'll examine you."

We walked to Dad's study. Mom pointed at the fainting couch.

"Lay down flat on the couch. I want to feel your stomach."

"Am I sick?"

"I hope not, just following the clues."

Mom lifted my sweater and T-shirt to expose my stomach once I laid on the couch.

"Is there any part of your stomach that hurts?" she asked.

"No."

She rubbed her palms together and then placed her right one on my stomach. "Don't flex it."

She moved her palm over my stomach, inch by inch, her eyes on my face.

"Breathe in."

I did, and she dug her finger a little deeper into my stomach.

I inhaled and held my breath. After about ten seconds I exhaled through my nose.

"I'm sorry," said Mom with a smile. "I forgot to tell you to breathe."

She now placed her left palm on my stomach and with her right middle finger tapped her left middle finger as she moved her left palm from left to right over my stomach.

"I will examine your groin area for lymph nodes, okay?"

She pushed her palms under my jeans a little below my waist and pushed her fingers down at the crease of my thigh. She did the same thing on the left side.

"Okay, I'm done." She looked at me and smiled. It wasn't her usual. Her eyes did not smile. I knew something was wrong.

47

Mom sat down beside me on the couch. I scooted over to make room for her. She took my hand and held it in hers.

She sighed. "Some of your lymph nodes are enlarged and so is your spleen. We have to get you to see a specialist and get blood work done."

"What does it mean . . . that my lymph nodes and spleen are enlarged?"

"Well . . ." Mom took a deep breath and squeezed my hand. She bent her head and tapped her forehead with our hands together. "Based on what you've told me and what I found . . . I'm suspecting . . . I'm just concerned."

Mom exhaled as she said the last word, as if attempting to cover up her word.

"How do you feel?" I could see the sides of her mouth quiver.

"Okay, just thirsty. Can I go get water?"

"Sure." She got up from the couch, "I'll call Dad. He should be on his way back."

I filled a glass with water from the fridge dispenser. Mom

had her cell phone in her hand, so I went up to my room. My laptop was on the table already open, and I turned it on.

Once the screen came alive, I Googled the causes of enlarged lymph nodes and spleens. Fingers trembling, I clicked through to the first website and read the first paragraph. My body went tense when I read the diagnosis.

48

Leukemia was what most of the articles suggested, a form of cancer. The more I read about it, the more symptoms I noticed I had experienced.

There were two types, acute and chronic. People my age are prone to the acute type, the article said. I might have leukemia. I couldn't wait to tell Jennifer.

There was a knock on my door.

"Come in," I said.

The door opened, and Dad walked in. Behind him was Mom. He smiled.

"How . . . how are you feeling?" he asked.

"I'm all right," I said, nodding my head.

"Your . . . your mom called while I was driving back." He sat down beside me on the bed. "I've already called one of my colleagues . . . he'll see us tomorrow morning."

"You called already?" said Mom. "Ben, check for yourself, maybe I got it wrong."

He then hugged me and held me tight.

I cried. I knew this was serious. Mom placed her hand on my shoulders.

"We'll leave you to get some rest," said Mom. "I'll fry plantain and heat up some rice and stew. I'll come and get you when it's ready."

The gurgle of the water filter got my attention. Faith glided happily, and I added a pinch of food. She swam to the surface to feed with no cares in the world. Feeling chilly and tired, I got into bed and covered myself with the blanket. I dozed off.

"Ngozi! Ngozi!"

I felt a nudge and opened my eyes. Mom's eyes were wide. She placed her hand on my forehead.

"You're burning up!" said Mom. "Your nose is bleeding again."

I tried to talk, but I choked and coughed. Blood splattered on my pillow, adding to the blood already there. I'd been bleeding while I was asleep.

Mom opened the door. "Ben! Ben!"

"Yes? What is it?"

She came back in and grabbed some Kleenex from the table. She wiped my nose and handed me some.

Dad's feet sounded like thunder as he ran up the staircase.

Dad did a quick assessment. "We have to take her to the ER."

"Should I call an ambulance?" asked Mom in a shaky voice.

"No, we'll drive."

At the ER, they took a history and did a CBC.

"The complete blood count suggests its most likely leukemia," said the ER doctor when he came back with the result. "But we would need to do a bone marrow aspirate to be definite."

Dad had chosen the ER of the hospital of the doctor we

were supposed to see in the morning, so they discharged me to his clinic.

In the morning, Dr. Brian Palmer, a pediatric oncologist, came to my room. He was a small man and was slow and deliberate with his words. He reminded me of the character in *Twins* played by Danny DeVito. I must have seen that movie a thousand times with Zainab. It was one of the few non-Nigerian DVDs they had, and it seemed to be playing whenever I came to their apartment.

"Well, Ngozi," said Dr. Palmer. He looked up at me and then at my parents, a slight grin on his lips. "I found a few things we will analyze further so we can identify exactly what we are dealing with. I've written out some tests, and we'll need a bone marrow aspirate."

His eyes darted from me and to my parents as if expecting questions.

Dad rubbed his hand over his head and nodded. "Okay."

"Once the results are in, we can come together again to come up with a treatment plan that will be beneficial to the patient," said Dr. Palmer. He pointed at me. "And everybody involved."

"So, what do you think?" asked Mom.

"Based on the history, signs, and symptoms . . . CBC, it could be some blood disorder, but I don't want to jump the gun. Once the results are in, we will know for sure."

"I have a question," I said. My voice was a whisper.

Dr. Palmer looked in my direction and smiled. "What would you like to know?"

"What exactly is leukemia?"

"Ah!" He leaned toward me. "Well, leukemia is a malignancy that can occur in children, teenagers, and adults. It is a cancer of white blood cells. The white blood cells fight infection in our bodies and keep us healthy. They are made in the bone marrow." He paused and looked at me.

I nodded. "So, cancer cells are abnormal cells that grow a lot?" I asked raising my eyebrows.

Dr. Palmer nodded. "In leukemia, the bone marrow produces abnormal white cells. These abnormal cells cannot fight infection. That's one strike against them making the patient prone to infection. Then they are continuously being produced, overwhelming healthy cells by competing with them for nutrients—"

"Does it have a cure?" I asked.

Dr. Palmer raised himself to his five-foot-and-nothing-inch frame. "Well, we now know a lot about leukemia in children, much more than we did thirty years ago. I've managed quite a few cases to complete resolution. So, there are treatment options that work, but it also depends on how the patient responds to treatment."

49

I was discharged and told to report back for the bone marrow aspirate. Mom called her office and told them she'd be taking the next few days off and why.

Dad said his team was more flexible. He would talk to them later.

"Where will they be getting the marrow from?" I asked on the drive home.

Dad answered. "In kids, it's taken from long bones such as the femur—"

"The thigh bone, right?"

"Yes, or they could take it from the iliac crest. Have you studied the skeleton in school yet?"

I caught his eye in the rearview mirror. I nodded.

"Do you know where the iliac crest is?" he asked.

I knew he was just teasing. "Crest toothpaste," I said and laughed.

"Silly. Well, just around the top of the hip bone there is an area called the posterior superior iliac crest. It's an excellent spot to harvest stem cells. That's where the needle goes."

I froze. "Needle? Nobody said anything about more needles." I was alarmed at the thought of being poked again.

"I don't like needles myself," said Dad. "But it's a necessary inconvenience." They'll give you a patch to dull the pain before inserting the needle."

"A patch? Like the ad on TV for people who smoke?"

"Yes, but this would be for pain," said Dad. He turned back to look at me for a second and then turned to face oncoming traffic. "They'll put you in a hospital gown, and numb the area over the iliac crest with a patch. Just like they did before taking blood for the CBC. Next, they'll inject a local anesthetic over the area to numb it more. By then you're already in the operating room on the operating table. They'll lay you on your side, the doctor will collect the bone marrow and send it to the pathologist to analyze."

"How long does the whole procedure take?"

"About fifteen minutes."

My phone vibrated. Thank God, something to distract me from thinking about needles. I fished it out of my jeans pocket. It was a text from Jennifer. I was giving her a minute-by-minute update about what was going on. She said she'd meet me at home after school.

I looked up at Dad. "Oh, we forgot to tell the school I would not be there today."

"Mom must have called them."

At the mention of school, I sent Jennifer a text that I wouldn't be in school today and tomorrow too. Ken was on my mind, but I felt the less he knew, the better off for him.

When we got home, I felt an urge to look at the family tree I had made again. I had put a silhouette with a question mark over the area where my biological parents would go. That all seemed like years ago.

The next day, Mom and I went to the hospital. We rode up

the elevator to the day surgery unit. They asked for my name and checked me up in the system. They matched me up to the doctor who would do the procedure and then told us to wait in the waiting room.

Some guy in scrubs came and talked to us about the surgery. It was just as Dad had described it. Then the prep for the operation began.

I woke up in the recovery room, drowsy.

Mom was there, staring out of the window.

"How did it go?" I asked. My mouth was dry, my voice low. I swallowed and spoke louder. "How did it go?"

Mom spun around and smiled. "Ah, you're awake." She came toward me on the bed.

I attempted a smile.

"The doctor said it went well," said Mom. "We'll now wait for them to analyze the bone marrow. How do you feel?" She pulled a chair closer and sat down. She held my hand and smoothed my forehead.

I still had a hospital gown on. "A little sore." I tried to adjust myself on the bed, felt a sharp pain, and stopped. I shifted again and the pain was not as intense. I guess I should take baby steps until the pain fades for good.

"It'll just feel sore for a little while," said Mom.

"Can we go home now?" I asked. I wanted to get out of the hospital.

"Sure," said Mom. "It all depends on you. We can stand up and try a few steps. Once you are steady on your feet, I'll help you dress."

Mom helped me out of the car when we got home. I was still out of it from the effect of the sedatives and the procedure itself. The pain was now a dull ache on my hip. Once my head touched my pillow, I slept.

I stayed home from school for the next couple of days. I

read the first few chapters of *Divergent*, a dystopian novel about a girl who had to make a choice—stay with her old faction or join a new one. It reminded me of the time when Mom, then my godmother, invited me to come to live with her in America. I was scared to make a move; I didn't know her.

In the afternoon of the second day, Mom and Dad came to my room.

"I spoke with Dr. Palmer," said Dad.

I took one look at them and knew. "Bad news?"

"The results are out," said Dad. He sat down beside Mom and me on my other side.

"It's a rare form of AML, acute myelogenous leukemia," Mom said. "We'd hoped it wouldn't be any of that . . . but . . ." Her voice broke.

Mom covered her face with her hands and cried. "Sorry, I wasn't going to do this."

Dad stretched his hand behind me and squeezed Mom's shoulder. "Dr. Palmer wants us to come in at once so he can begin treatment."

Dad hugged me. I felt a growing painful lump in my throat. It wouldn't go away no matter how much I swallowed.

Dad continued, "He said the sooner we started treatment, the better the prognosis."

There was a long pause. We were all deep in our own thoughts.

Dad broke the silence. "Ngozi, we'll fight this together."

50

We arrived at Dr. Palmer's office, and he wanted to know if we had questions before he started with the treatment options. Dad assured him we had none.

"Our working diagnosis is acute myelogenous leukemia," said Dr. Palmer. "I have handled cases that went into complete remission with chemotherapy. Some we treated with high-energy radiation. Where the standard treatment is not an option, then we go for a bone marrow transplant."

He paused, looked at my parents, then at me. "Every treatment comes with its own difficulties and sometimes the unexpected. In most cases, it's nothing we can't handle."

Dad nodded. "So far so good," he said and sighed, looking more nervous than his usual calm self.

"Good," said Dr. Palmer. "For chemotherapy, we would begin with induction, which could go one to three rounds. If everything goes as we expect, we would then follow with a consolidation phase, which could run another three rounds of chemo. After consolidation, we would then do a second bone marrow biopsy to track the progress of the treatment."

A smile appeared on the doctor's face.

"If it's in complete remission, then you're designated NOD," continued Dr. Palmer.

Dad released a breath. "No evidence of disease. That would be great." Dad's lips quivered as if they were debating whether to smile or laugh.

Dr. Palmer nodded. "The options are straightforward. Start with chemo and track the response."

The discussion had been going on as if I wasn't there. I liked it. What was I going to say, anyway? I wondered what the side effects would be.

"There are side effects to chemo too," said Dr. Palmer. "Apart from the bread-and-butter side effects like nausea, vomiting, and diarrhea. Others like hypersensitivity reaction to the medication are individually based and only become clear after we start treatment."

As we waited in the waiting area for my room to be ready, I called Jennifer and told her about the diagnosis.

Jennifer was quiet.

"Ngozi, I don't know what to say. My mom's sister died a few years ago from cancer. She had leukemia or maybe breast cancer, but she was sick." There was a pause. "Ngozi, I know cancer is a bad disease, but I'll always be here for you."

I felt overwhelmed in a good way. Jennifer had always been good to me. I didn't want to cry and make her cry. I stared down at my empty hand. "The doctor said I'll be out of school for some time."

"How long?" asked Jennifer.

The tears were threatening to come. I needed to say something, otherwise I would crumble. The hospital reception area wasn't a place I wanted to cry in. I sniffed. "They divide the treatment into phases, I think. The first one is called the induction stage, takes about three to six weeks."

"Induction?" asked Jennifer in a shaky voice.

My eyes were blurry. "They start the first round of chemo and then look at how I'm responding, whether the tumor cells are being killed." I rubbed my eyes with the back of my hand.

"Oh, man, you'll be getting chemo?" asked Jennifer.

"Yes," I said, my voice tearful.

Jennifer let out a nervous laugh. "That's good-bye to your hair. Maybe you'll have half an eyebrow left at the end." She giggled.

I pictured myself with no hair and half an eyebrow and laughed. "What a sorry sight that would be."

Jennifer stopped laughing. "I can't believe we're laughing about something like this."

"What else can we do? We've been sad, we've cried, and then we laugh! We've gone through all the emotions. We can't just look sad, for looking sad's sake."

"So, after the induction phase, you're done?" asked Jennifer.

I told her all Dr. Palmer said at his office about the induction phase and consolidation phase and tracking the progress of my treatment.

"So, what it means is that if, God forbid, chemo fails, then you would need bone marrow from a donor?" said Jennifer.

"Yes."

"I always hear about bone marrow donations," said Jennifer. "It's funny, something you hear about all the time and don't pay attention to. It's only when it affects you personally or someone you know that you care."

"I know," I said. "Always somebody else's problems until it affects you."

"I think we should get on the Internet and learn more about this bone marrow transplant thing."

I could hear typing from Jennifer's end. "Are you there? What are you doing?"

"Still here, Googling bone marrow transplant," said Jennifer. "Listen to this . . . if chemo fails, one has a better chance of being cured by getting bone marrow that matches theirs from a relative than a stranger."

Induction better not fail then, I said to myself.

51

Mom and I sat in the room watching TV and taking in our surroundings. An infusion pump stood next to a comfortable leather chair with a TV hanging down from the ceiling. *A sweet spot for long chemo infusion sessions*, I thought. A sharp knock drew our attention to the door.

"Hello!" said a nurse as she walked in, clipboard in hand.

We exchanged introductions, and she talked about what to expect while I was in the hospital. She showed us the control for the TV and thermostat.

"Do you have questions?" inquired the nurse.

I was about to say no when I remembered and smiled. "Do you have Wi-Fi?" I blurted.

The nurse smiled. "You brought your phone and computer? Almost all our teenage patients ask that question. That would depend on Dr. Palmer. He will assess your situation as you receive medication. The side effects could be an issue, but it all depends on him. The rooms are all wired."

"I'm glad to hear that!"

"We also have tutors," continued the nurse. "If you need

them. They'll work with you so you don't miss a lot of schoolwork. There is a call button beside you on the bed and whenever you need help, just use it." She showed us the button.

The nurse took my vitals and told Mom there was an air mattress and some sheets in the closet. As soon as she left, Mom called Dad to let him know we were in a room. He said he would drop by on his way back from work.

Dr. Palmer arrived soon after we settled in. "How are you today, Ngozi? I brought my whole team with me."

"Okay," I said and looked down. There were so many people in lab coats, and I was the center of attention.

"How are you doing, Dr. Obi?" he asked. His head tilted in Mom's direction.

"Good," Mom said and smiled.

Dr. Palmer turned around to his team, "Dr. Obi is an attending at the nephrology department. I'm sure some of you are wondering why she's so familiar."

Dr. Palmer looked back at me. "All right, young lady, do you have questions?"

I shook my head.

"The first leg of the induction will last for twenty-nine days," said Dr. Palmer. He rattled off the names of the drugs they would use. "We'll start induction treatment tomorrow."

Most of what he said went in one ear and left through the other. I got interested when he talked about possible side effects and hair loss, but he assured me it would grow back.

"IV line or port surgery?" asked Dr. Palmer.

I agreed to port surgery after he described what it was. They insert a catheter beneath my skin to a major vein, and I receive the medication, fluids, and transfusions through it. That way I wouldn't be poked multiple times.

The next day, induction started on schedule. Mom was by

my side all the time and Dad came and went. I reminded him to feed the fish at least once a day.

I spent my time watching TV and reading. We alternated between Mom's show and what I wanted to watch. Mom brought reading materials too, medical journals and a novel. I saw reruns of *The Voice* and *American Idol*.

"Ah, so this is what they modeled *Nigerian Idol* after," I said out loud while watching one singer.

Mom's eyebrows shot up, "There's a *Nigerian Idol*?"

"Yes, and it's popular too."

"Hmm, I didn't know," said Mom.

I called Jennifer after watching TV. "Hi."

"Can I see your hair?" she asked, cutting me off.

"Why?" I asked.

"Never mind! Ken said he's been texting you and you're not returning his text."

I told her I would text him. But that was a lie. Since the day I realized I was the girl with the oranges, I'd felt like an impostor, not worthy of anybody's attention. Sometimes I felt angry with the world. Why me? What did I do to deserve all these bad things happening? Maybe I'd talk to Dr. Walters about it next time I saw her. Jennifer and I talked a little more, and she hung up.

By the fifth day of therapy, I felt so tired and out of it that even getting up to go to the bathroom or to the infusion chair was now demanding. Each time I placed my foot on the floor, I would get terrible headaches, as if someone was banging a coconut on my head. My calves and thighs would burn with every step. For the first time since I was diagnosed, it scared me that the outcome might not be positive.

"The pain and fatigue are some side effects we see early with the chemo," explained Dr. Palmer. "We'll give you something for the side effects. Let us know at once of any discomforts so we can counter them. We want you to be as comfortable as possible."

I detested nausea and throwing up, and I thought somehow I had kept those two at bay by my dislike for them, but by the second week of treatment, they came knocking. Like a storm, they gathered in the depth of my stomach and then surged to the surface like molten lava, only to stop short of erupting. It would tease me, enjoy my agony, and then take me by surprise, spewing my most recent meal all over my clean hospital gown.

52

The nurses were always nice when they came to clean after I threw up, which Mom would start.

"We'll get you a bucket for next time," said one nurse.

Dr. Palmer prescribed a medication that put an end to nausea and vomiting, for which I'd forever remain grateful.

By the beginning of the fourth week, I was not doing well. I woke up fatigued, and an hour later I was exhausted. Even though I had Wi-Fi, I didn't have the energy to do much online. Classmates and teachers sent "get well soon" messages. People I didn't know. It would take a while to get through all the e-mails and texts. But each one I replied to, I always got a fast reply from the person I sent it to.

That morning, I had woken up late, as was now the norm. I guess the nightmare had taken a backseat, as something more ominous was present. As I ran my hand over my head, two braids came off. As tired as I was, fatigued or not, there was an adrenaline surge.

"What!" I gasped. I stared at my hair in disbelief. I shuffled to the bathroom and faced the mirror. It was clean hair removal, right from the roots, and I had felt no pain. The bald spot shimmered in the yellow light of the bathroom bulb.

"Are you okay?" Mom asked as she walked into the bathroom. She must have heard.

I lifted my hand and showed her the jet-black braids clutched in it.

"Oh, sweetheart, don't worry, it's just a minor setback. It will grow back," she said and gave me a hug.

Even though I'd expected it, it saddened me. I sent a text to Jennifer after I had calmed down and settled back on the bed. "FaceTime me as soon as you can!"

She called me within the hour, "Hello, Ngozi, are you home?"

"Haha, very funny," I said and smiled. Her smiling face filled up the screen. "Not yet. Can you see me?" I asked.

"No, I see a pillow," she said.

I adjusted the camera until she could see. "Now watch this!" I steadied the phone with my left hand. Or rather, I tried to steady the phone with my left hand. My hand seemed to be fluttering in the air. I grabbed a chunk of hair with my right hand and pulled.

"Oh my God!" Jenifer gasped. "Your hair is falling off!"

"I'll have the whole thing removed today, so by the end of the day I'll look like that one girl with a shaved head on *America's Next Top Model*."

We talked for a little while, and then Jennifer had to go because she was in school.

"Are you sure you want it all off?" asked Mom. "It will take a while to grow back."

I nodded, and Mom cut my braids off as low as she could go with scissors. Later, when Dr. Palmer and his team came by, they commented on my new look, and all claimed they loved it. Dr. Palmer looked at my charts and addressed us.

"Tomorrow will be the twenty-ninth day of treatment. At that point, we assess the progress."

Mom nodded, lips pursed.

"How is that done?" I asked.

"MRD?" asked Mom, looking at Dr. Palmer.

Dr. Palmer nodded. "Minimal residue disease test. It gives us an idea of how Ngozi is responding to treatment, how well the chemo is destroying the cancer cells. And this we do by measuring the number of cells left in your bone marrow."

My eyes widened. "I'll be getting another bone marrow tap?"

"Afraid so," said Dr. Palmer. But we'll make sure you have the least amount of discomfort. Based on the MRD result, we can decide on the next step."

"So, what's a good MRD result?" I inquired.

"Well, there are two ways to look at this. It could be negative or positive. A negative result means there are no more detectable leukemic cells, but they are still lurking around, so we'll then come up with a medication strategy to mop them up. A negative value validates our treatment choice."

I nodded, even though I didn't understand.

"A positive result means we must reevaluate our choice of chemo. Then, depending on the value, we'll determine whether we would recommend a different regimen or . . . stem cell transplant."

The pause was not lost on me, neither was it lost on Mom. We had hoped it wouldn't come to that.

"So there's a possibility she might need a bone marrow transplant?" asked Mom.

Dr. Palmer pushed his glasses back and folded his arms in front of him. He had a faint reassuring smile on his lips. "Yes, but pending the outcome of the MRD test. So, in the next couple of days, we'll know exactly where we stand."

Dr. Palmer and his team left, leaving Mom and me to our own thoughts. I wondered what would happen if I needed a bone marrow transplant. I had no idea who my biological parents were.

Mom called Dad and told him the news. She was anxious and had dark circles under her eyes. They seemed to have come from nowhere. She always appeared calm, and it never occurred to me my ordeal would not be easy on her. I turned on the TV—the default channel was CNN—and let it play, drowning out Mom's hushed voice.

I must have fallen asleep because when I woke up, the time on the clock was already after three in the afternoon. Mom sat on the chair, a book in hand. She put the book she was reading down.

"Hi," said Mom. "You were exhausted. You've slept for a while. You usually don't sleep for this long in the afternoon."

"I guess so," I said and rubbed the sleep from my eyes. "What's for lunch?" I asked out of habit. I didn't have much of an appetite.

Mom pointed at the menu. "The usual. Do you want me to order you something?"

"No, I'm not ready yet. Maybe I'll wait for dinner. With luck, I'll have a bigger appetite by then. I'll just drink water."

My phone vibrated. I'd turned the ring tone off so it wouldn't go off when we had company. I picked it up and saw Jennifer's name on the screen. "What's up?"

"Can you talk?" she asked. She sounded excited.

"Yes," I said and sat up. "Just Mom and me in the room. What's going on?" My eyes narrowed. What could it be? Did something happen to Ken?

"I want to show you something. Can you call me back on FaceTime?" said Jennifer.

I hesitated. "Sure, what is it?"

"Just call." Jennifer hung up.

I dialed her back on FaceTime. She answered on the first ring.

"Can you see me?" Jennifer blurted.

"Yes," I said slowly. I could see her smiling and waving at me, but something was wrong.

53

"**M**y God!" I gasped. My hands flew to my mouth, my eyes wide with disbelief. "YOU SHAVED YOUR HAIR!"

Mom rushed out of her chair and ran toward me. She took one look at my phone. "Jesus, Jennifer! What did you do?"

All we heard was laughter and giggles as Jennifer twirled around showing off her bald head.

"Do you like it?" Jennifer asked. She looked like she was having a lot of fun.

"I can't believe it!" I croaked. I felt the tears roll down my cheeks.

"Ngozi, I can't be there with you, but I can be there with you in spirit and in likeness. I told you, we'll fight his together."

"Oh," said Mom, clutching her hands to her chest and smiling.

Jennifer's gesture made my day. She brought me up to speed on things that had been happening in school and what she had been up to. I also told her about the MRD test and what it signified. She wished me well and promised to call back.

After she hung up, I sat there and stared into space. The full impact of what I was facing hit me. When would it ever end? Whenever things seemed to be working in my favor, life tapped me on my shoulders with yet another load to carry. I looked at Mom. I would rob them of their greatest wish—they only wanted to be parents.

Fresh tears rolled down my cheeks. A sob escaped my lip.

"Are you okay?" Mom asked, looking up from her book. "That Jennifer girl is something, isn't she?"

I signaled to her I was all right. She went back to her book, not knowing there was more to the tears than Jennifer's gesture. I'd never wanted to pull through more than ever. The more I thought about it, the more obvious it became that finding out who my biological parents were would play a huge role in determining whether I beat this disease or not.

The orderly took me to the operating room the next morning where I went through the same procedure I'd had done a few weeks before to extract bone marrow. This time, I wasn't as apprehensive because I knew what to expect. I willed myself to hang in there and be strong. The patch that would numb the area was a no-brainer, but I still felt the first injection a bit. The rest of the procedure would be fine.

They extracted the marrow and took it to the laboratory for analysis. I stayed in the recovery room for thirty minutes before they wheeled me back to my room.

Dr. Palmer did not show up to my room that morning. Instead, he came in the afternoon with his entourage. The look on his face and that of his staff suggested a problem. From what I'd discovered in the past few weeks he'd been treating me, he believed in delivering news fast.

"Ngozi, Dr. Obi, the test is out, and the result is positive," said Dr. Palmer.

My hands clenched into fists. I felt like the rug was yanked out underneath me. I glanced at Mom. She struggled to keep a calm composure, but she came out looking like someone had punched her in the stomach.

Mom's eyes glistened with tears. "We'd hoped for a different result, but it is what it is." She paused. "What are your recommendations?"

I had to give it to her, her voice was solid, not shaky.

Dr. Palmer pursed his lips. He took a deep breath and sighed. "We have two options. The first is increasing the dose of chemo. That could cause more side effects and possible collateral damage."

"How effective would that approach be?" Mom asked.

Dr. Palmer shook his head. He looked like he was in pain. "I can't say. The other option is a stem cell transplant. As you already know, it is a process that wipes out the immune system, which then has to rebuild itself." He paused and glanced at us. "Finding a match is the first hurdle. The most promising source is a sibling, and the next best would be a close relative."

I tuned out. I had neither. My mind went blank. Maybe I didn't understand the full implication of what was going on inside my body. But I understood pain and when my body didn't feel right. I wished I could click a button and restore my health to what it had been a few months ago.

A while ago, Jennifer had downloaded free music from the Internet, and her computer had crashed. She had restored her laptop to an earlier date with the click of a button. Click a button. Restore health. A faint smile crossed my face.

Dr. Palmer must have caught the smile. He looked at me,

and his eyebrows shot up as if asking a question. Then he continued.

"The normal cells are being attacked at a faster rate than we've encountered before. This is a more aggressive type of leukemia." Dr. Palmer lowered his voice to a whisper. "Nkechi, at this rate, in two weeks, there won't be any more normal cells left. I'm sorry."

Dr. Palmer and his people left Mom and me to think about what he had said. The stem cell transplant option seemed to be the most promising, if we could find a close match.

Mom shook her head. "We have less than two weeks or . . ." Her voice caught as she spoke.

Her lips quivered. I'd never seen such a sad look on anybody before. She looked like her entire world was falling apart. I couldn't blame her; I was no good.

Mom called Dad and told him the result. She put the phone on speaker. "Ngozi is here."

"Ngozi, I heard we had a setback," said Dad. He sounded tired and sad. "Don't worry, we are in this together, and we'll fight and beat it. I'll be there soon."

"Yes, Dad," I said, agreeing for his sake. My hands went limp beside me. I was glad Dad wasn't there yet. I didn't want to see the disappointment on his face. I'd let them down. What else could go wrong today?

"That's my girl. Emmm . . . Ngozi, the goldfish has been swimming upside down . . . is it a trick?"

After Dad hung up, Mom and I sat on the bed and appreciated each other's company. We said nothing.

Mom stared out of the window, deep in her own thoughts. The room was calm and peaceful. The TV was on but with the volume on mute. I could see the CNN afternoon news anchor with gray hair and beard speaking into a microphone.

Dad had tried to lighten up the mood by telling me something positive. But it was no trick. Faith was dead. I wouldn't be far behind. I thought of Jennifer and Ken and picked up my phone. There was no need. I had to end it with Ken. I typed the text.

54

———

Me: *Dear Ken, I got bad news today. Induction failed and I have about two weeks left unless I find my biological family or compatible stem cells. It is over. I think you should make up with Mary Ann and forget about me.*

Tears rolled down my cheeks. I didn't know what else to write. There was a knock on the door. I pressed my finger on "Send." The message left with a whoosh sound as Dad walked in. I put the phone away.

"My princess," said Dad in a low voice. He hugged me, and I cried. "We'll fight this together, we'll always be there for you." His voice cracked.

Dad wouldn't stop apologizing about Faith.

"It's not your fault," I said. "I should have told you. I learned the hard way too. Some say fish keep on eating as long as there's food in the water, while some say the decaying excess food produces ammonia toxic to the fish. Just one pinch a day."

"Guilty of both," said Dad. "I thought I could kill . . . two birds with one stone." Dad slapped his forehead with his palm. "I better stop talking."

The three of us sat on the bed, me in the middle and Mom and Dad beside me. We focused on the TV, not talking about the big python in the room, enjoying each other's company until I drifted off to sleep.

A constant pelting sound woke me up. I opened my eyes. A distant flash of lightning illuminated the room and faded. Outside, the rain was hitting the window in sheets. As my eyes adjusted to the dim light in the room, I saw Mom on the mattress, but Dad wasn't there. He must have left after I'd fallen asleep.

The events of the previous day hit me anew like a thunderbolt. I pressed my hand against the bed. The throbbing in my head sounded like a roaring river to my ears.

What was I going to do? I looked at Mom and wondered if she cursed the day she set eyes on me in that neonatology unit many years ago—fifteen years ago. Or maybe I should hate her. If she hadn't intervened, my life would have taken another course. I would have remained at the hospital and become a ward of the hospital. Maybe I would have contracted another illness, which would have ended my life a long time ago.

I wanted to hate Mom, not because of who she was but because of what her being in my life was making her go through. Ken's song came to my mind. *Of all the girls in the world, it's you that has captured my heart.* Of all the children in the world, she adopts me. Why?

Another flash of lightning illuminated Mom's face. She looked calm and peaceful in sleep, the worry lines gone. But I knew once she woke they would return, all because of me. My anger dissipated just as it had come. I couldn't hate her, she was only following what she felt inside.

But we cannot stop dreaming. We must follow our dreams. I remembered as a child right after Matron passed and I went to live with Uncle Thomas. I wasn't used to him, and I dreamed that my father was a big man with a big job and a big car, and one day he would come and take me away from here. Instead, my uncle, who loved me as his own child, perished in a car accident, leaving me at the mercy of Auntie Halima and my cousins Maryam and Peter. After all, a beggar has no choice.

But I felt I had a choice. Auntie Halima owed me nothing. She could have thrown me out, but she had pity on me. Fatima was there to guide me, but I didn't see it. Instead, my eyes were on the other side of the fence, the greener side of the fence. Where I thought I would be free. I'd made my move and learned that the grass is not always greener over there.

My phone buzzed and lit up. It was a voice mail from Ken. The time on my phone was 3:00 a.m. My God, he was still awake. I picked up the phone. There were many notifications. Texts and voice messages from Ken and Jennifer.

I didn't want to read Ken's messages or listen to his voice mail. It would break my soul. He should understand that I was protecting him. He didn't understand how damaged I was. I didn't even know the extent. Who knew what else I would uncover when I returned to therapy with Dr. Walters. That is, if I returned.

I could hear Dr. Palmer's whispered words to Mom again as if he were there. *Nkechi, at this rate, in two weeks, there won't be any more normal cells left. I'm sorry.*

My phone buzzed again. This time it was a text from Maryam. "Maryam," I whispered out loud. I never returned the last message she sent me. It wouldn't hurt to drop her a few words. I read the first sentence.

Her: *Cousin Ngozi, how are you? I haven't heard from you in a while. Is everything fine? Text me.*

I chuckled. This was a girl that would rather die than say I was her cousin. Now she couldn't mention my name without attaching "cousin" before it. And from what we knew now, we were not biological cousins.

I heard a sound and looked up. Mom had stirred in her sleep. I typed a reply to Maryam.

55

ow did Maryam know I was adopted? I wondered. Maybe her mother or Uncle Thomas had told her. Maybe Auntie Halima knew a lot more than she ever let on. She always had her anger in check.

Me: *Hi, Maryam, sorry I didn't get back to you earlier. I've been sick, and I need your help.*

Her: *Cousin Ngozi! What's wrong? Do you have malaria?*

I chuckled. I'd almost forgotten. Once you don't feel well in Nigeria, the first culprit is malaria. My fingers hovered over the phone. Do I tell her? I had to if I expected her to help me.

Me: *Not malaria. I'm on admission. I have leukemia.*

Her: *Ha? Wetin be that!*

I laughed at Maryam's "What is that?" in Pidgin English. My phone rang. I turned the ringer off and glanced at Mom. She was still sleeping. Maryam had just called. She wanted to talk?

Her: *I flashed you!! Call me. This is serious.*

Me: *I'll call in the morning. It's still 3:10 a.m. here. I need your help. I need to find my biological parents. Do you think your mother would know?*

I waited. The word "typing" came up in italics under Maryam's name. I waited. Was she consulting someone? Maybe her mom? My pulse beat faster.

Me: *Are you there?*

Her: *I'll flash you later in the day. I'll talk to Mom.*

Me: *Okay, bye.*

Air rattled out of my lungs as I exhaled. Even though we were thousands of miles apart, just the thought of Auntie Halima thinking about me put me in panic mode.

With daybreak, the rain stopped. I had toast for breakfast and drifted in and out of sleep.

"You look tired," said Mom. "Did you sleep at all?"

"The rain woke me," I said. Should I tell Mom about Maryam? Maybe I'd wait until I heard from her.

"Try to sleep this morning. I'll take a walk later to clear my head."

Dr. Palmer was a no-show that morning, but his team members came. It was a regular ward round. They planned to give us enough time to evaluate the options that they had laid out and remind us that every day was crucial. After all, it was a matter of life and death.

The rest of the morning was a blur. I drifted in and out of sleep. Each time I looked at my phone to check whether Maryam had flashed, I would see a text from Ken. It made me so sad. I would have to call him or maybe write him.

Around noon, Maryam's name flashed on my phone. Sleep vanished from my eyes. She sent a text to call her in one hour—she had news. My pulse raced as if I was in a one-hundred-meter dash.

I looked at Mom. She sat on the couch reading a novel, glasses in place. I didn't want her to know what I was up to yet. As the time approached, I thought of going into the bath-room. She would still hear and feel sad. If I went for a walk, she would come with me.

My phone buzzed, and I almost jumped out of my skin. It was a text from Jennifer.

Her: *Are you all right? Send us a text. We are anxious. You know we still can't visit.*

Me: *I will.*

I didn't want the phone to be tied up. My fingers trembled as a scrolled through my phone to Maryam's number. This was the first time I had done any meaningful thing about finding my biological parents. My stomach was tied in knots. I didn't know what to expect. Maryam picked up on the third ring.

"Hello, Maryam, it's Ngozi." I smiled. "I hope this is a good time."

"Wow, your voice has changed. You are now speaking Americana!"

"I sound the same." Mom glanced up from her novel.

"Expect my text. I'll send it once I'm done talking to my mom."

The line went dead.

"Who was that? Jennifer?" asked Mom.

"No, Maryam in Nigeria."

"Your . . . cousin?"

Mom still called them my cousins even though they were not.

Mom's eyes went back to her novel. "How are they? I'm sure they are knee deep in elections now."

"They are fine," I said.

My phone buzzed. It was Maryam.

Her: *My mom said Auntie Matron told them about you before the adoption. She will send Peter and me to the teaching hospital in Kano to see if we can talk to some people that were there when Auntie Matron worked there.*

Peter? My sadistic cousin? I remembered how he used to hit me and call me names when we were kids. It felt strange that now they all wanted to help. The screen showed she was still typing. I waited, but the "typing" status remained there. Maybe she was typing and deleting. I got impatient.

Me: *Thank you so much! When are you going?*

Her: *My mom gave us the names of some people to talk to when we get to Kano.*

I stared at the screen. Auntie Halima is helping? A woman that had terrorized me for most of my formative years? I remembered the look on her face when she accused me of stealing. The fear in her eyes after I'd said terrible words to her. Right now I wished I hadn't said them.

Me: *Thank Auntie Halima for me.*

56
———

Later that night I sent a text to Jennifer. I told her all that was going on. How I was looking for my birth parents and what I'd done so far. She'd called, and it went to voice mail. I didn't think I could talk on the phone.

Mom and Dad needed to know about my discussions. I'd have to tell them. Who knew how they would take it? By the time Dad dropped by later that night, I'd decided not to. Tomorrow I would, when I had more information.

In the morning, there was no Dr. Palmer. His team members came for a round, examined me, and said they'd let us know once there was a match on the database they were looking at.

"I'll walk off my breakfast," said Mom after she finished eating.

"Not after lunch?" For the past few days, Mom had been going for walks along the corridor after lunch.

Mom walked to the door. "I'll go then too."

"Okay." I looked at the toast I'd buttered. I still wasn't hungry.

"See you." Mom shut the door behind her.

My phone vibrated. I'd silenced it last night when Jennifer was trying to reach me. It was Maryam.

"Hello," I said.

"Ngozi, how are you?" said a deep and hoarse voice. "This is Auntie Beatrice! You don't know my voice again?"

I sat up. My mind's gear engaged. Auntie Beatrice? Who was she again? Auntie Halima's younger sister, rough around the edges. Yes!

"Hello?"

"Oh, Auntie!" I looked at my watch, "Good evening, how are you doing?"

"I'm fine! You've forgotten all about us. You are there enjoying America."

I turned the volume on the phone down. Why did Nigerians scream a lot on the phone?

"Hello? Hello?" Auntie Beatrice yelled.

I cleared my throat. "Yes, I'm still here."

"You're lucky Maryam told me about your problem, and I decided to help. Peter drove us to Warawa near Kano," she said. "Ngozi, I can't talk. I'm about to meet with the night watchman on duty the day they dropped you off. He is now retired. I'll flash you once I'm done."

I couldn't believe my ears. "What?"

"Stay by your phone. Bye."

"Okay, Auntie, thank you so much. God bless you." The phone went dead. Auntie Beatrice was in Warawa? I was beside myself with excitement. Auntie Beatrice was effective when she's on your side. "Oh my God, I'm going to know," I said through trembling lips. I felt happy, sad, and scared at the same time.

There was a knock on the door.

"Come in," I said.

"Hello." It was the ward maid. She pointed at the break-fast tray. "Can I remove it?"

"Yes, thank you." I stretched out my hand and grabbed my toast. My appetite came back. The ward maid picked up the tray and left.

Pumped with energy, I went to the bathroom, splashed water on my face, and toweled it dry. My phone rang. Maryam's name flashed on my screen. I grabbed the phone and pushed it against my ear, so hard that my ear throbbed.

"Hello, Ngozi?"

"Yes, Auntie." I held my breath.

"Ngozi, you won't believe what I went through the entire day for your sake! The man said he remembers the event as if it were yesterday."

"Yes, Auntie," I said, hanging on to her every word. I couldn't wait for her to deliver the story. *Hurry*, I screamed in my mind.

"The man said that it was early in the morning and he was doing his rounds, and he saw a man by the main entrance. As he approached, the man left. He finished his shift and went home. It was only after he came back to work later that night that he heard it was a baby."

There was a pause. I looked at the phone. Was it still connected? "Hello?" I said.

"I'm here," said Auntie.

"Who did he see?"

"Don't rush me. I'm the one telling the story."

I bit my tongue. Auntie Beatrice hadn't changed.

"The man said he lost his job and had been unemployed for the past six months. He said he'd only exchange the infor-mation for money."

At the mention of money, I felt like I'd been kicked in the stomach. "Auntie, how much is he asking for?"

"It comes to about fifteen thousand dollars based on the current exchange rate," said Auntie Beatrice.

I gasped. "Fifteen thousand dollars!"

"I told him no way. That he should be ashamed of himself asking for money to do a worthy act."

"How . . . how do we know the information is authentic?" I asked. "He could say whatever he likes."

"Ngozi, I asked him the same thing, and his reply was that if I wanted the information, I'd have to grease his palms."

Within seconds my high hopes had evaporated. Fifteen thousand dollars! Where was I going to get that? My shoulders slumped.

"Hello! Hello, Ngozi, are you there?"

"Yes, Auntie," I said. She must have noticed the dejection in my voice.

"Ngozi, listen, don't lose hope. Let's see what I can do. I'll negotiate with him and see if he'll agree to a smaller amount, okay? Don't worry, he must tell us who he saw!"

"Can't he tell us . . ." I whispered.

"Let me talk to him more. Hang up. I'll flash you."

"OK, Auntie, bye." I sat on my bed and stared at the phone for a long time. Things had gone from hopeful to hopeless. What was a guard going to do with that much money?

I lay on my bed thinking of how to persuade him to give up the information without money. *Don't be naïve*, I said to myself. This is his moment. He'd had the information with him for so many years and nobody cared about it until now.

Maryam flashed me, and I called back.

"Ngozi, baby!" Auntie Beatrice sounded excited. "I spoke with him again. It wasn't easy. We talked and talked, and at the end I got him to agree to ten thousand dollars. I think it's reasonable. You can handle that."

"I . . . I . . ."

"Why are you stammering? You don't have any dollars? Isn't there money everywhere in America?" she asked, the surprise evident in her voice.

"No, Auntie, I don't work yet."

"All right, Ngozi, I . . . I don't know what to say. We have tried for you. Why don't you ask the doc?"

I searched my mind for a smart thing to say, but nothing came to mind. "Okay, Auntie, I'll talk to . . . the doctor."

"Call me. It's already past midnight, but I'll be awake. We'll leave for Lamija tomorrow."

Later in the evening when Dad came to the hospital, I told them the whole story.

Mom exhaled. "Ngozi, I don't think it's authentic. As soon as people know you want something, and you are in America, all they see is dollar signs, and they find six ways from Sunday to exploit you. I think the watchman or Auntie Beatrice, or both, are trying to extract money for themselves."

"Did you talk to Mrs. Bashiru?" asked Dad.

"Auntie Halima? No." I shook my head.

"And it was she who sent them to Warawa?" asked Dad.

"Yes," I said.

"And they go back to Lamija tomorrow with or without the information?" asked Mom.

I nodded. "That's what Auntie Beatrice said."

Dad looked at Mom. "If it's real, that would help." He exhaled and ran his hand over his head. "It's been many years . . . you know how Nigeria is, a lot of decent people, but a few sophisticated tricksters mess everything up . . ."

Dad's voice trailed off, I could tell he was weighing all options. I felt bad.

Dad tapped his lips and looked at Mom. "We can tap the emergency fund." A loud laugh escaped his lips. "It is an emergency."

Mom nodded her agreement. I knew they'd reached a decision.

"Give me Beatrice's number. I'll call her to take care of this," said Dad.

57

I woke up tired and dejected. I went to the bathroom to ease myself and brush my teeth. I caught my reflection in the mirror. Bald, sunken eyes, skinny; a total stranger. That couldn't be me. I rubbed my hand on my head, and the stranger did the same. Cancer had stolen whoever Ngozi Obi had been. I sighed. Sometimes I wondered if there was a need to continue.

"Good morning, Mom," I said as I shuffled into the room.

Phone pressed against her left ear, Mom looked at me and signaled to keep quiet. A minute later, the call was over.

"Hi! Did you sleep well?" Mom smiled. She seemed to be in a better mood. "That was Dad. Beatrice talked to the man. He refused at first, but he later agreed." Mom walked over and gave me a hug.

"Did he provide the information?" I asked. I felt the adrenaline surge through my veins. Maybe there was hope.

"Going to, in the next few hours," said Mom. "Dad has just wired the money. Once Beatrice receives it and gives it to him, he'll divulge the info." She beamed. "Beatrice seems to be very capable. We'll have her trace the person and hopefully find the right donor."

I'd never seen Mom so happy. I was delighted, blown away. This was great.

"Ngozi, things are again looking hopeful," Mom said.

I took a deep breath and exhaled. Ten thousand dollars! I didn't think I was worth it. "But, Mom, it's a lot of money."

"And . . . you are priceless, Ngozi!" Mom said. "I think we're close to getting tangible results. The next step would be to convince the person to come here. We would have to call the US embassy or get in touch with the attorney, Mr. Fulbright, in Nigeria to explain the situation and expedite the visa processing. I feel hopeful. Come, let's watch some TV."

Things were moving so fast. Even Mom babbled.

She looked at her watch. "Nigeria is five hours ahead. Everything being equal, we should hear from her soon. What do you want to watch?"

We settled for Mom's favorite, some women's celebrity gossip show. We lay side by side on my bed. The show hostess appeared on the screen. All big. Big smile, big hair, everything big. She shook hands with the people in the first row, like most TV talk show hosts do, and then went into her celebrity gossip routine.

"She still looks like a man in drag, no matter what you say," I said.

Mom laughed. "She's just a big lady."

Two hours later, Mom's phone rang. "Go ahead, Ben, you're on speaker."

"Hi, Ngozi." Dad sounded upbeat. "Hang in there, everything will be all right, okay?"

I smiled when I heard his voice and felt encouraged. "Okay, Dad."

"Beatrice has picked up the money. She is now on her

way to see the night watchman. I'll call back as soon as she calls."

Dad came to the hospital and left late at night, but Beatrice hadn't called. We called and texted her, but she didn't answer.

I was awake for most of the night, but Dad never called back, meaning that Beatrice hadn't called him. In the morning, I'd fallen asleep, and it was now noon by my phone. Mom was napping on the couch with a book resting on her chest. I staggered to the bathroom, brushed my teeth, and got myself ready for the day.

I walked toward the window where Mom was sleeping. It was a beautiful and bright day. Mom's cell phone vibrated. I bent down and touched her shoulders. She woke with a start and stared at me for a few seconds. I pointed at her phone.

Mom rubbed her eyes and yawned. "Hi, Ngozi." She sighed. "I must have fallen asleep. For a second I didn't know where I was." She picked up the phone. "Hello, Ben." She put it on speaker and held the phone in front of her.

"You won't believe what I heard!" Dad's voice boomed through the speaker. He was angry. "Beatrice, can you repeat what you said again?"

Dad had her in a three-way call.

"He wants five thousand dollars more before he can release the information!" came Auntie's rough voice.

"What?" Mom barked. The sleep left her face. "More money for what? This is just a straightforward thing, tell us who you saw so we can find them and make a lifesaving decision!"

"People . . . look!" Beatrice stuttered. "You're trying to kill the messenger here. I'm only delivering the information I got from the man. Don't kill the messenger—"

"Put him on the phone!" Mom yelled, cutting her off. "He

needs to be straightened out. We've kept our own end of the bargain, and it's now his turn, and he's asking for more money!"

It was a frightening and tense moment. If Beatrice were right here in the room with us, Mom would have had her for brunch. I never knew Mom had such a hot streak in her.

"The man is not here!" said Auntie Beatrice. Her loud and hoarse voice exploded through the speakers. "I gave him the money and told him I'd see if I could get the rest!"

"You what?" Mom and Dad exploded at the same time.

"Please, don't you 'what' me now!" Auntie Beatrice yelled back.

"Since you people have the money to throw around just because Ngozi wants to know who her biological parents are . . . um . . . um . . . I'm just playing along with that."

Her words enraged Dad. "Is that what you think the information is for? Just to satisfy our daughter's curiosity? Well, you are wrong!"

"Beatrice, listen!" Mom interjected. "I'm in Ngozi's room at the children's cancer center. Ngozi has cancer of the blood. So far, the treatment she's receiving hasn't worked. We're moving on to the next step, which is a stem cell transplant. We need to know her biological parents so we can get a stem cell donor."

There was a pause. A long break. "Beatrice? Beatrice, talk!" Mom yelled.

"Yes, I was just thinking," said Auntie Beatrice, her voice calm and deliberate. "This Ngozi girl has always been bad luck to everybody that encounters her. Look at Matron, my sister-in-law. Once she took Ngozi into her home, that was it for her. She became sick, lost her job, and died. Nurse Balogun, dead, a car accident. My brother-in-law Thomas, dead, a car accident. Halima, my sister, only God will save her."

"What?" Dad said. His voice was loud. He spat out his words. "Beatrice, you are out of your mind! Will you—"

Beatrice cut him off. "I'm not out of my mind," she snapped. "You have to call it what it is. This girl is *bad luck*! Look at you. You and your wife had a good relationship going for you. No worries, no hiccups, everything was working smoothly, until you brought her into your life. Now she is wasting your money! Why . . . why don't you just let her die?"

58

The silence was deafening. It felt like the devil himself walked through the room and shushed everybody.

"Shut up! Shut up!" Mom cried. "What . . . what has that got to do with what you're supposed to do! Kindly collect the money from the man and wire it back. You're a despicable human being. You have until tomorrow morning to do that. Otherwise, we are reporting you to Interpol. This is nothing but advance-fee fraud!"

Mom was shaking. The veins in her neck stood out. "And . . . and, Ngozi heard everything you just said. What type of human being are you? You . . ."

Mom's voice tapered off, defeated. She did not wait for Beatrice to reply; she hung up. I didn't expect much from Auntie Beatrice, but she shocked me with her new low. I sat down on the bed thinking of what she had just said. Maybe I was indeed a liability. Damaged goods—that's exactly what I was. *Why don't you just let her die* kept ringing in my head. Wishing death to someone is one thing, but vocalizing it to other people is another.

I now understood why even Auntie Hamila never had so much faith in her sister. Auntie Hamila never criticized Auntie Beatrice in front of us kids, but her body language and the way she talked about her gave me the feeling she tolerated her because they were siblings.

When Mom mentioned Interpol, everything became clear. There never was a night watchman or any sighting of who dropped me off. Auntie Beatrice must have convinced Maryam and Peter to join her and extort money from me, and then from Mom and Dad. How could she be so mean?

Mom came over, sat down, and hugged me. I hugged her back and sobbed. Mom cried too. We said nothing. We held each other, the true meaning of what had just happened not lost on any of us. The hope we had in finding a lead to any information about what happened that night had just evaporated. We were back to square one.

"Ngozi, remain strong," said Mom. "This fight is not over. As one door closes, another even larger one opens. Something will come up, I can feel it."

I felt guilty for putting them through this. They should have left me in Nigeria. I shouldn't have agreed to leave Nigeria. Seeing Mom like this devastated me. I got up from the bed and headed for the bathroom. Once inside I shut the door and leaned against it. Why, God, why? Why must I be the source of so much sorrow? My body trembled. All the frustration I'd ever felt, the suppressed emotions, all came bubbling to the surface.

I felt sorry for myself, for Mom and Dad. Since birth, I'd been a liability to anyone who came in touch with me. I left heartbreak and sorrow in my wake, just as Auntie Beatrice said. Even the woman who gave me life did not want me. She discarded me like something broken. Maybe I was cursed and not meant to be.

At last, the end had caught up with me. I clasped my hand over my mouth to suppress the sobs that erupted through my throat. Tears flowed. I cried for a while, and then I stopped.

I looked at my face in the mirror. My eyes were red. There was no mistaking that I had been crying my eyes out. I turned on the sink and splashed cold water on my face. It felt good. I dried my face and blew my nose loud so Mom would know I was fine.

As I grabbed the door handle to open it, Mom's cell phone rang. I don't know why, but I stopped and pressed my ear to the door.

"Hello? Ben!" I could hear Mom loud and clear. She was crying again. "What did we do to deserve this?" There was a pause, then Mom spoke amid sobs, "Oh God, Ben, I'm not going to be a mother anymore. Children bury their parents, not the other way around. God should take me instead . . . less than two weeks . . . only days!" she sobbed.

In the bathroom, I sank to the floor and drew my knees to my chest and held my head in my hands.

59

I pulled myself together, opened the door, and entered the room. Mom spun around when she heard me. She had some Kleenex in her hands, and her eyes were red. She walked over and hugged me, told me she loved me no matter what.

I took a deep breath, stepped back, and looked her in the face. "Mom . . ." My voice broke. I felt a lump in my throat.

"Yes," said Mom in a low voice. Her eyes wide, she looked scared.

"I'll never forget that day at the police station. I didn't know what to do. I was afraid, alone . . . and without hope. I'd given up on life." My voice cracked. "Then . . . then the door burst open, and you appeared." I laughed amid sobs. "You looked more scared than I was." A tear rolled down my cheek, and I wiped it off. "And I said to myself that if I had a choice for who my mother should be, I would choose you."

Mom hugged me tightly. "Ngozi."

I buried my face in her shoulder. "No matter what happens, you will always be my mother."

60

I thought about my life up until now. I'd always believed there was something else, someone else, an error somewhere, an explanation. As a little girl, I would ask Matron where my dad was, and she would say, "We'll talk about it later," and we left it at that. But she ran out of time.

When I moved to Uncle Thomas's after she died, I heard the whispers. Then they became loud after my uncle died. *She has no father, no mother. In fact, she was discarded, thrown away as rubbish.* That was when I realized there might be some truth to the adoption story.

But still, I would challenge anyone and fight to disprove them. If I were stronger, the person wouldn't repeat it. If they were stronger and beat me up, I would challenge them again and again until they stopped.

But I didn't want to believe that not only was I adopted but nobody knew who my parents were. When I felt maltreated, I would long for my father or mother to show up in a big car and whisk me away to their mansion and beg for my forgiveness. I wanted to believe there was a fairy-tale story out there. It never happened.

Then I would sink to the other side. I would get angry, my anger directed at my biological parents. *Why? Why did they give me up? Why did they abandon me?*

But that wasn't a way to live. I'd helped Ken see why his parents worried, and he adapted. I helped Mom see she was already a mother no matter the outcome of our predicament. Now I must help myself. The facts are the facts, and I must accept them to move on.

I was discarded at birth. Abandoned by parents who feared I was damaged from meningitis, but rescued by not one, not two, but three loving women who transcended their tribal differences to give me a chance. Matron, Nkechi, and Nurse Balogun gave me a chance. Mom lost her baby and her womb as a young woman. She'd been robbed of the possibility of having her own children, but she had the heart of a mother.

She found a man that loved her the way she was, unconditional love. By a twist of faith, they adopted me, and now they were about to lose me.

I wouldn't let that happen without a fight, but I must stop running from who I am. I am a child abandoned in the emergency room. Some kids are born with a silver spoon in their mouth, some with a wooden spoon. For me there was no spoon at all. All I needed to survive was love, and it had always been there inside me, but I refused to embrace it.

I wasn't a prayerful person, but I closed my eyes and said a prayer, asking God to bless all those who had come into my life and helped this once discarded girl survive and gave me the courage to accept myself the way I am.

After the prayer, I didn't feel like a massive boulder had been lifted off my shoulders, but I felt better. Like doing something you've been putting off for a long time.

I still couldn't sleep, and I decided to watch TV, but Mom

was asleep and I didn't want to wake her by turning it on. I grabbed my computer instead to watch a movie and use head-phones. Dad's name popped up as always whenever I turned on my laptop. It seemed like so many years had passed since he gave me the computer, but it had only been a few months. The screen filled with a pop-up from membership sites Dad subscribed to, another reminder of who the computer used to belong to.

I slid the mouse back and forth and closed some of the tabs. One of these days I would delete them. I yawned. The time on the computer was almost 2:00 a.m. I should get some sleep. I read the title of the remaining website; it was on Facebook; "University of Kano Teaching Hospital Alumni Group." By now I was so sleepy that maneuvering the mouse to shut the laptop was a challenge. I gave up, lowered the screen, and put the computer on the bedside table.

61

Our dreams are made up of our concerns. A cackle of hyenas had chased me all the way to the University of Kano Teaching Hospital. I woke up with a start to the smell of coffee.

"Sleepyhead, you're awake," said Mom with a smile as she brought her mug to her mouth and took a sip.

"What time is it? I must have overslept."

"It's 8:00 a.m. I'm going to walk over to my office to pick up a folder. Will be back soon."

I nodded.

"Ngozi, why don't you want to see Ken or talk to him?"

I tried to smile. It was too early to talk about such things. "Mom, where's this coming from?" My smile faltered. I turned away, weighted down by guilt. The same questions had crossed my mind so many times. Mom's eyes met mine.

This time Mom looked away and adjusted the sleeve on her blouse. "He's been coming here every day after school you know."

"It can't be. I told him not to. We are over."

Mom smiled. "He does his homework in the lobby, then leaves after saying hi to your dad when he comes."

"What?" I narrowed my eyes. "How do you know? Ah," I said with a smile. "All those frequent walks you take, going to your office." I nodded.

Mom glanced at me. "You forgot to tell us about the bet—"

I shook my head. "I didn't forget—"

Mom raised her hand, cutting me off. "Remember the story I told you?"

I frowned. "Which story?"

"After I found my boyfriend with the nurse, I wanted revenge. I went to the party and hooked up with a guy in my class I knew liked me. I got my revenge, but it didn't make me feel any better. After I lost the baby, I felt it was the punishment for what I'd done. A few years later I met that person again. I kind of used him and dumped him, but he forgave me."

Despite the sound of the TV in the background, I focused on what Mom was saying.

"Maybe, if he hadn't accepted that bet," said Mom, "he would never know you for who you are. Two wrongs don't make a right."

"I already forgave him," I whispered. "I'm damaged . . . and dying . . . we don't have a future . . ."

"He knows about Sambisa, and you are still living."

My head shot up. "Mom, you shouldn't have."

"I know . . . I'm sorry. I wanted to chase him away."

Shaky laughter escaped my lips. "Good, now he won't come back."

Mom smiled. "I told him last week. He still comes."

Mom pushed the envelope toward me. "He said I should give you this."

I hesitated, then took the envelope and placed it on my laptop. I watched Mom walk away, and my thoughts drifted to all the good times I had with Ken. The day he took me to the movies and we discovered the swings. Mom was right. That someone had done something terrible to you is no justification to act similarly. The only thing he did wrong was fall in love with a damaged and dying girl.

My pulse raced. He was still coming even though Mom had told him about Sambisa. But I was still dying.

I smiled and stared at the envelope. I opened it and found another sealed envelope addressed to me but with Ken's address. The return address was the DNA company. I looked inside the envelope for a note or something. There was nothing.

Disappointed, I opened the drawer of the bedside table and threw the envelope in. I picked up my laptop. There was nothing the DNA would tell me I didn't already know.

I picked up my laptop and opened it. It was just like I'd left it last night; a pop-up for the University of Kano Teaching Hospital Alumni Group was still there on a social media site. I was about to close it but stopped.

Something occurred to me. This could be the one thing that would make a difference. I logged in as Dad. His username and password were saved on the computer.

It was a group of over two hundred active physicians, all alumni of Dad's medical school, now scattered all over the world. Somebody must remember something. It was tempting.

I signed in and felt hot all over as the thought of mischief pumped adrenalin through me.

As I looked around Dad's in-box, I noticed a letter he had written a few hours earlier in the draft in-box of his account titled "My Daughter." I opened the draft and read it.

.   .   .

Dear Colleagues,

Fifteen years ago, a beautiful baby girl was abandoned in the neonatology unit of our beloved teaching hospital. I was doing my house job then and rotating through the pediatric department when she was there. My now wife, Nkechi Amadi, became godmother to this baby girl back then. Over the years we lost touch with her.

As providence would have it, less than a year ago, we came across her again. My wife and I adopted her, and she moved to America with us.

Today she is fighting for her life at the oncology unit of Children's Hospital, here in New Jersey where we live. Ngozi was diagnosed with a rare form of AML. Induction failed, and the only option we have is a bone marrow transplant.

Some of you must have gone through the neonatology unit while this baby was there. We are seeking any information that would guide us to her biological parents for a shot at getting a compatible transplant tissue. Time is of the essence.

I know that memory fades as time passes, but any information you can provide will be appreciated.

Regards,

Ben

Dr. Benjamin Obi.

I FELT A LUMP IN MY THROAT. I'D NEVER THOUGHT ABOUT how Dad felt. He was always upbeat. For a full minute, I sat there and stared at the screen, not knowing what to do. Dad had written the letter, but never sent it. Did he forget or was he still going to get to it?

I closed my eyes. *Think, think, think,* I implored myself.

What should I do? Call him and ask him about it or show Mom and seek her advice? I didn't find either of the options appealing.

I clicked on the tab with Dad's information. With trembling hands, I moved the mouse to the saved drafts folder and selected the message. For a moment, I found myself back on the truck, the night I jumped into the night to freedom. An effort is a decisive step in putting any dream into action. A cold shiver ran down my spine, and I hit the "Send to all" button.

I exhaled. The air rattled as it came out of me. I'd sent the message. I stared at the screen for what seemed like a long time and checked the time on the lower right corner; it had only been five minutes since I hit send. I continued to stare at the screen. My mind was empty. I didn't know what else to do. These words from a Nollywood movie I'd seen came to my mind: "From dust we came, and to dust we shall return."

I clicked the refresh button on Dad's account. The screen disappeared for a fraction of a second. When it reappeared, messages flooded Dad's in-box. I panicked and slammed the laptop screen shut.

62

———

My fingers ended in my mouth, and I bit my nails. Were those replies? No, they couldn't be. Too soon. I went to the bathroom to kill time. *Ngozi, what have you done?* I asked myself.

I did everything else but go back to my laptop. I went to the window and looked outside. We were several floors up. I stood there and enjoyed the warmth of the morning sun. Then I walked back to the bed.

My hands trembled as I reached to lift open the laptop screen. I raised it up and jerked back as if it were a trap about to snag me. The computer flickered on. Dad's alumni page was still open, and messages had poured in. With trembling fingers, I guided the cursor to the right place and clicked on the mail.

Some messages were from Dad's classmates who hadn't seen or heard from him since they'd left medical school. They were happy to know he was all right and wished his daughter a complete recovery. Some doctors explained they'd already graduated or were in the preclinical stage when the baby incident happened, so they couldn't help but all the same wished me a fast recovery.

I stared at the laptop screen as a tightness encircled my chest. The door to my room clicked open, and Mom walked in.

"Are you all right?" asked Mom.

Before I could answer, her phone rang.

"It's Dad." She put him on speaker. "Hello."

"Sweetheart, my e-mail box is going crazy, and everybody is calling me about Ngozi!"

Mom's eyebrows shot up. "What are they saying?"

"They said they saw my post. I posted nothing anywhere."

I felt terrible. What would Dad say? Now he would know I didn't delete his profiles as he had instructed me to. I didn't want to be a disappointment in any way. "Dad, I think I know what it is."

"Ngozi?" asked Dad.

Mom lifted her head to look at me, her eyebrows narrowed.

"Yes, Dad, I . . . I was on Facebook and I saw your draft message, so I sent it. I'm sorry."

"Oh, that makes sense. I was wondering how all those people remembered me all at the same time. But . . ."

There was a pause. I thought Dad was still confused about how I'd done it.

"I see, I see," came Dad's voice over the phone.

"See what?" asked Mom.

"My computers, phones, and tablet are all synced together . . . Ngozi, you didn't delete my account on your laptop, right?"

I'd never been so embarrassed in my life. Dad would wonder what else I'd been doing.

"Wow!" exclaimed Mom, looking at her phone. "This is crazy! My account has exploded too." She giggled like a little girl as she tapped her phone now and then. "People I haven't spoken to in years are writing on my wall!"

Dad's phone beeped. "I have an incoming call. I must hang up. I'll be at the hospital in the next twenty minutes. See you guys soon." The phone went dead.

Mom walked over to the chair and sat down. "I have a lot of messages to sieve through here. Maybe we'll find something useful. Dad was supposed to delete his stuff before giving you his laptop. I guess it was meant to be."

I watched Mom. Her eyes never left her phone as she spoke. My prayer was that something good would come out of my invasion of Dad's privacy. There would be a talk later if all ended well.

"This would be better to wade through on a bigger screen and with a printer," said Mom. "We don't have the luxury of a second pass at all this information. My office would be a good place to go through this."

Boredom was about to kill me, reading the messages one after the other. It must have been exciting for Mom since she knew these people and could relate to their anecdotes. I dozed off and, bit by bit, the fingers of sleep pulled me away.

63

"Hi," said Dad in a low voice. "How are you feeling?"

I must have drifted off to sleep. I opened my eyes to see Dad's smiling face. All I wanted to do was sleep more. I nodded, attempted a smile, and shut my eyes. I could still hear the TV.

"Ben, good . . . you're here," said Mom.

"Shhh . . . she's sleeping," said Dad.

"Listen, I have to go to my office," whispered Mom. "I need to print these messages out."

"All right, I'll be here," said Dad.

I heard shuffling feet, and then the door opened and shut. Moments later, Dad's phone rang and he answered it.

"Hello, it's Ben. Sorry, I drove through an area with a bad signal and lost you. You are in New York for political engagement? Emmm . . . it's unnecessary. What type of information? . . . About my daughter? I think someone mentioned it. Please accept my condolences. You know something? Okay, Children's Cancer Center. I'll be expecting you."

It felt like I'd heard Dad talk to someone in a dream. Who

could it be? I wanted to know more, but it was now quiet. I drifted in and out of sleep, hearing the television.

My eyes shot open when I heard three quick raps on the door. Must be the food lady. I wasn't that hungry. I shut my eyes as I heard Dad walk over to the door.

"Hamza!" said Dad.

I heard the snap of fingers, the high point in a casual handshake among Nigerian friends.

"Good to see you. Come on in," said Dad, lowering his voice.

"Good to see you too, Benjamin," whispered a deep rich voice. "What about Nkechi?"

"Oh, she's fine. She went to her office," said Dad.

I heard footsteps come closer, stop, and then walk away.

"Sorry, I almost forgot . . . Mr. President," said Dad. "Congratulations on winning the election. I know you'll do a fine job."

"Thank you so much. Nigeria is a tough place, but we'll put a team together that will move us forward."

"My condolences again on your loss. Your father's passing was Nigeria's loss."

"Thank you. That's actually why I'm here."

Mr. President? Hamza Tarbari? I was wide-awake now but kept my eyes closed, my ears sharp. They must be sitting on Mom's usual couch.

"Ben, I'm sorry about your . . . daughter," said Hamza. "I pray she makes a quick recovery. I needed to see you face-to-face. I've learned a lot since being in politics. Politics is not for the faint of heart. No detail is too small to be overlooked." Hamza paused. "We haven't seen each other in a while, but we go back a long way. I don't think I should have anything to worry about, right?"

"Of course not," said Dad. "But what is it all about?"

I could hear the tension in Dad's voice.

"I saw the e-mail you sent out to our alumni forum this morning. Since I was already here in the States, I had to come."

There was a long pause, so I opened my eyes a slit and saw them sitting. The man in the black suit opposite Dad was Hamza Tarbari, the president-elect of Nigeria.

"How did you get to adopt her?" Hamza asked.

"My daughter?" asked Dad, surprise in his voice.

Dr. Tarbari must have nodded because Dad told him about Matron adopting me, her passing and that of Uncle Thomas, and the kidnapping at Akarika."

Most people reacted with shock when they heard I was at Akarika, but not this politician. I continued to listen, not moving a muscle.

"But before then. You must have known her before then. Could you start from the beginning when she was a baby?" asked Hamza in a shaky voice.

I opened my eyes and saw Dad just looking at him, then he started from when I was at the ER and all the way to when they rescued me from the police station.

"You're a better man than I am," said Hamza when Dad finished the story. "Your daughter's name is Ngozi right?"

"Yes," said Dad.

"Ngozi," said Hamza. His voice was low, as if savoring every vowel of the word. "Befitting name."

Dad exhaled. "Mr. President, you were two years ahead of us, and you were already pursuing your residency when Ngozi was in the hospital. You didn't meet her. Where does helping my daughter fit into all this? We have less than a week to save her life."

Hamza wrung his fingers together, and gloom descended over his face like a dark curtain. "If my father were still alive today, we wouldn't be having this discussion." He paused. "Ben, what I'll tell you now is between the two of us and must not be shared."

Dad nodded. "Sure."

"My father was a piece of work," said the president-elect. "I admired and hated him at the same time. He had great foresight. He wasn't educated, even though he had the opportunity, but through hard work, keeping his eyes and ears open, and hobnobbing with the right people, he extended his inheritance into a multibillion-dollar business and a huge network of people in the public and private sectors who he could call on for favors when the need arose."

"Okay," said Dad. "But that's public knowledge."

"I agree," said Hamza. "He had dreams for himself but knew he had limited himself with a lack of formal education. Nigerians would never vote for an individual that never saw the four walls of a secondary school. He decided he could still achieve his dreams and aspirations through his children. My brother was the designated heir apparent, but we lost him in a car accident and . . . it fell on me."

I opened my eyes again a tiny slit to see what was going on. Hamza Tarbari was now standing facing the window.

"During my house job, when I found out that my girlfriend then was pregnant, I knew the right thing to do was marry her. But after I told my father, he had other plans."

Dad clapped his hands together. "So, you're Ngozi's biological father?"

64

M y heart pounded so loud, I expected both men to turn around and look.

Hamza Tarbari didn't answer Dad's question. "My father thought it was not the right time, nor was she the right person. It could jeopardize his plans for me. My girlfriend had a difficult delivery, which worked in my father's favor and helped solidify his plans. When the baby came, she was stillborn . . . or so my girlfriend and everybody else was made to believe. My father had made it happen."

Hamza Tarbari just stood there, as if trying to decide on what choice of words to use. "Have you ever heard of Dr. Lambert Muzo?"

"The name sounds familiar. Was he in the news?" asked Dad.

"He used to consult at the teaching hospital now and then. He was my mentor when I was in school. Yes, he died about a year ago in his office," said Hamza. "We were supposed to meet the next day. The media had a field day. I was under suspicion just as the presidential primaries loomed. In fact, he was murdered. All I'm telling you now are things I found out in the past four weeks since my father died. My father, for some unknown reason, believed in keeping meticulous records of all his dealings, good and bad."

"This sounds like a scene from Mario Puzo's *The Godfather*." Dad chuckled. "But still, how is it connected to my daughter?"

I could hear the nervousness in Dad's voice.

"I've destroyed all the documents—"

"Why?" asked Dad.

Hamza brushed off invisible lint from his suit. "For political reasons, just in case they get into the wrong hands." He cleared his throat. "My father, or Malam as his associates knew him, arranged for the baby to be delivered in Dr. Muzo's private hospital and had planned with him, after the exchange of a large amount of money and settlement of his gambling debts, to terminate the baby after birth if a girl, but to keep him if a boy."

My pulse raced. *Oh my God*, I said to myself.

"However, from my father's journals, there were complications during the delivery. Uterine bleeding-"

"The baby died, and Nkechi lost her uterus," said Dad, cutting him off and completing the story. "Otherwise she would have bled to death."

"No," said Hamza and held up a finger. "According to the journal, Dr. Muzo had lived up to the bargain. My girlfriend and I went our separate ways; we couldn't survive the tragedy. However, in another journal entry about two years from the last, Dr. Muzo came back and told father the baby was alive, that he had not carried out his request. He had dropped her off at the motherless babies' home in Warawa. He had asked for more money, or he would go to the media. The baby had been adopted by one of the nurses from the pediatric unit."

Adrenaline coursed through me. *Oh my God, Matron.*

"Blackmail?" asked dad.

"Yes. Chief gave him money, but things did not go well for Dr. Muzo. His wife had been pushing him to report to the authorities. Soon after, he lost his family in a car accident."

Dad's eyes almost bulged out of their sockets. He sat there stunned.

Hamza Tarbari cleared his throat. "Another entry showed that Chief sent monthly allowances to this nurse's bank account through a dizzying array of surrogates. For about fourteen years, everything was quiet. No more mention of the girl until last year."

Hamza Tarbari was my father? And that monster was my grandfather? A cold shiver ran down my spine.

"You've heard of Boko Haram and the 290 girls kidnapped by them at Chibok?" asked Hamza.

"Yes," said Dad. He sounded hoarse.

"A copycat kidnapping happened soon after that, but this time at Akarika Girls—"

"Akarika Girls? That's Ngozi's school!" said Dad, anxiety in his voice.

Dad turned to look at me, and I shut my eyes.

Hamza continued. "By this time, I was on my way to securing my party's nomination for the presidential ticket. But Dr. Muzo found himself in financial straits again and this time raised the stakes. He approached father and again threatened him with blackmail. He was supposed to meet with me the next day. I can't say for sure what for. But I'd kept him as a personal physician to make sure he was well taken care of, out of my fondness for him."

Hamza walked closer to Dad and turned to look at me. I shut my eyes tight. His voice dropped to a whisper.

"To make sure there were no hiccups and to tie up any

loose ends, my father had set things in motion, using a guy called Gambo who my brother had rescued a few years earlier from Libya." Hamza Tarbari's voice broke. "In an entry in his journal last year, he wrote about sponsoring the attack at Akarika Girls Secondary School. To . . . to . . . murder his own granddaughter, my . . . daughter, so that all loose ends are taken care of in my climb to the presidency. For the sake of power. My . . . my daughter."

"My God!" said Dad.

My eyes were wide open. Hamza Tarbari faced Dad. Both men stared at each other. The shock on Dad's face and sorrow on Hamza Tarbari's face was unmistakable.

"You're Ngozi's biological father," Dad whispered.

Hamza nodded, a pensive look on his face. "I'm . . . I'm not my father. The past is the past. We can't change it; the future we can shape. Ben, you gave me your word. What you heard must not leave this room."

This was too much information. My mind was numb and at the same time alive. At least we had a breakthrough. One sharp knock drew everyone's attention to the door. It opened, and Mom walked in.

"I didn't find any—" Mom stopped in her tracks, her eyes wide, mouth agape, a picture of bewilderment and distress. "Hamza?"

"Nkechi," whispered Hamza.

"Ben, what's Hamza doing here?" Mom's hand flew to her chest. She looked like she'd seen a ghost.

My eyes went from Mom to Dad and Hamza Tarbari. Mom was hyperventilating, bordering on hysteria. The papers she'd printed fell on the floor.

"Hamza is Ngozi's biological father," blurted Dad.

"No, no, no," screamed Mom. "It can't be. She died. They showed me where they buried her."

"Nkechi, I'm so sorry, I only found out after my father died."

Mom collapsed on the floor, her body wracked with sobs. "Oh my God," sobbed Mom.

"I have to go now," said Hamza. "Sorry for the . . . Please let me know any way I can help."

Hamza Tarbari exited the room fast. I jumped off the bed and walked over to Mom. I kneeled on the floor beside her. Tears flowed down her face and down my face. She looked up at me. The corners of her lips quivered as they tried to cry and laugh at the same time.

"Mom . . . it's all right," I said.

Mom cupped my face with both trembling hands. "My daughter . . . my daughter, the fruit of my womb."

65

While Mom and I had been on the floor, lamenting our shock, surprise, and good fortune, Dad was several steps ahead. He had put everything aside for now, and his focus was on the reason we were in the hospital.

After the excitement had died down, Dad told us he had run after Dr. Tarbari. He knew that once he left the hospital and New York, it might be difficult to get him back to do HLA typing.

Dad was happy to describe what that was after I'd asked.

"HLA is the acronym for human leucocyte antigen," said Dad. "It's a marker present in the blood that, if similar to yours, increases the likelihood of the blood owner being a potential donor, and we could move on to more tests and then bone marrow, stem cell, or peripheral blood stem cell harvest."

I nodded.

Dad continued. "I called Dr. Palmer, and a member of his team met us at the phlebotomy unit. He took care of the paperwork, and they drew Dr. Tarbari's blood. The result for that takes five days, so we should get that in two days. However, the rapid paternity test result we get today. That one takes only three days."

The team had also come to the room and taken blood samples from Mom. They already had mine, they said. Dad had swabbed Mom's cheek and mine, then sent the kit off to the lab.

"I still don't understand why he agreed to do it," said Mom in a whisper. "He has changed. I guess he is his own man now."

That day Dr. Tarbari showed up, Mom had gone into shock. I mean, everybody else was in shock too. Mom and Dad knew him. He was just another wealthy politician I saw on the news now and then. I didn't know he was the boyfriend Mom had been talking about. The man would be the next president of Nigeria, and he was my father? It was too much.

Mom was sedated to calm her down. In fact, they had wheeled another bed into my room for her. The bed was now gone, but since that day, Mom hadn't fully recovered. She stared a lot into space as if she had something on her mind.

"Apparently," said Dad, "Dr. Tarbari and his wife have no children, and maybe once he found out what his father had done, plus the e-mail from Ngozi and the possibility he has a child out there, he jumped at it." Dad shrugged. "It was the right thing to do too."

"Are you sure the test is coming in today?" asked Mom.

"Yes," said Dad." It takes three days. They'll send a text when it's ready, and we'll log into the account." Dad brought out his phone, and his finger went back and forth on the screen. "No text message from them yet."

I looked at Mom. She was biting her lower lip. "Mom, it will be fine." This was the third time Mom had asked.

"Until there is scientific confirmation," said Mom. "We might be back to square one." She closed her eyes and sighed. "God works in mysterious ways."

"Hamza wouldn't come here if he wasn't sure," said Dad. "At least with your bone marrow, Ngozi has an excellent chance."

There was a sharp knock on the door, and Dr. Palmer's face peered in.

"Good morning, everybody," said Dr. Palmer. "I see we're all here today." He looked at me. "How are we doing today, Ngozi?"

"Fine," I said, smiling.

Dr. Palmer picked up my chart at the foot of the bed and flipped through. "Good, good. The screening test will be ready in two days, and we'll take it from there." He looked at me and smiled. "Questions?"

I shook my head. Dr. Palmer looked at Dad, who was looking at his phone, and Mom, who had her hands clasped together, staring into space.

"I'll get going then," said Dr. Palmer. "See you soon with good news." He and his team exited.

"It can't be," said Dad. His eyebrows narrowed as he stared at his phone screen. "The paternity test report is out . . . I don't understand."

Dad rubbed the back of his head with his free hand. His eyes darted from Mom to me. "There's no DNA connection at all between Ngozi and Hamza."

Mom sprang to her feet with so much force that the chair toppled over behind her. "What about the maternity test?"

"It's positive!" said Dad. "Nkechi . . . what happened here?"

Mom sank to her knees, her hands clasped together as if

in prayer. I heard the hurt in Dad's voice. Mom suddenly looked older than her age. Tears streamed down her cheeks.

"Is . . . is there something else we need to know?" asked Dad.

"Ben . . . Ben," said Mom through sobs. She got up and walked toward Dad, her out-stretched hands shaking. She clasped him on the cheeks. "Ben . . . she's our baby."

EPILOGUE

One year later, as I strolled the corridors of my school on my way to my next class, I had a big smile on my face. The last MRD test was negative so far, knock on wood, which meant my leukemia was on its way to complete remission.

Dad was the guy Mom had gotten her revenge on Dr. Tarbari with. That day, I had pulled out the DNA analysis Ken had sent. I read the report, and it blew me away. It showed that I had two DNA matches in Bergen County, New Jersey.

1. THE CRITERIA PARENT/CHILD.
   Confidence: Extremely high
   Relationship: D138657 is your father

2. THE CRITERIA PARENT/CHILD.
   Confidence: Extremely high

Relationship: T918766 is your mother

To unlock the names behind who I was matched to, I would have to contact the account owners. We did that later, and they confirmed it was Mom and Dad. I kept on wondering how things would have turned out if I'd done this the first time Ken urged me to.

Ken and I were still together. I apologized to him about my insecurities, and he understood. He got accepted to study music at Princeton University, and his parents are okay with that.

Dr. Tarbari was sworn in as President of Nigeria. According to the newspaper, in the one year he'd been in office, he had been dismantling the country's endemic corruption problems. One newspaper quoted him as saying:

"A civil servant or politician's priority is to serve the people and represent their interests as laid out by the government department or branch they serve in. By impeding the process in any way, they are no longer serving the people, but their own interests, and should be held accountable. Their integrity as an individual is what would be on the line, not their religion or ethnicity. Neither the civil service nor political office is the place to seek your fortune; that is why there's a private sector."

∽

News coming out of Aso Rock said President Tarbari and the first lady were expecting their first child.

Over the months, as I told and retold my experience, Dad said Zainab must have been addicted to the codeine in cough syrup and looking for money to feed her addiction. That could have been her motivation for agreeing to work with Danladi. Even though I ended up in school due to reasons, Dad thinks Tarbari senior could have given them my information. They'd put two and two together and approached Zainab.

Some days later, while watching CNN Africa, there was a report about a suicide bombing in Abuja that killed hundreds of people. Footage captured by an innocent Nigerian on his cell phone showed the terrorist, a young girl with big round eyes, just moments before the bomb went off. A single tribal scar ran along both cheeks. She could have passed for my childhood friend, Zainab, whom I never saw nor heard from again.

The Nigerian Army stormed parts of Sambisa. They rescued some girls. Kaka, Gambo's grandmother, and her friend Baruwa, chaperones for the kidnapped girls who later forced them into illicit marriages, are still at large. Just like Faith, a good number of the rescued girls were ostracized by their families. Some nongovernmental agencies set up shelters for such girls where they were rehabilitated back into society. Some of the girls had no choice but to go back to their terrorist husbands. After a year as hostages and getting married off to the terrorists, most of the Akarika girls were now dubbed Akarika mothers.

Bala, who rescued Faith and me after we escaped the terrorists by jumping off the truck, and later delivered us back to them, was picked up by the Nigerian police after I wrote my long-overdue report. He and his accomplice were placed in police custody, charged with the murder of Joy Okafor, the Christian girl who was kidnapped with me in Sambisa.

Preeti Kumar explained to me that she stayed away because she knew from her mom how I felt about receiving visitors and wanted to remember me the way she knew me. That was fine with me.

Jennifer Davis, my best friend, and Preeti are itching to visit Nigeria. Jennifer wants us to co-write a book about my experience and visit where it all happened for firsthand information. I told her she would have to go alone. It's only in American movies that I see people running toward danger. She should watch Nollywood movies, where people run away from danger. Bottom line, I wasn't about to visit Nigeria any time soon.

Maryam and Peter denied collaborating with Auntie Beatrice. They said Auntie Beatrice had borrowed Maryam's phone and disappeared with it for a few days.

Auntie Beatrice herself is recovering at Lamija Hospital with a broken leg after she fell off an Okada motorbike while escaping from armed robbers that came to loot what she had looted.

Auntie Halima has still refused to talk to me. I sent my regards to her through cousin Maryam, who I text now and then.

Fatima was said to have left soon after I went to America with no forwarding address. They suspect she went back to live in the village. She was my guiding angel.

One day, I rode with Ken in his car when he came back for the weekend from school. We were headed to the movies. After that, we'd hang out on the playground with the swings.

"I have something to say to you," said Ken, a crooked smile on his lips. "Well, you must listen."

"Okay, I'm all ears."

He tapped his phone screen a few times, and his car

speakers came alive with music—2Face's "African Queen." Ken sang along to the lyrics.

"I love you," said Ken when the music ended.

I threw my head back and laughed. "I love you too."

THE END.

AUTHORS NOTE

I hope you enjoyed One Thing After Another, as much as I enjoyed writing.

For more books from me, join my newsletter below.

Thank you!

NEWSLETTER

Join my newsletter list and download a HOT Freebie at www. ifeanyiesimai.com

ABOUT THE AUTHOR

Ifeanyi Esimai enjoys listening to folklore and loves to read across different genres, which he argues, tongue -in- cheek, qualifies him to write thrillers, science fiction, and fantasy.

He was born in Nigeria, and trained as a physician. Outside of reading and writing, Ifeanyi loves to spend time with family at their home in New Jersey.

 facebook.com/ifeanyiesimaiauthor

 twitter.com/IEsimai

 instagram.com/ifeanyiesimaiauthor

www.ingramcontent.com/pod-product-compliance
Lightning Source LLC
Chambersburg PA
CBHW060244100726

47907CB00003B/765